RISK

By Briana Michaels

COPYRIGHT

Dedication

For those who love an audience: May every scene end with a standing O.

Chapter 1

Leah

"That feels so good." I tip my head back, getting into it more. "Mmmm."

"My good girl likes making me happy, doesn't she?"

I bite my bottom lip and nod eagerly. "Mmm hmm." I playfully squeal while sticking my other foot in the shallow container. No, I don't enjoy what I'm doing, but this guy has paid five hundred bucks to watch me slather my pedicured feet in a vat of peanut butter, so I will happily fake my pleasure. "It's so creamy."

His bright blue eyes intensify with desire. Seeing how turned on he is, how his yearning translates to lustful excitement when I do things for him in our private sessions, empowers me.

"I love your toes painted pink." He repositions, likely so he can pull out his dick, and leans into the camera. "Give me a closer look, Daisy."

Most guys don't let me see their face, but Mr. C always does. He's not bad looking, maybe mid-thirties, dark brown hair clipped tight to his head, brilliant blue eyes, nice mouth. The veins in his temple always pop out when he's close to coming, so I can tell he's about a minute away from blowing his load.

I tip the camera, making my feet take up the entire screen and wiggle my toes. Groaning like it's going to give me an O, I run my fingers through the peanut butter and smear it up my ankles. "I wish you were here to lick all this off me, Mr. C."

He grunts as he orgasms, and I kind of wish I could see his face right now. To watch him come undone at the sight of my little piggies slathered in creamy peanut butter, while he fantasizes about touching them, licking them. Sucking on them. Bet it's hot. He sounds sexy when he comes. I'm an aural girlie, so listening to people come drives me wild.

I'm never one to kink shame, and though not all kinks are my cup of tea, I enjoy having a connection with my patrons like this. It's fun.

And lucrative.

However, being dressed as a pink-haired bunny with my toes slathered in PB has me questioning if I'm charging enough for these sessions. Foot worship is one of the most popular kinks out there and I need to capitalize on it better.

"Such a good little bunny," Mr. C says, out of breath. "I'll see you next week, right?" The lift in his tone at the end breaks my heart a bit. Bless him, I think he's getting attached. And damn me, because I'm happy to have a steady client who pays so well.

The bangs of my wig fall into my eyes as I tip the camera back up to my face. "I'll be counting down the days."

He flashes me a big, post-orgasm smile. "Thanks, baby."

Blowing him a kiss, I wave goodbye and end the chat.

That was my first session for the day, but my next one isn't until tonight. Mr. C is the only one who gets me at the ass crack of dawn, and since it's only a couple days out of the month, I'm not about to complain. But how the fuck am I going to get all this mess off my feet now?

Fucking damnit, I left the towel in the kitchen when I was preparing for this session!

Sliding onto the floor, I crawl into the kitchen with my feet up as high as I can get them. In my bunny suit.

"*Ching*!" The sound of Mr. C's tip coming through makes up for it.

After getting most of the peanut butter off my feet and out from between my toes, I wash them thoroughly in the kitchen sink, then strip out of my outfit, pull off my wig, and rewash my entire bottom half in the tub. I don't have time for a whole scrub down because this call took longer than I thought it would and now it's time for my other job.

Shoving into an old t-shirt and shorts, I pluck my cell off the floor and check my messages on the app.

Mr. C: *Next week I want honey.*

Great. That's going to be so sticky and messy. My annoyance fades when I see he's tipped me another five hundred for this morning, though.

A grand for a half hour of slathering peanut butter on my feet? Not too shabby. Bet I can up it to two grand next month and he'll pay it.

Some people may wonder why I clean houses for a living when I make bank being a camgirl, and the truth is I need a backup plan. Something reliable and enjoyable that pays my bills.

Hey, I like being watched. I like sex. I like being wanted and adored and fantasied about. I like it when other people get off. But this line of sex work isn't sustainable. One day my clients will move on, or I'll get bored, or I won't be desirable anymore. Coming up with fresh content all the time is fucking exhausting, too.

House cleaning is hard work, and it's not for everyone, but I love it. It satisfies me in a way nothing else does. Why not capitalize on that and charge rich people lots of money to clean the homes they barely use any way?

Case in point: Today I go to Mason Finch's condo. It's huge, modern, and basically empty. He's rarely there but insists on it being cleaned once a month. I've never seen this guy in my life, but I picture him as a skinny old dude who spends a lot of time in opera houses and has an extensive collection of bow ties. No clue why. That's just how my imagination works. All I know is, he's the easiest house I'm going to clean all week, and he never fails to make his payment and give a sizable tip.

My cell rings and it's my bestie, Mak. "Good morning, gorgeous."

"Hey, you off to work yet?"

"Just about to leave." Grabbing my keys, I head out and lock my front door.

"How many houses you got today?"

"Four." Which is why being punctual or early is important.

"Want to have dinner with me and Carson later?"

"Hells yes!" I love hanging with them. Carson's a blast, and I'll never say no to Mak. "When and where, baby?"

"There's a place I'm dying to try called Maestros."

"Ohhh that fancy place on the east side?"

"Yup!" Mak chirps. "Seven okay?"

"Can we make it like seven thirty or eight? I'll need to come home and shower the scuzz off me and will probably hit traffic."

"Eight it is. See you then."

"Hey wait." I scramble towards my car. "How was the sex club last night?"

"Ahhh-maaaa-zzzzing."

"Nice!" I wish my sex life was as fantastic as my bestie's, but for the past couple of years it's just been me, myself, and my online audience. "Tell Carson I said hi. Love you."

"Love you too."

After hanging up, I fly down the road and end up having to park half a block away from the café I love, which means I'm sprinting to the nectar of the Gods. Hey, nothing's stopping me from getting my daily double espresso, even if I'm crunched on time. I have priorities, people.

With a little speeding, I still make it to Mason's condo five minutes early.

Pulling out my collapsible cart, I load it with all my preferred cleaning supplies and head inside the swanky building.

"Hey!" I wave at the doorman. This guy knows me. I'm here every month. Why's he looking at me weird? "Cleaning Condo 207."

"Uhh. Yeah. Go on up." Why does he look so amused?

I don't know what he thinks is so funny about a woman pulling a heavy ass cart around. I'm already sweating, and I haven't even started. Annoyed, I drag my shit to the elevator, flustered because now I think he's making fun of me for being a housemaid.

The doors open just as I'm about to hit the button and out pops a gentleman in a suit that likely costs over three months' rent for me. Our gazes meet and he gawks for a moment, then moves past me as if I have the plague.

Asshole.

Time to dig out my music and put myself in a better mood because clearly the double espresso hasn't kicked into my system enough for all this bullshit.

Earbuds in. Playlist on. Time to clean house.

The instant I open the door to Mason's condo, the scents of bergamot, cloves, and leather hit my nose. Damn, did he put a candle or something in here since the last time I cleaned? It smells divine. This place is beautifully built but lacks décor and color. Unless you call that signed baseball jersey framed in the foyer artwork, there's nothing here to make it homey.

Shutting the door, I wheel my cart into the galley kitchen and get to work. Spray, scrub, swipe, repeat. I make my way through the kitchen quickly and head to the bathroom next. This is one of my favorite houses to clean because the owner rarely uses this place, which means it's never dirty.

Unlike the house I have after this, that has four kids, two dogs, and six cats.

Singing into my microphone—the mop handle—I bump and grind to my tunes.

The bathroom is bright and sweet smelling. Deep in my zone, putting on a full performance with twerking and air humping, I squeeze my eyes shut and belt out the high notes until I've run out of air.

Nailed it!

Popping my eyes open, my reflection scares the shit out of me. Screaming, hands flying, I accidentally knock the earbuds out of my head.

Dear god, I'm still wearing the makeup and whiskers from this morning!

And that's not the worst part.

Someone else is in this bathroom.

And he's *huge*.

"Stay back!" I swing my mop like a baseball bat at him. The guy catches it with ease, and I can't rip it out of his grip. Fear spikes in my system and I scramble back, tripping on the rug by the sink. Arms pinwheeling, I gasp, pitching backwards.

Before my ass hits the tile floor, the man catches me. "Easy does it," he says in a low timbre. He shifts me so I can stand again and cocks his eyebrow. "You good?"

Not at all. I'm horrified. "You're…"

"Mason Finch."

I shake my head as my eyes sail south. "No, you're… you're naked."

And his big dick is as hard as steel.

Chapter 2

Mason

At first, when I heard someone singing, I thought my bluetooth speakers had somehow turned on. Then I remembered the cleaning service was scheduled for today, and assumed they'd realize I was in the shower and would leave cleaning the master bathroom for last.

Apparently not.

Can't say I'm mad about it.

This woman's about five-foot nine, with long dirty blonde hair, big doe eyes the color of cognac, and a lush mouth. She's fucking stunning. Seeing her barge into my bathroom singing into her mop just before dry humping the damn thing is a sight I'll never forget, either.

Fucking adorable.

The whiskers on her face are a little confusing, though.

And can we talk about her swing? My hand still stings from catching the mop before she could decapitate me with it. This woman's strong with fast reflexes. Good thing mine are faster, which is the only reason she didn't fall into the vanity when she tripped on my rug.

And now here we are. Her in whiskers. Me in my birthday suit. Awkward as fuck.

Can't say I'm thrilled about this, but the way she's gawking at my dick inflates my ego substantially.

Between the dancing, singing, and the sight of her ass in those little booty shorts, I'm turned on enough to lose my mind. It's been a long time since I've had a good hard fuck, and my dick is in a constant state of "pay attention to me".

Too bad she's off limits.

"Sorry." I snatch the towel off the floor to cover myself up with. "I dropped the towel trying to make sure you didn't take my head off with that mop."

She looks furious. "You should have locked your door!"

Is she trying to put the blame on me here? "I don't lock doors inside my own home. Especially since I'm the only one living here. Maybe *you* should have knocked before you came in."

Her brow furrows, as if she's trying to find an argument for that. "I didn't think you were home. You're never home."

Isn't that the truth. "Well, I am today."

"And I would have known if you at least used a light!"

Is she for real? "There's enough sun streaming in from the windows to not warrant a light on."

She snaps her fingers. "Steam." The woman has the nerve to step in closer to me. "There should have been steam from your hot shower and there wasn't. How could I have known you were in the shower when there's no steam?"

"I don't take hot showers."

Her eyes widen. "Only psychopaths take cold ones."

Or sexually frustrated businessmen. "I'm not a psychopath."

"I bet that's what all psychopaths say." Her eyes are smiling while she says this and I have no idea how she managed to defuse a very awkward situation, but I'm feeling less and less frustrated by it now.

"Well." Keeping the towel over my junk to cover it, I flash her a disarming grin. "I'll leave you to it in here." Walking backwards, I enter my bedroom and shut the door.

Fuck me running! What am I going to do now? My mind's already going into damage control. I can't help it. I'm hard-wired to think of every angle something can backfire and taint my name.

Is she going to report me to her company for sexual harassment? How's that going to look when it gets out? I can see the headlines now: "Big Tech Mason Finch Exposes Himself to Innocent House Cleaner."

My family will have a collective coronary and that's a headache I'm not in the mood to get right now.

Except she doesn't strike me as someone who would run to tell her superiors about this incident. In fact, the way she handled this was far better than what I would have been able to do if the tables were turned.

It was just an unfortunate timing issue. A big, weird, embarrassing accident.

But hard-ons don't happen by mistake. I was turned on looking at her. *And I wanted her to see it.* Holding her in my arms when I caught her only made it worse.

Swiping a hand over my mouth, I stare at my carefully laid out suit on the bed. I feel bad being here, startling her the way I did. Wait a minute. Why do I feel like I'm trespassing on *her* territory when it's *my* goddamn condo?

Fuck it. It doesn't matter. What happened, happened, and now it's done. I just have to focus on getting out of here before I do something stupid like ask for her number.

God, my dick won't deflate. I blame the twerking. I'm a sucker for woman with confidence and the one in my bathroom right now has it in spades. Palming my hard-on, I know if I don't blow off some steam, I'm going to choke at the meeting I have at eleven o'clock and that can't happen. I'm so close to getting all I want, and this little diversion can't slow me down.

Glancing back at the door separating me

and that sexpot, I debate on locking it. But my naughty side wants to play and, honestly, I doubt she'll barge in on me again.

No matter how much I want her to watch.

Spitting in my palm, I slide my hand over the hard length of my cock and close my eyes. The only image that appears is of that cleaning woman. Her ass. Her hips. The way she dances.

I latch onto the fact that she had whiskers and fill in the gaps of what she'd look like, dressed as a cat with ears and a long-tailed butt plug. My strokes speed up. What would she look like cleaning my house naked? The image of her on all fours, scrubbing my kitchen floors, her tits swaying, ass up in the air with her bare feet tucked under her, makes me groan.

I'd approach from behind, squat down and eat her pussy in that position. I'd eat her ass too. Fuck, I'd devour every bit of her sweet body I could get my tongue on and then drive my cock inside her swollen cunt. Make her take every inch of me until her pussy stretches around my girth. Then I'd have her beg me to move my hips and fuck her like an animal.

My orgasm builds, and builds, and builds until I can't hold it back anymore. The noises I make when I come aren't loud. But they aren't quiet either. *Can she hear me?* I watch myself in the mirror, still jerking off until my dick is spent, and ignore the hollowness in my chest because pleasuring myself alone all the time is getting old.

Dragging my towel across the carpet to wipe up the mess I just made, I clean up and get dressed in dead silence.

Before I set out, I lean against the bathroom door and listen. Water's running, so I assume she's working on my sinks. Knocking once, I open it, prepared to say something ordinary and aloof, so I can read her mood before I worry about what she'll say about all this later. "Hey, I just wanted to—"

"Please don't report me," she says with bright yellow gloves on. Holding the toilet brush over the bowl, she looks at me with flushed cheeks. "I don't want to lose this house."

What? "You didn't do anything wrong. Why would I report you?" The fumes from bleach and lemon-scented cleaners make my eyes water the closer I get to her. "What are you talking about?"

"I'm so sorry I barged in on you earlier. I honestly didn't know you were here."

Guilt ripples down my chest. "If anyone should apologize, it's me. I should have rescheduled you. Or at least let you know I was here beforehand. I forgot you were coming. I've got a lot going on and hadn't realized what day it was."

Not that it would have mattered, because I don't schedule my cleaning service. My secretary does that shit for me.

"You're not mad?" She looks up at me with her big, beautiful eyes and pouty mouth, and it's all I can do to keep myself from cupping her cheek and kissing her.

Okay. Whoa. I need to back the fuck off immediately. I didn't release enough tension in my bedroom if my first instinct is to kiss this woman instead of getting out of here and doing my job. "What's your name?"

"Leah."

I feel like a jerk because shouldn't I at least know the name of the woman who cleans my toilets once a month?

"Nice to meet you, Leah." I hold out my hand, and she rips her glove off to shake it. What would that grip feel like wrapped around my d—

"I gotta go. Lock up once you're done."

"Yes, sir."

Oh. My. God. She's killing me and doesn't even know it. "Mason," I say. "Just call me Mason."

"Okay."

I nearly smack my head on the doorjamb, trying to get the hell out of my bathroom and away from her after that. Jumping out of the window wouldn't get me out of this building fast enough.

Jesus Christ, what's wrong with me?

"Mr. Finch." The doorman in the lobby opens the glass entrance for me. "Nice to see you again."

I wave without even looking at him and rush outside. Only then do I suck in fresh, warm air and actually *breathe*. Car, car, where's my —

Dropping into the driver's seat, I tug on my tie. It's too tight. Everything's hot and tight and —

"Yes, sir." Leah's voice assails me even when she isn't around. My dick's hard again and pinned down in my pants.

Glaring at the clock, my heart pounds because I've got twenty minutes to get to my meeting. That's not enough time to run back up there and ask her to dinner. It's definitely not enough time to convince her to let me fuck her. And I can't jack off again because I'll make a mess all over my suit.

Drive, Mason. You're not here for a good time. You're here to get your life in order.

I've got twenty minutes to get it together.

But first, I'm going to schedule Leah to come back and clean again as soon as possible.

Chapter 3

Leah

"So, there I was, cleaning and singing my ass off, with no clue I still had on the whiskers."

Mak laughs so hard at my misfortune that she practically falls on Carson.

I stuff a breadstick in my mouth and talk around it. "I'm glad my pain amuses you."

"More wine?" the waiter asks. Don't think it's escaped me that this dude's staying close enough to hear my dramatic tale of house cleaning.

"Yes. Thanks." I snag my glass and hand it over.

Carson leans back and crosses his arms over his chest. "I'm still stuck on the peanut butter part."

"It was a *grand*, including the tip!" Mak tips her head up and stares at the ceiling. "I'd slather molasses on my ass and make choo-choo train noises for that much cash."

Carson lifts his brow. "I'd pay double."

"Sold!" Mak claps. "Show starts at midnight, Big Boy."

Carson shakes his head and chuckles before bringing his attention back to me. "How did you get it all out from between your toes?"

I lean in with my shoulders slumped. "It took forever, man. That shit's not easy to get off and it leaves an oily residue, so I had to wash my ankles and feet like *ten times* before I could go to work. It took an entire container of sugar scrub to get it all off."

The server hands over my full glass. "Thanks." I wait for him to leave and when he doesn't, I flash a huge cheesy smile and make it awkward. He finally gets the hint and walks away, thank God. "So anyway, that's why I didn't get out of my full makeup. It just slipped my mind. Then there I am, at the condo for my first cleaning of the day, wondering why the doorman was acting so weird when he saw me."

Mak's eyes light up. "Ohhh, was it the fancy condo with the ten-person marble shower and disco lights?"

"No. It's the condo with the guy who's never there." I drain my glass halfway. "I'm just jamming out, you know, minding my biz and doing my thing, and I go into the bathroom and scare the absolute *shit* out of myself when I see my reflection with those damn whiskers."

Mak cackles, and I swear everyone in the restaurant turns to stare at us.

"This is the best story *ever*," she says.

"It gets worse."

Her eyes widen. "How can it get worse?"

Part of me doesn't want to tell them the whole story, but Mak's my best friend and, honestly, Carson's just as close to me now. If anyone gets to share my pain, it's them. "The client was home, and I didn't know it."

"Oh noooo." Mak covers her face. "Tell me he's hot, single, and loves bunnies."

"He's hot and huge and..." The rest jams in my throat because it's like talking about that guy has summoned him from the lost city of Atlantis. My entire body freezes as Mason Finch saunters across the restaurant and over to a table in the back corner.

"Leah," Mak says cautiously. "What's wrong?"

My mouth waters. I can't pull my eyes from him. My jaw drops. When Carson and Mak both turn to see what's enraptured me, I hiss, "Don't look!"

Mak doesn't listen. "Who are we not looking at?" she whisper-yells back.

Carson sighs. "I have a feeling Mr. Hot and Huge is here, isn't he?"

"Yup."

"I don't think he sees us," Mak whispers.

Carson places his hand on her head and turns her back around. "You're being obvious."

To prove Carson right, Mason takes a seat and looks right at me from clean across the restaurant.

This can't be happening.

"Oh shit. He's looking at you, isn't he? Your cheeks are turning bright red."

I want to die.

Mason's gaze lingers for only a couple more seconds, then it drifts around the rest of the room and falls to the table setting. He's got a drink in his hand already, and as he sits alone, he runs his finger along the rim of the glass.

Throughout dinner, I keep flicking my gaze over to him. I can't help it. He's just so pretty.

And looks so lonely.

"Would anyone care for dessert?" The server pulls out his pen and pad. "The tiramisu is incredible here. As are our gelatos."

"I'm stuffed." Carson rubs his belly. "You ladies want something?"

Mak wipes her mouth with a napkin. "No, I can't put one more thing in my body."

"Pity," Carson mumbles playfully.

"Just the check, please." I grab my purse to dig out my wallet.

"It's on me, Leah."

Of course, Carson would want to pay. He does whenever we go out. "Can't I pay just this once?"

"Nope." He takes the bill from the waiter before I have the chance.

My gaze drifts back to Mason one more time and my stomach drops when I see he's no longer sitting there. Where did he go?

A few minutes later, Carson escorts Mak and I out of the restaurant. I never feel like a third wheel with them. They're family to me. But it makes me almost wish I had someone to go home with every night.

I said *almost*.

I'm not really a relationship kind of girl.

Valet brings Carson's car around first, and I give them both a hug goodbye. Standing at the curb, I smooth out my dress and dream about how great my bed's going to feel when I crawl into it. It's been a long day and I'm ready for it to be over.

This is definitely a double bath bomb, hottest-water-I-can-stand in the tub kind of night. I've earned it.

"No more whiskers?" asks a man behind me.

I spin around to find Mason with his hands in his pockets and a sexy smile plastered on his face. God, he's gorgeous. Jet black hair, stormy grey eyes, clean shaven, sharp jawline. This man's the epitome of main character energy in a romance novel. My brain immediately fills in the image of what's under his three-piece suit.

The vision of his abs and dick this morning is going to live rent free in my head for life.

"Ummm. Ha. Ha. Nope, no whiskers."

"That's a shame. They looked adorable on you."

I'm good at spinning things around to make

me more, or less, the object of attention. "Nice suit. I see you left the towel at home. That's a shame. It looked so good off you."

Wait, that's *not* what I meant to say! My brain, pussy, and mouth aren't on the same page. There's been a miscommunication. A glitch. I need to back away, or maintain professionalism, or at least play hard to get for crying out loud. "Come here often?"

Fuck. My. Life.

Why am I botching this so badly? And where the hell is my car, damnit? This valet guy sucks.

Mason stands next to me, almost brushing my arm, and a wicked little smile plays on his mouth. "Unfortunately, I don't come anywhere often."

"Only when you're alone in your room," I mumble under my breath as I face away from him.

Yes, I heard him jerk off earlier. I couldn't help myself! Besides, I swear he was being loud in there on purpose. It was almost like he wanted me to hear him.

Okay, fine, I might have peeked too. Not that he noticed. Mason was so caught up in his orgasm, he blew his load all over the place and let me tell you, it was molten lava hotness to watch. I've been wet from it all day.

So when he came back into the bathroom, I immediately felt like a criminal who got caught.

It made me panic. Apologize. Get desperate. I'm just glad it all worked out, and he didn't have a clue I spied on his self-love moment.

Except now I feel like I've violated his privacy and part of me feels terrible about it.

Not enough to out myself, though. Fuck that.

After Mason left the condo and I straightened his barely touched bedroom. There were ropes of white across the front of his dresser and faint wet spots on the carpet too that he must have missed while cleaning up. Or maybe he hadn't cleaned any of it up and left it there on purpose for me to find. Thinking that was a likely possibility also had me hot and bothered all day.

He frowns. "Alone in my room?" Then it dawns on him.

My cheeks blaze because I know I shouldn't have said that. I also shouldn't have watched. And I definitely shouldn't have relived it on repeat all day long.

"You saw me." Mason's not asking.

I can't tell if he's insulted, embarrassed, or worried, so I send the conversation in another direction again. "If I didn't know any better, I'd think you were following me."

One downside to being a camgirl is that I have to be extra cautious of who I let into my private life. I've never had a problem with a stalker online, but sometimes I think it's just a matter of time before I do. I wear costumes and exaggerated makeup to keep myself safe. My identity is concealed, my name is fake, my hair is fake, my personality is fake.

What Mason saw this morning was the real Leah. The goofy, loves to clean, sings too loud, dances too crazy, big personality *me*. I'd have put on my best professional smile, spoken respectfully, and kept my head down and done my work if I'd known he was there when I came in this morning.

Jesus, how often do I fake who I am just to get through the day?

To make it worse, I'm flirting with him. A client. A man who, many might say, is way out of my league. And I can't seem to stop.

There's a chemistry here I want to explore.

Besides, he approached me first. That must mean he feels it, too.

"I could say the same about you." Mason flashes another heart-stopping grin. "Maybe you followed *me* here, Leah."

"I was at this restaurant first."

"How do you know I wasn't at the bar when you walked in?"

Fair point. "Were you?"

He shrugs. "Maybe we were at the same place at the same time."

Possibly. Okay, probably. "You booked me again for next week. Why?"

Earlier today, I got a notification saying Mason scheduled another cleaning. My calendar is packed every day, and he's booked me for this coming Saturday. I still need to accept the job or decline it, and if I do the latter, it'll bump him to another maid on the roster. I haven't decided what choice to make yet.

"How long have you worked for the cleaning company?"

"Five years." Why would he care? "You were actually one of my first clients."

He nods and stares at me like he's calculating something. It makes me twitchy. Then his gaze drifts down my body and back up. "What else do you do, Leah?"

"Excuse me?"

"You're carrying a five-thousand-dollar purse from Dolce and Gabbana."

"So?"

"You aren't making that much on a maid's salary."

"First off, fuck you for assuming I don't make bank cleaning." He, for one, left me a gigantic tip on the kitchen counter this morning. *Probably so I don't tell everyone about his huge dick.* "And second—"

"They pay you thirty an hour."

He looked it up? Nosey weirdo. And now I feel defensive. "I got it on sale."

Mason doesn't relent. "What else do you do, Leah?"

"It's not your business."

How the fuck did we just downward spiral

so fast? Time to turn the tables. "What do *you* do, Mason Finch?"

He has the audacity to laugh. "Don't act like you don't know."

What the hell does that mean? "I don't." And his arrogance and nosiness are getting on my nerves.

The valet finally shows up with my car and hands me the keys. "Have a good evening, Miss."

"Thanks." I need to get out of here, ASAP.

"Hold up." Mason rushes forward and takes my hand. "We're not done talking yet."

"Yes, we are." Snagging my hand away, I look him up and down. "Have a nice night." I can't get into my car fast enough.

"Leah, please wait!"

Against my better judgment, I halt with my head down and hand on the door handle.

His footsteps get louder the closer he gets. "I'm sorry."

"For what?"

"Prying."

Good. He should be. "What's it matter what I do?"

"It doesn't." Mason's expression softens. "I just want to know everything about you and I'm too direct for my own good sometimes."

And too observant. "How the hell did you know how much my purse cost?"

"Because I bought my sister the same one in red for Christmas two years ago."

Oh. I'm only slightly less annoyed now. "Well, have a good night, Mr. Finch."

"Wait." He steps closer. "Let me take you out to dinner."

"I just ate."

"What about tomorrow night?"

I'm flattered and extremely tempted to take him up on his offer. "I'm busy."

"Breakfast?"

His persistence makes me laugh.

"Coffee?" He sounds hopeful, even as I get in my car. "Cocktails? A movie?" He talks faster. "Craft fair? Deep sea diving? Wait, do you like baseball?"

A laugh bubbles out of me. He's adorable. "See you around, Mason." I drive off with that luscious man in my rearview mirror.

I can't believe he looked me up like that on the cleaning site.

"I just want to know everything about you," he'd said.

Well, two can play this game.

Chapter 4

Mason

I'm a fucking idiot. Why couldn't I just let things develop naturally? I think it's my delivery. Spending my whole life barking orders and asking direct questions—because time is money and I have a lot of one and little of the other—I think I've become desensitized on how to woo a woman.

God. Damnit. This is why I don't date.

I've never had a real girlfriend. Any romances I've had were brief, surface-level quickies offering temporary relief to a stressful life. And those trysts were secret, which is a joke because there are no secrets in my social circles. Only deals, lies, leverage, and affairs exist in my world.

Leah's a fresh shot of adrenaline in my long dying soul. I love how vibrant she is. How quick she can recover from an awkward situation. Her confidence really gets my blood pumping and the fact that she holds her ground and doesn't seem easily flustered is intoxicating. It's not every day you meet a woman like Leah, and I've barely scratched the surface.

Our both being in the same place tonight was purely a coincidence, but I had been sitting at the bar earlier, waiting for a table to open up because I hadn't made reservations. Then Leah walked into the restaurant, and it was like the entire establishment held its breath in awe of her.

Her little black dress hugged her body that had, earlier this morning, been concealed in her oversized T-shirt. Her tits swelled out of the top, the stilettos that I'm dying to feel dig into my back and ass defined her leg muscles, and then she sat down like a motherfucking queen and captivated her audience with some kind of animated story.

Leah's mouth moved a mile a minute, her hands flying around as she talked, her thighs showing so much decadent skin when she crossed and uncrossed her legs that it should have been criminal. I spilled my fucking bourbon all over my tie when I took the first sip because I couldn't get my brain to function properly with her in my orbit.

I wasn't the only one looking, either.

The bartender and two waiters—including the one who served her table for the night— drooled over her. I loved it. I enjoy when someone admires something I have.

Except I don't *have* Leah.

And though my mind raced with fantasies about how to make her mine, my ears strained to hear even one sentence of her story, seeing how enraptured her friends were as they laughed hysterically. But I was too far away to catch any of it. Even her server couldn't drag his sorry ass away from her tale.

This woman can captivate her audience with expert skill.

I like that. A lot.

Now I've likely blown my chance with her before I even got out the gate. She rejected me so fast I'll likely never recover. Or maybe not. I mean, I did make her laugh. And I saw her smiling as she looked back at me in her rearview mirror. Maybe she wants to be chased? Shit, maybe she'll go home and rethink her answer. She knows where I live, so the ball is in her court.

"Your car, Sir."

I stare down at a scrawny valet attendant holding the key to my Maserati. "On second thought. I'm not finished here." Handing him a hundred-dollar bill, I clap his arm. "Keep it close. I'm heading back in for a bourbon."

Hopefully, another drink will help take the edge off my growing tension. I'm not ready to go back to my empty, boring condo, and I sure as shit don't feel like driving around the city looking for something to do.

My cell vibrates in my pocket as I walk through the door and head to the bar. I can only imagine who this might be or what they want from me. What I wouldn't give to chuck my phone in a trash can and never answer it again, but that's not how rich people maintain being rich.

One glance at the screen has me groaning before I answer. "What is it, Grace?"

"Mom wants to know if you're still buying a table for the gala."

"I always buy a table." This is a manipulation tactic. I just can't tell if it's Grace's doing or my mother's. "I'm sure my secretary sent the check already, correct?"

"Oh yeah, yeah. But Mom wants you to fill the table this time. *And* show up yourself."

I drop onto a bar stool and flick my finger to catch the bartender's attention. "I'm busy that night." I don't even know when the damn thing is.

"Don't be an asshole, Mase. She's still mad about you-know-what as it is."

"Good. That makes both of us."

"*Mason.*" Grace sighs heavily, as if I'm the problem here. "Come on. This is an easy way to get back onto their good side."

Her words make my chest tighten. Grace will bend over backwards for our parents, and so will my brother. But I'm the black sheep of the family because apparently wanting things and getting them on my own is disrespectful and rebellious to the family name.

"For me?" She asks in a sweeter tone.

Pushing back on my family is instinct, but I always cave for Grace. "Fine. I'll come. When is it?"

"At the end of the month."

I hang up before saying something I'll regret. My mother is such a piece of work. If she thinks I've forgotten our little argument where she called me a disgrace and biggest disappointment in her life, and is now trying to use Grace to get me to step one foot back into her web...

It's worked.

"Fuck my life." Burying my face in my hands won't hide my shame, but it helps keep my temper under control. I hate that I knowingly let myself just get played.

"What can I get for you?"

A one-way ticket off this planet would be nice. Sudden exhaustion has me glancing up slowly. "Old Fashioned, please."

Today was absolute shit. First, my meetings were rough, then dinner alone, then rejected by the most gorgeous woman in the universe, and now I'm roped into attending a gala I have zero interest in.

"I'm telling you it was her," says someone behind me. "Had to be."

"No way," argues another person.

"She was talking about putting peanut butter on her feet for a grand!"

My ears perk up.

"So? That proves nothing."

"It proves she's in the business."

"No, it doesn't. You're delusional. That woman looked too old to be Daisy Ren."

"Anyone can look young in bunny ears, wigs, and makeup. I swear to you, that's her. They have the same big eyes."

I glance over my shoulder to see two young men staring at a cell phone as they debate.

"Her tits look the same. That's about it."

"Same pretty mouth, too. Daisy's stunning. That woman was her. No way it wasn't."

Now they have my full attention.

"You're just crushing so hard you see her everywhere you go. Time to touch grass, man." The waiter pats the other guy on the shoulder. Then he looks at me and blanches as if they've just been caught watching porn in church. "Come on, table five needs a fresh bottle of champagne and thirteen needs appetizers brought out."

They split off just in time for my drink to show up.

One sip.

Two sips.

Three sips and I'm looking up *Daisy Ren* on my cell.

Annnnd spit that third sip out in a spectacular spray of smoked citrus rind and top shelf bourbon.

Hello, Leah.

I can see why they were arguing. The woman staring back at me online has purple contacts, pink hair with matching bunny ears, and a corset that lifts her ample tits nearly up to her chin. She looks barely legal. But there's no mistaking her mischievous smile. It's the same one Leah gave her friends earlier during dinner.

It's the same one she gave *me* when she turned me down.

Fuck me running, this woman is hot in every way. From the over-sized T-shirt this morning, to the knockout cocktail dress tonight, to this crazy fetish outfit on her profile pic—there's no denying she's a smoke show. The longer I stare at her big doe eyes, the harder my cock gets. Bet the lip gloss on her pouty mouth is fruity flavored and would leave a nice pink ring around the base of my dick as she sucked me off.

Before I realize what I'm doing, I'm halfway out the door, stuffing my phone in my pocket.

The valet still has my car parked out front, and I stuff another fifty in his hand as I snatch the keys from him.

"Have a great night, Sir!"

I plan on it.

The drive home takes me ages instead of the normal fifteen minutes. I barrel into my condo, rip off my suit jacket, loosen my tie, and drop down at my desk so I can see my beautiful creature on the biggest screen I have.

Signing in with a fake name, I pay the top tier price on her site without batting an eye. She's not charging enough for the privilege of looking at her photos, let alone have a live chat.

Part of me hopes seeing Leah in action, just this once, will scratch the itch I've developed today.

The other part of me worries this is only the beginning of a new obsession.

Chapter 5

Leah

Tossing my purse on the couch, I kick off my heels and strip out of my dress as I stumble into the bathroom. I'm exhausted. Geez, even taking a bath feels like more effort than I want to give tonight. But I know how good it'll feel to soak my bones, so I turn the faucet on anyway, add a bath bomb, and light a couple candles.

You know what would make this better? A good audiobook. A smutty, funny, no major drama story to lighten me up. Except I'm fresh out of those and don't feel like online shopping for a new one.

I'm a mess.

The entire way home, I couldn't get Mason out of my head. I can't believe he looked up what the cleaning service pays. But the madder I try to get at his prying questions, the less it seems to matter. I think it's because he wasn't shaming me or talking down about my career choice. Instead, he was trying to figure out how I got money for a purse and practically begging for a date.

That's weird. Right?

After soaking in the tub for a few minutes, my self-control breaks, and I grab my phone. "Okay, Mason Finch. Let's learn about you and what *you* make per hour, fucker."

Google pulls up articles and images and I sit up so fast water sloshes out of the tub. Holy shitballs. Photo after photo after hot, professional photo flood my screen. The more I scroll, the hotter they get.

"*Mason Finch, founder of BanditFX, makes new waves in Big Tech.*" Words blur because I'm scanning the article too fast. "*Mason Finch breaks barriers with his innovative security...*" Holy crap. "*BanditFX lures best in the tech world to Finch's door with unmatched salaries...*"

My heart pounds in my chest as more photos with Mason smiling at the camera pop up. My god, does he not have a bad angle? Some pics are of him with a group of stuffy looking older people. Another is of him handing an award to someone. Or maybe he's getting the award, I can't tell. And there's another where he's shaking hands with —

"Is that Henry Cavill?" Holy crap, it totally is.

A few more swipes and I'm down a Mason Finch rabbit hole where I learn that he's not only a die-hard Red Sox fan, but that his great-grandfather on his mother's side was an oil tycoon in Texas. His father's family is in law. His mother's name is Scarlet. His dad's name is

Thomas. It looks like Mason also has a brother, Jackson, and a sister named Grace.

Before I can deep dive and go into full stalker mode, a notification pops up on my screen from the site my sexy persona makes bank on.

A bunny's work is never done, am I right?

Clicking on it, the app opens and brings me directly to the chat room I have set up for my online fun times. Hey! I got two new top tier patrons today. Sweet! For as tired as I was ten minutes ago, I'm now energized—thanks to snooping on Mason.

I don't know what that says about me.

Going into the chat group, I post a few winky faces and type, *How about a quick live in thirty?*

I set my phone down and lean back, listening to the dings go off as some of my patrons get online and respond. They're used to my sporadic lives, so this is nothing new to them. After I've finished my soak, I dry off and get to work.

Instead of going heavy with makeup tonight, I put on a black, half-face mask that's got long, straight bunny ears attached to it. The bottom of the mask reaches the tip of my nose and is made of a soft, leather-like material. It covers enough of my face that I don't have to worry about being identified, and all I really need to complete the look is lipstick.

Snagging a black silk robe from my closet, I

tie it in a way that lets some of my cleavage show enough to make them thirsty for more. Then I sit in my chair with ring lights aimed at me.

Shit, I forgot lipstick! Running a deep red color over my lips quickly, I open my laptop and log in.

"Hi," I say in a flirty, cute voice. "What is everyone up to tonight?"

Seven patrons are logged in already, which is pretty decent for a last-minute thing like this. Oop, another one just joined. Avatars pop up as they fill my chat with compliments and flirtations. Two have already sent me kisses, which are ten bucks a piece.

Ty407: "No plans tonight, Daisy?"

"Nope," I lean back and squirm in my chair. "I'm enjoying a quiet night all by myself." I twirl my hair around a finger and make a pouty face.

Mr. C: Awww. I'd keep you company.

"I've been so busy today. It's nice to just..." Leaning back, my loose robe shows off a little more skin around my collarbone. "Relax, you know?"

Keeping the giggles and teasing going for another ten minutes, I talk about mediocre bullshit and ask them if they like my new lipstick, even reapplying it so they can get a good look at my mouth. "Mmmm, this needs lip gloss. What flavor should I do?"

They eat this shit up. These guys love picking lip-gloss flavors, even if they never get to taste it.

"Watermelon? Okay." I pump the tube of lip gloss suggestively before slathering it on my bottom lip. Then rub it in and pucker for them. "Mmmm, how's that look?"

I've had no less than ten more kisses fly across the screen. A hundred bucks for putting on lip-gloss? That's the definition of working smarter, not harder.

Another notification pops up on the right side of the screen.

X would like a private chat. Do you accept?

Hmmm. This is one of the new patrons that joined today. I really don't have the energy to give him my best, but I also don't want to lose him so soon by declining. Rejecting one man today was enough.

"Well, guys, this little bunny needs to go to bed. Thanks for keeping me company. Good night." I blow the camera a kiss and log off the live chat screen. Yawning, I accept X's request.

The only thing that shows up on the screen are his legs in black suit pants. He's stretched out on what looks like a white couch.

"Hi." I lean back in my chair. "You're new."

X: You're gorgeous.

"Aww. Thank you." I cast my eyes down for a moment, then look back at the camera sheepishly again. "How was your day?" I have no clue yet how shy this guy is, or if he just likes anonymity. I also don't know if he likes a confident or meek woman. I'll figure it out.

X: Busy.

"Ugh, life gets so exhausting, doesn't it? Always go, go, go with no time to take a deep breath and just... *be*." I sigh loudly.

X: Long day for you too?

"Yes. I'm always running around for work. It's nice to just be home."

X: You should get in bed. Relax a little. You deserve it.

I really like when someone gives me orders in the bedroom. Part of me melts because I don't have to think. I just do. But Daisy Ren can't afford that luxury. I only give the illusion that I'm submitting to what they want me to do. I'm still forever on guard and steering conversations where I want, though. It makes conversations like this tedious because I'm constantly running a million situations in my head to improvise our interaction in a way that benefits me more than them.

But sometimes, I just want to let go. Give in. Obey like a good girl.

"Mmmm." I stretch my arms over my head and arch my back. "Getting in bed sounds soooo good."

I don't normally leave this room, but occasionally I've taken a patron into another part of my house. It makes me more personable and easier to converse with, even though I don't like how they get to see more of my personal space.

But sometimes the littlest things turn into a deeper connection. And sometimes those deeper connections turn into big cash rewards.

A guy once paid two hundred dollars to watch me clean dishes in just an apron. Another wanted me to play video games with him while dressed in my pink glitter bunny outfit and paid me a grand for it. And plenty pay for me to talk dirty to them while they get off on just seeing me squirm in my chair.

I have mixed feelings about it. On one hand, I like the power, control, the exchanges we have. I like being watched and enjoyed. Sometimes I pretend to use a vibrator to get off with while they're jerking themselves. But they never see the action on my end. I haven't gone that far yet.

And part of me wants to, really bad.

Exhibition kink? Yeah, I have one.

Voyeurism? *Definitely.*

It's been a strange, self-discovering journey over the past couple of years. Sadly, I haven't found a partner to have fun with. It's not as easy as one may think. Lots of people like almost getting caught.

I *want* to get caught.

There's been a few opportunities to join a sex club, but I keep chickening out. For someone who's so bold with everything, I've really backpedaled on diving into the kind of sex I like.

I fell into this gig on a whim one night. Impulsive and frustrated, I dove headfirst into being a camgirl. Never thought I'd be good at it. I definitely didn't expect to like it so much either. The hint of intimacy is enough to satisfy my guarded heart. Plus, I get to see men come undone over something I do for them, which is so fucking addictive.

And lucrative.

No one's seen me fully naked online yet, but it's just a matter of time. If I can't find a way to boost my viewer's pleasure, I'll likely lose them because they'll get bored with me and move on to the next shiny toy.

That's a problem for another day.

"How about I take you to bed with me, X?" Holding my cell at eye-level, I walk away from my set up and over to my comfy queen-sized bed. My robe opens a little more as I climb onto the mattress, and I catch it just before one of my tits falls out. "Oops." Playing it off like it's an accident, I giggle and lay on my side, propping my head with my hand. "That's better."

X: Comfortable, Princess?

"Yes." I can't lie. Being called "princess" does something to me. "What about you, X?"

X: My dick's too hard for me to get comfortable.

Talk about straight to the point. I like his directness. Sometimes these warmup, teasing conversations get old. Especially when I'm dying to hang up and watch old reruns on TV. "Well, maybe we can do something about that." I bite my bottom lip. "Would you like a little relief?"

X: Yes.

"Slip those pants down for me."

The screen shifts as he obeys and suddenly the view of his ceiling pops up. "What next, Princess?"

The smile that spreads across my face hurts my cheeks. His voice is sexy as hell.

"You like being called princess, don't you." It's not a question, it's a confirmation.

"Yes."

"Good. Then that's what I'll call you. It's how I'll treat you too."

He's not the first one to make claims like that, so I let it roll off my back. "It's nice to finally hear your voice, X."

His deep chuckle makes my thighs clench.

Did I mention how sexy his hands are? They're big and veiny. Bet they'd feel amazing in my pussy.

When X pulls his dick out of his pants, it takes up the entire screen. My mouth waters with half-anticipation, half-dread. The only way I get through calls like this is imagining they're someone I like. Or worse, someone I'm attracted to. I've already painted this man as Mason Finch, which is terrible. If I screw up and call him the wrong name, I'm done for.

Jesus, why am I even considering liking Mason in the first place, much less fantasizing about him now? I really need to get my head on straight.

"What's going through that pretty head of yours, Princess?"

"Daisy," I say quickly. Then I clear my throat because I'm getting off track and need to separate my thoughts of Mason with the hot sounding dude on the screen. If not, I'll go all in tonight with this stranger and that's not how I saw my first online orgasm going. "How about you call me Daisy tonight."

"Whatever you want, *Daisy*."

Even the way he says my fake name sounds hot. I must really need to get laid if I'm fawning all over men today. "Let's relieve some of the stress you've built up, X."

"Will you relieve some of yours with me?"

Excitement skitters down my spine even as my heart pounds in panic. "Yes." This might kill three birds with one stone. I can make this guy happy, perform my first actual sex act online, and, in a roundabout way, get Mason out of my system. "Want to pick out a toy for me?"

"No. Use whatever you want."

I pout even though I'm relieved.

In my experience, guys don't normally have a clue what a woman needs to get off. Bless them for trying to learn, though.

Would Mason know how to make me come? I desperately want to find out.

Would he ever join a site like this? That's laughable. He doesn't strike me as the type to pay

47

so he can watch a woman act like I do on here. He probably has as many women fawning for him as he does zeroes in his bank account. And they're all probably just as filthy rich as he is.

"What's got you blushing, Daisy?"

"I was just…" *Thinking of someone who isn't you.* "Admiring the spectacular view, X."

When he places the phone on the side of the sofa, I can see a bit more of his waist and legs. His pants are down to his ankles, and his cock is huge and veiny. He rolls his sleeves up and my mouth waters. God, his forearms are yummy. Shadows dance across his lower abs, too. He's stacked. I seriously hit the jackpot with this man. He's so hot, maybe *I* should pay *him* for this chat tonight.

"I like what I see, X."

"Good." He spits in his palm and glides it along his shaft, running his thumb along the head of his dick. "You gonna make me play all by myself, Daisy?"

Hell to the no. This man's sexy with a capital S-E-X-Y. My pussy aches and feels all puffed out. I'm so turned on and needy, if I don't come soon, I might go loco.

Am I seriously taking this next step in the world of Daisy Ren tonight?

Impulsivity wraps around my throat, making it hard to swallow the truth.

Yes. I am.

Excitement cuts my nerves to shreds. When I go all in with something, I'm one-thousand percent in. Life's too short to have regrets. I'll make a million and one mistakes and have a blast until the day I die. I knew this day was coming. Why prolong it a minute more?

I grab a vibrator from the top drawer and prop the cell up so he can get a delightful view. Turning my toy on, I place it between my thighs. My pussy clenches immediately.

"That's my good girl." X says in a gruff voice. "I like a woman who goes for what she wants and doesn't play around."

My breath shudders out of me. Bet that's something Mason would say.

Stop thinking of Mason!

"I wish I was there between your thighs, Daisy. Licking that needy little pussy." X jerks himself in long, slow strokes while I watch. My mouth waters. "If you were mine, I'd have you riding my face every fucking day."

"I'd saddle up whenever you beg me."

"You'd be the one begging, Daisy." His hips thrust up as he fucks his hand. "I'll eat your pussy until you beg me to stuff my dick inside you."

Moaning, I run the vibrator over my clit. "Which hole would you stuff first, X?"

"Your pretty little mouth. I want that red lipstick to stain the base of my dick. Then I'd shove it in your cunt, stretch you, fuck you until you can't breathe. Then I'd pull out and work my way into your ass."

The vibrator and his filthy words are doing

a great job of bringing me closer to a release.

"If you were mine, I'd fill you with my cum and make you spread your legs so I can eat it out of your pussy."

Felching is definitely on my list of things I want to try. While X fills my ears with a dirty visual, my mind's painted Mason as the one doing it all to me.

"Do you want that, Daisy?" X growls. "Want me to cum all over you and lick it off?"

"Yes. God, yes." Slamming my legs together, I pin the vibrator against my clit with one hand and grip my pillow with the other. "Oh my god." I arch back and ride the long wave of pleasure until my thighs shake.

"That's my good fucking girl." His voice drips down my body like warm honey.

I climb out of my orgasm induced fog just in time to see X blow his load. Groaning loudly, he thrusts upward, and suddenly, his phone falls to its side and lands tilted towards the wall.

"Shit," he mutters, quickly flipping it over so the screen goes black.

I'm too stunned to speak. Too confused to move.

Holy moly, I think I've lost my mind.

In the time it took X to move his phone from the floor, I saw something hanging on the wall.

It's the framed, signed jersey Mason has in his living room.

Chapter 6

Mason

I've never paid for the privilege of coming before. My pride's torn in two about it. On one hand, that was the single hottest moment I've ever experienced with another woman. On the other, it was over too fast and likely faked on her end.

Once my phone fell over, I closed the chat before she could say another word and shot her two grand.

That's when confusion set in.

Did I pay my maid to make me come over the phone?

Did I get off on the slim chance that she actually orgasmed with me?

Am I really considering buying the site she uses just so I can own a piece of her?

Wow. I'm a dick.

The worst part about all this is the shame I keep waiting to show up. It's been a week since I had that live chat with Daisy Fucking Ren and still all I feel is desire to do it all over again. Humiliation and embarrassment haven't hit at all. Probably because I used a fake name, and she didn't see my face.

I'd never reveal my identity on a site like that. Shit, my entire social circle would keel over if they knew the kinks I have.

On second thought, maybe I should out myself and let them drop like flies. It would make my life so much simpler.

When I hear the elevator door ding, my focus doubles down on the business proposal I've been staring at for over an hour. I'm going to Hell for the shit I'm about to pull, but I can't help myself. I want to see if I can catch Leah's attention, and this is my piss poor way of attempting that.

My front door opens and in walks Leah with her cart of cleaning equipment. Instead of coming straight to me, like I fantasize, she heads to the kitchen first. I suck at playing pretend, so acting like I don't care that she's here isn't something I'm capable of.

Leah walks by the massive bouquet of daisies with her name on them that's sitting in the center of my kitchen island.

Hope inflates my chest until she ignores the display and keeps her back turned towards me.

That's irritating.

The sound of her cart rolling across the tile irks me, too.

Is my condo always this quiet in here, or is Leah's mere presence making it extra loud?

Pushing away from my desk, I make my way into the living room. Leah turns around and I'm not sure who's shocked more.

Her, seeing me. Or me, for what she's fucking wearing.

"Damnit, Mason!" Leah plucks her earbuds out. "You scared the shit out of me! *Again*. Are you trying to give me a heart attack or are you that much of a creeper?"

All I can do is stare at her.

"Hello. Earth to Mason." She waves her hands in my face. "What's wrong with you?"

"I should ask you that." I jab a finger at her outfit. "Tell me you only wear that abomination because you use bleach all day."

She smooths the jersey down over her phenomenal figure. "What? You're not a Yankees fan?"

My gaze narrows. "Don't even mention them in my house."

The smiles she's failing to hide cues me in that she did this on purpose. Which means she knows I'm a Red Sox fan. And the only way she'd know that is if she researched me.

My dick hardens.

"I'm in the middle of a good book, so I won't disturb you today with a concert, Mr. Finch." Leah grabs her dust rag and gets back to work like I'm not standing here with my jaw on the floor.

I zero in on her shapely legs. Is she even wearing shorts under that fucking jersey?

I don't want to know. I'll turn into an animal about it, regardless of the answer.

This sneaky minx thought she could ruffle me by wearing that jersey, and it's worked. Everything about this woman cranks my lust into high gear. I'm hungry for her. Starved.

Fuuuuck. Eating her would be so—

Nope. Don't go there, Mason. You just opened a door you need to slam shut and padlock.

Dragging a hand over my face, I count to ten and force myself to sit at my desk and get back to work. Leah has a job to do and so do I. She'll see the flowers I bought her soon enough. Maybe when she does, this pathetic game we're both attempting to play will end and the real fun can begin.

Minutes tick by and it gets harder and harder to sit still. She isn't in the living room anymore. Where has she gone? I strain my ears for any noise she'll make.

Stop being so desperate, Mason. You're better than this.

I used to have more patience than this. Fuck it. I'm going for her.

Pushing out of my chair, my heart jumps at the sound of glass shattering.

"*Leah!*" I run out of my office faster than lightning.

Chapter 7

Leah

This is karma.

While the narrators in my ear are having hot, enemies-to-lovers sex, I quickly crouch down and pluck the broken glass off the floor. Mason races into the kitchen, yelling something I can't hear thanks to how loud the volume is on my audiobook.

Pulling out my earbuds, I look up at him. "I'm so sorry." My voice shakes. "The vase slipped out of my hands when I moved it to wipe the counter. I'll pay for it to be replaced."

"Are you hurt?"

"No." I stare at the mess all over the floor. I can't believe I did this. "I'm so sorry, Mason."

"No, it's fine. It's nothing."

Nothing? There are probably a hundred gorgeous daisies in this bouquet, with *my* name on them, and he says it's *nothing*?

"Please don't touch it," Mason kneels down and tries to grab my wrist.

"No, no, I've got it. Really." Dodging his hand, I pick up more pieces. "Ouch!" A shard sticks into my palm.

"God damnit." Mason scoops me up in his arms and carries me out of the kitchen.

It happens so fast; it takes my brain a minute to catch up. My mouth takes even longer. "Mason, it's fine."

"You're bleeding. You're definitely *not* fine."

I think he's mad at me. Great.

I planned to fuck around with him possibly being X today, and even if he wasn't, I wanted to push his buttons just for fun by wearing this stupid jersey. I don't even like the Yankees. I just wanted to snag his attention. I wanted him to ask me out again so I can say yes, this time.

The more I thought about it all week, the more convinced I became that Mason was X. If that's the case, and he's cool with dating someone like me, I want to try. Just one night won't hurt. No feelings. No deep connection. No big plans. I just want to have fun with someone who might be into the same kinks as me.

One date. One fuck. That's it.

But seeing my name on a tag attached to that vase of my most favorite flower in the world stunned me. I picked them up to move them to a safer space, and that's when I saw the tag. The bouquet and vase were so heavy, it slipped out of my clammy hands and smashed on the floor.

This is definitely not *nothing*.

Now I'm in his bathroom and I have no clue

how to get out of this situation.

Mason carefully inspects my cut. With a steady hand, he plucks the small shard out and blood wells. "I don't think it needs stitches." Mason pulls his phone out and starts dialing. "I want it looked at by a professional, to be sure."

"No, it's fine." I'm not about to pay an astronomical medical bill just for a couple stitches. "Let me just—" I make the mistake of looking at the cut. Blood covers my palm. My legs give out and I see stars. My ears start ringing. My vision closes in.

"Oh shit," I hear him say before it's lights out.

• • •

My stomach rolls as I focus on the bright white ceiling. I'm no longer in the bathroom.

"There she is," Mason says, sounding relieved.

My gaze drifts until it latches onto his grey eyes. "What happened?"

"You fainted."

Mason looks like he's going to be sick, which alarms me. "Are you okay?"

"*Me*? You're the one who got hurt. I'm so sorry, Leah." Mason holds my hand to keep pressure on the cut. "If I hadn't tried to play games, this never would have happened. I should have just told you I was X."

His admission makes me feel a lot of things at once—relief, guilt, annoyance, confusion.

Lust.

Pulling the hem of my jersey, I admit, "I wore this knowing you were a Red Sox fan. I wanted to rile you up with it."

"Well, that's a relief. I was going to have to find a new house cleaner if you said you were a true Yankees fan."

His joke falls flat, and we both know it.

And though my hand stings, my pride hurts more. "How did you know I was Daisy Ren?" It's been a while since someone recognized me.

"I heard the servers at the restaurant talk about how you looked like Daisy Ren. So, I looked you up."

Shame digs its claws into my pride but doesn't last. Mason might know what I do for extra cash now, but he also just outed himself as the man who got off seeing me orgasm.

He's famous. I'm a nobody.

Which one of us would be in bigger trouble if our secret got out?

Mason rubs the back of his neck. "Did you know I was X the whole time?"

I shake my head. "I saw the framed jersey when you dropped the phone after you… came. I knew it had to be you."

He's as still as a statue next to me on the bed.

There's terror in his eyes. His face drains of color. He's probably reliving our session, remembering all the dirty things he said, how he jerked off in front of a camera, how he came so hard it splattered all over his crisp black pants and abs.

How he paid me for it.

The sex industry is a mighty large grey area. Where's the line separating flirt and a sex worker? How does a gracious tip become an actual payment? When does fake become real?

I crossed a line with Mason that night and neither of us can go back now.

Shitty thing is, I'm more scared for him than I am for myself. He's popular in a world I'm not part of. His name is everywhere.

"I won't tell, if you won't," I promise. "I'll sign an NDA if that makes you feel better."

His jaw ticks, and I look down at my lap. The towel around my hand has a little blood on it. At least my guilt has squashed the pain I was in.

A knock at the door has Mason standing fast, like he's been caught doing something he shouldn't. That hurts my feelings too. "I'll be right back." He marches out of the bedroom and comes back seconds later with another man. "This is my neighbor, Chase."

"Hi, Leah. Nice to meet you."

"Nice to meet you, too. I need to uhhh…" *Get out of Mason's bed.* "Get back to work."

"Stay still. Let him look at you." Mason puts his hand on my shoulder, gently pushing me back on the bed. "He's a surgeon."

How convenient.

"Let's have a look." Chase sits beside me on the bed. "May I?" He points at my hand.

I feel cagey. "I'm sure it's fine."

"Let's be extra sure, okay?" Chase carefully unwraps my hand. I look away because the sight of blood makes me queasy, and I don't want to faint again. "Can you make a fist?"

No problem.

"Good. Can you feel all your fingers?"

"Yes."

He tips my hand back and forth, examining it. "You cut it on glass, correct?"

"Mmm hmm." My cheeks heat because I feel Mason staring at me. This is awkward.

Chase frowns. "It's a bit deep."

Fear spikes in my system. "Does it need stitches?"

"Mmmmm. Given the location, I think butterfly closures will work. We can also glue it." Chase covers the gash with the washcloth. "Is this your dominant hand?"

"No."

"Good. Okay. I'll be right back with supplies." Chase leaves, and Mason and I stare at each other.

I don't feel the pain in my hand anymore. With him looking at me like this, I barely feel anything but the heat pooling between my thighs.

Without warning, Mason moves closer.

"Tell me to stop."

"S-stop what?"

"Stop thinking what I'm thinking."

"I don't know what you're thinking."

He leans in until we're dangerously close. "Yes, you do, Princess."

My thighs clench. He's right. I do. Because I'm thinking the same thing.

"He's coming back any minute," Mason says, half in warning, half in temptation. His hand slides up the back of my leg. It's like being set on fire. "Does it still hurt?"

I shake my head. "I can't feel anything when you're this close to me."

Did I just say that out loud? I must be in shock. It's the only thing that explains my sudden stupidity.

"You don't feel *anything*?" Mason's dark brow arches. "Not even this?" He leans down and kisses my inner thigh.

My stomach flutters. "N-no."

"What about... *this.*" He nudges my legs open and seals his mouth over my cotton shorts, blowing hot air on my pussy.

I shake my head. My eyes dart to the door. Chase is coming back any second!

"Hmmm." Mason slides my shorts and panties to the side and runs his finger along my exposed pussy. "What about this?"

"A little." I shrug as if it's not that big a deal. But inside I'm screaming. Every touch, every breath, every miniscule move he makes on me is amplified by the fact that we could very well get caught by Chase any second. My gaze flicks to the door again, then back at Mason.

His eyes glint with humor. "How about this, Princess?" He shoves his finger inside me and hits my g-spot on the first try.

I groan and glue my eyes on him.

"My girl likes to play games, doesn't she?" He hits the pleasure point over and over.

"Yes."

"Then let's play." He pumps into me faster. "This game is called, How many times can my girl come before we get caught."

My heels dig into the bed, and I open my legs more for him. It feels so good. So bad. So wrong. So exciting.

I don't know if I want to get caught or not, but I want to come.

"You're so wet, Princess. Does this excite you?"

Biting my bottom lip, I glance at the doorway and nod. Now I kind of want Chase to watch.

"Use your words."

My eyes roll when he adds another finger. "Yes."

"Yes, what?"

"Yes, Mr. X, Sir." I'll call him Daddy if he just keeps going. Holy shit, this is thrilling.

Mason fingers me faster. "He's coming

back, Leah."

"Don't stop." I grab his arm. "I'm so fucking close."

His wicked smile does me in. I hear the door shut as Chase enters the condo and my pussy clamps around Mason's fingers as I come. My mouth drops in a silent scream.

A second before Chase enters the room, Mason pulls out and I slam my thighs shut.

"Here we go." Chase rests a first aid kit on the mattress. "This will only take a minute."

"Take your time, Doc." Mason stands back to give him room and sucks his fingers into his mouth, down to the last knuckle. My cum is all over them.

I can't stop staring at him.

"It's already stopped bleeding, so that's good." Clueless about what we just did, Chase cleans the cut, and all the pain in my palm comes back three-fold.

"I don't feel good." My mouth fills with saliva.

"Look at me," Mason orders. "Eyes on me, Leah."

I'm not sure how, but the moment our gazes collide, I'm enthralled by him again. I swear I still feel his touch on me. Inside me. While Chase patches my hand, I sink into a daze while staring at Mason. He's a stunning specimen of a man. His expression shifts from worry to hunger to amusement to lust while I ogle him. I think he likes being my focal point.

"There we go." Chase closes his kit, and I finally blink, bringing my attention back to my hand. "Keep it clean and try to be careful you don't hit it on anything. It could bust back open if it doesn't have time to heal properly."

"She'll be careful," Mason says.

Chase smiles at me. Can he tell I just orgasmed? Did he hear me when I came? Is he playing it cool or really that clueless? "I take it you're a house cleaner?"

"Yeah."

"Wear a glove to protect it, okay? Don't let any chemicals touch it."

"She's not cleaning any houses while she's injured," Mason says, like he's my fucking boss.

I glower at him, the enthrallment spell broken. "I still have a job to do. And I'd appreciate it if you didn't speak for me."

Mason crosses his arms. "You're hurt. You're not working."

"It's all better." I wave my bandaged hand in the air. "I don't feel a thing."

Chase looks from me to Mason and back to me. "Okay, then." He gets up and clears his throat. "It was nice meeting you, Leah. Mason, any chance you can score me two tickets to the opera house this weekend? It's my wife's birthday."

"Consider it done." Mason might sound cheery, but he's scowling at me.

"Thanks, man."

Once Chase leaves, I climb out of bed so I can get back to work.

"Where the hell are you going?"

"To the kitchen." I blow out an exasperated sigh. "Then the office. After that, I'll do the two bathrooms and your bedroom."

"You're not cleaning my condo in your condition!"

"I'm fine!" I bark back. "And I have *two* more places to clean after this, so I can't waste any more time or I'm going to be behind for the rest of the day."

Flustered and still wet from my orgasm, I slip past Mason to head back into the kitchen.

He catches my arm and presses me against the wall in the hallway.

Mason's eyes bore into mine, setting my skin on fire. My palm thuds around my cut because my heart's racing so fast.

"You're too good at this," he growls. It doesn't sound like a compliment.

"I haven't even done anything." I'm not sure what he's talking about, but I can fake it until I figure it out.

"You're driving me insane."

Honestly? He's doing the same to me and I can't understand how.

"Good," I shoot back, quickly gathering my sensibilities.

Mason's eyes flash with indignation. "You

didn't tell me to stop."

I tip my head back and smile, too horny and reckless for my own good.

"You should have told me to stop, Princess."

"Why's that?"

"Because now I can't." He crushes his mouth to mine and pins my body to the wall.

Chapter 8

Mason

Every cell in my brain screams for me to back the fuck off and yet, when I kiss Leah, it's as if I've been shattered and my final form rises out of the broken fragments like a god.

Dramatic as fuck, yes, but this isn't just some kiss that hardens my dick.

It's a connection I feel from the base of my feet to the roots of my hair.

Leah's nails scrape my scalp as she takes over, and it makes my toes curl. Jesus Christ, what's gotten into us? Before losing what's left of my control, I gently place my hand on her throat and bite her bottom lip before pulling back.

Leah's flushed and gorgeous when she says, "Harder, Daddy."

The little air left in my lungs evaporates. "Fucking hell." I kiss her again, my restraint snapping like taut cords severed by a knife. Leah's that knife. "I want to fuck you."

I'll be careful so I don't accidentally break her cut open again.

"Take this fucking shirt off." I hate the

Yankees almost as much as I hate myself.

When I lift her shirt, Leah smacks my hands away. "Fuck me with it on."

Excuse me? I inch closer to her face, our mouths nearly touching. "I *hate* the Yankees."

She doesn't back down. "Show me how much."

This woman takes my aggression and turns it into an aphrodisiac.

Growling, I smash my mouth to hers again and we're both ripping her shorts down and getting my pants off. Suddenly, Leah hisses in pain and I jerk back. "Shit, are you okay?"

She looks down at her palm and I swear my dick deflates instantly. That my greedy goddamn nature might have caused her more harm makes me sick. Without saying a word, I pick her up and carry her over to the couch. I don't trust myself to put her back in my bed. "What can I do?"

"Nothing. I'm fine." Leah cradles her palm. "It just stings a bit."

My throat feels tight, and it's hard to swallow. I glance in the kitchen and realize there's still glass, water, and flowers all over the floor. I look back at Leah and see she's staring at me like a hawk.

"I'm torn between taking care of your needs and cleaning that mess up, so it's safer in here for you, Princess." Every time I call her that, she visibly melts a little.

"I'm perfectly capable of doing it myself,

Mason."

I know she is, but I don't want her cleaning up my messes. Leah cleaning my shower and mopping my floor suddenly sits badly with me, too. This insane urge to spoil and keep her is going to get us both into a heap of trouble.

I have to be careful.

"When is your next job?"

Leah's brow furrows. "You mean after I'm done here?"

She's done here already; she just doesn't know it. "Yeah."

"Two o'clock."

"Where?"

"South Side. At Sampson Hill."

One glance at my watch tells me she only gives herself three hours to clean my condo and get over to the other side of town. When does she eat? "Come on." I help her stand. "I'll take you."

"What? No. Mason, that's not necessary."

"Yes, it is. You're done cleaning here." The look on her face cuts me to the quick. Does she think I'm firing her? Shit. "It's not even dirty." She still doesn't look pleased. Is it the money she'll get for cleaning? "I'll still pay you for the allotted time, don't worry."

She yanks away from me and shoves me back. "God, you're such an asshole."

What the fuck? "What did I do?"

"You just throw money at everything like that makes it all better, don't you?"

"That's not what I was doing."

"You just said you were paying me for my time." She jams her finger in my chest. "I'm *not* Daisy Ren right now, Mason. You can't pay me to have your way and finish with a fat tip and think that makes me happy when it's really only to ease *your* conscience."

Hold up.

"I know you're not Daisy right now, Leah. And I'm not throwing money at anything to make you happy or ease my fucking conscience. I'm simply paying for the time allotted to clean my condo because that's business. And instead of wasting your time cleaning an already pristine home, I'm going to get you a nice lunch, drive you to your next two jobs, and help you because it's what I want to do."

She freezes. "*Help* me?" Leah has the audacity to look me up and down. "Help me how?"

"Clean, obviously." I give her the same look she just gave me, but Leah bursts out in this awful fake laugh that makes my blood boil. "What's so funny?"

"Something tells me, Mason Finch, that you've never scrubbed a toilet in your life."

She's right. "So?"

"Oh, my god. Just stop." Leah shoves past me and I let her this time because I don't want her falling or tripping and hurting herself more. Instead of marching out my front door, she heads back into the kitchen.

I barge in and snatch the broom and pan from her cart before she can get to it.

"Damnit, what is wrong with you?" She stomps her foot. It's fucking precious. "I'm trying to earn my living and I don't like handouts. Let me do my damn job."

"Sit," I growl. "And let me take care of this." Worried I'm coming off a little too dickish, I soften my next words. "Please, Princess?"

She looks at the mess, then back at me. "Fine." Leah pokes her finger at me. "But when you're done cleaning up in here, I'm finishing the rest of your condo on my own."

I don't like it, but I admire her tenacity. "Deal."

A half hour later, she's in the hallway mopping and I pull out the vacuum from my spare bedroom closet to start on the rug in my living room, even though she cleaned in there already.

Leah storms in with her hands up in the air. "What are you doing?"

"Practicing," I snap back.

She storms back into the bathroom, mumbling under her breath.

Damn, her ass is delectable.

The electricity between us is palpable. I think I like having her annoyed with me. My dick sure enjoys it.

Surprisingly, vacuuming turns out to be

quite soothing. I like the lines it makes in the carpet. The repetitiveness is calming.

Wow. I have no clue what this says about me.

New kinks unlock every day.

Not that this shit turns me on, but it is oddly satisfying.

A knot forms in my belly as I mentally tally all the maids my family has been through. Being nice to the help got me in trouble a lot. Psht, just talking to them got us in deep shit.

The household staff were to be silent and invisible.

So were us kids.

Leah giggles in the bathroom. Other than her giving me shit for vacuuming, she hasn't said a word since I cleaned up the kitchen floor. In fact, she'd stuffed her earbuds back in her head and hasn't even danced. I don't like that today's Leah is so different from last week's version.

She was so vibrant and carefree when she thought no one was around last time. Even as Daisy Ren, she's charming and sweet and fun and sexy as all get out. Today, however, she's different. Feisty and bossy but closed off.

I'm not a fan.

It's my fault. I know that. Still, I'm dying to see Leah in her natural state. What's her home like? What's her favorite food? Does she watch movies or read books in her spare time?

I know her kinks include almost getting

caught and being praised. She made that really fucking obvious. God damn, this woman has no clue what she's doing to me. The push and pull between us is driving me bananas.

Being around Leah is like landing in paradise after getting shipwrecked. Excitement, fear, curiosity, relief swirl in my gut. That's a red flag, right?

Fuck if I know.

She gasps in the bathroom and then cackle-laughs. Something warm blooms in my chest and I sneak down the hall to catch her leaning against my sink, her hands curled against her cheeks. This beautiful smile spreads across her face and she laughs again, cupping her mouth and shaking her head.

Then she catches me watching and her smile drops. Spinning around, she scrubs the sinks harder and really puts her back into it.

I lean against the door, enjoying the view. She likes cleaning. It's so obvious.

"What?" She pulls her earbuds out.

I didn't say anything, and I bet she knows it. This woman's testing me again. "No singing today?"

"Audiobook." She goes to put her earbuds back in, but I snag one from her.

"Hey!" Her hands rest on her ample hips. "You're gonna regret that."

Doubtful.

Pushing the earbud in, a man's deep voice

booms, " — *presses his cock against her wet pussy. I'm gonna fuck you so hard, my little cum dumpster.*"

My eyes widen with shock and Leah laughs so hard she holds her stomach and doubles over.

I can't believe she walks around with a straight face while smut pipes into her ears. "You've been listening to this for the past hour?"

"You just missed the good part where he had to prep her for his knot."

"His *what*?"

"Knot. It's this extra thing at the base of his dick that swells when he's about to blow his load."

Damn. That's... hot.

"I told you you'd regret—"

"Shhhh." I just missed the dude's next line. "I want to hear this."

I'll google what knots are later.

The next forty-five minutes pass by with both of us in different rooms, listening to the same story. We laugh at the same parts. I hear her squeal twice. My dick gets rock hard during this one scene where the hero bends his human mate over a boulder and rims her before fucking her ass with his tail.

"You ready?" Leah asks, pulling her yellow gloves off.

My dick's tenting my slacks and I'm all sweaty. Holy hell, I had no clue audiobooks were like this. Or that I'd be into whatever this genre is. "Yeah."

Leah heads over to grab her cart from the hallway. Chapter Fourteen starts up in my left ear as I rush to grab the cart handle from her. She's not wheeling this thing herself. Anything I can do to help, I will.

"This guy has the best voice, doesn't he?" She holds the door while I drag her shit out of my condo.

"Definitely."

Her gaze lands on my hard-on. It's easy to see in these pants. I love that she can't pull her eyes off it.

The door shuts, closing us in the elevator, and Leah blindly smacks the button for the lobby.

It only takes her three steps to reach me. With our gazes deadlocked, she closes the space between us and the narrator in our ears says, *"You make me crazy, you filthy little bitch. And I'm unhinged enough to fuck you until you can't walk away from me ever again."*

I lick my lips. Leah's gaze drags to my mouth.

Then she slams me against the back wall and kisses me.

Fuck. Yes.

While the couple in our ears fuck, we ravage each other in the elevator. Our hands are all over the place, groping, sqeeezing every body part we can touch. But the instant we reach the lobby, and the doors slide open, we break away panting.

My heart's in my throat. I feel lightheaded

and floaty.

What the hell is she doing to me?

Leah seems to know *exactly* how affected I am by her, because she's still blocking my way out.

"Turn around, Princess."

"Why?"

"Because I want to stare at your sweet ass while I fix my hard cock. I can't have it punching a hole through my pants for everyone in the lobby to see."

"Maybe they'd like to see it." Her eyes are lit with a fire that makes my cock twitch.

She looks down and gropes my dick, grazing her nails over the fabric of my pants and I groan. "Maybe you should tuck it," she says teasingly. "We wouldn't want anyone to trip over this massive thing and break their leg."

"That would be tragic."

Giggling, Leah turns around, but she's not big enough to hide my bulk. Not that I thought she would be. It's just a great excuse to stare at what I plan to fuck, lick, and worship later.

Chapter Fifteen starts up in our ears, but she pauses it on her phone. The silence makes all the regular noises seem like an intrusion on our fantasy. She steps out of the elevator first, and I follow, lugging her cart behind me. My dick's still hard, but that's not going to change. As long as I'm around this woman, I suspect I'll be in a constant state of *I-wanna-fuck-her*.

After loading her things in my car, I check the time. "We have forty minutes to get there. What do you want for lunch?"

"You," she teases with a wicked smile. This woman is wonderful for my ego. "But I'll settle for a Mexican bowl."

I hold the door for her while she slips into my passenger seat. The animosity between us has vanished. I still feel her kiss on my lips and my dick's dying for a turn.

"Start that audiobook back up, Princess." Revving my engine, I throw it in reverse. "I have to see how this all ends now."

"Ohhh you're invested, huh?"

"Yeah," I drag my gaze down her body. "I am."

Chapter 9

Leah

I have no clue what I'm doing with this man. Or what he's doing with me. This is beyond weird, right?

Why would a man like Mason Finch tag along with his housecleaner? The cut on my hand isn't *that* bad. I think we both overreacted about it. If he's feeling guilty for my accident, that would be silly. He owes me nothing. And I'm sure he's busy, so why waste time with me cleaning?

Staring at the dashboard to his Maserati Ghibli, I'm suddenly at a loss for words. The audiobook is still playing in our ears, not that I've heard a single word of it since we got on the road after lunch. I can't concentrate anymore.

Stealing a glance at Mason, I fall into a trance.

His profile is beautiful. Sharp angles, bold features—He looks like a Greek god. Jet black hair, dreamy eyes, perfectly sloped nose, sexy mouth, clean-shaven face, and stupidly sharp jaw line. He's main character energy all the way.

Ugh. Why do the worst ideas have the best jawlines?

Mason hasn't noticed me staring at him, so I don't stop. His broad shoulders fill out his button-down shirt nicely. His black suit pants hug his thick thighs, and that Rolex makes his skin look extra tan.

He looks like a mafia boss.

A billionaire boss man.

A luxury I can't afford.

Dropping my gaze to my lap, I'm painfully aware that I do not match his caliber of sophistication. I'm in a stupid Yankees shirt and cotton shorts that have a hole in one pocket and stains all over them. My black Converse have faded from years of use and I'm missing a gromet on one of the lace holes. I know in reality we're both from the same planet and put our pants on the same way in the morning, but...

We're not the same.

At all.

What is he trying to get out of this?

Is it foolish to think he's as attracted to me as I am to him?

Being a camgirl has jaded me. Many men only have the capacity to think with one head at a time. For Daisy Ren, it's the one in their pants. Is Mason different, or does he see a fun time and is taking advantage of it?

It would explain him fingering me before his neighbor came back.

It would not, however, explain my behavior when I made out with him in the elevator.

Stop it, Leah. You're overthinking. What happened to having all the fun with no feelings hookup? Just shut up and enjoy the ride.

Mason laughs, startling me out of my thoughts. "He shouldn't have done that."

Done what? I've fallen behind on the storyline of the audiobook.

"This guy's a real dumbass if he thinks he can bully her into that deal." Mason shakes his head in disappointment. Pulling into the parking lot, he slides into an open spot and turns the engine off. "What's a nest?"

"Huh?" I'm really struggling to focus here.

"They keep referring to a nest, but I don't get what that is."

A laugh escapes me, taking my anxiety down a couple of notches. "It's her own private space. Comfy bedding, lots of pillows. All kinds of cozy warmth and luxury piled around her so she can feel safe and relaxed."

He nods, but his brow furrows a bit. "So, it's like a blanket fort?"

"Sort of." I better get out of this car and back to reality. "Thanks for lunch and the ride, but you really don't have to stay."

"I'm helping you for the day, Leah. That's not up for negotiation."

Now I'm annoyed. "Why?"

We both hop out of the car at the same time.

"Because..." he says, slamming his door shut. "I like spending time with you."

That's not the answer I was expecting.

"Look, if this is about you being X online, privacy is just as important to me as it is to you."

"It doesn't bother me," Mason says. "Much." Popping his trunk, he digs out all of my stuff. "I like you, Leah."

He doesn't even *know* me. He probably can't even separate me from Daisy Ren. "Request another private chat if you enjoy my company so much."

Mason slams the trunk shut. "I'd rather take you to dinner."

"I'm busy," I lie. There's no way he's making the moves on me for real. We've just been pushing each other today for funsies because we both thought we had something on each other.

Dinner is *not* on the agenda.

"Breakfast tomorrow then." He flashes me a smile as he lugs the cart up to the front door.

"Busy then too."

"Really?" He holds the door. "Tell you what, how about I book you for every night you're not busy. Just tell me when and I'll clear my calendar for it."

I think he's serious. My heart actually swoons a little.

Nope. Nope. Nope. He's playing me.

"I'm busy every night." Blasting past him, I storm to the elevator and hit the up button.

"Every single night?" he asks suspiciously.

"Yup." I don't look at him. "For the rest of my life."

I thought I could handle a date with him, but it's too much. He's too easy to be around. Too fun. Too addictive. Those are red flags.

"Breakfast it is." Mason gets into the elevator with me. "I know a place that makes amazing omelets."

What a pushy little shit! "Jesus Christ, Mason. Why are you doing this?"

"Doing what?"

"This!" I wave my hands around. "The cleaning. The lunch. The dinner and breakfast. The *persistence*."

"I told you..." He leans into my face. "I like being with you."

"You don't even know me."

"That's why I was hoping we could go on a date." He slams his hand on the *close door* button and holds it. Then he presses into me until my body is flush against the wall. "Am I not your type, Leah?"

"Nope. Not at all." The breath that shudders out of me gives my lie away.

His toothy grin is so prideful I want to slap and kiss him at the same time. "Liar."

"It's true. You're too pretty for me. I like my men dirty."

"How dirty do you want me, Princess?"

Fuck. Me. He's too good at this.

"Ugh!" I shove him back. "Seriously, dude, you're a Big Tech Bagillionaire. Why are you pretending you're into me?" Then it hits me. "If you think that, all because you got a show online last week, you can rent me for a night to get in your bed, you're *very* mistaken."

He backs off immediately. "I'm not trying to rent you, Leah. I'm trying to date you."

Mason has the audacity to look stricken that I suggested he pay for the pleasure of my company. When, in fact, that's exactly what he's done.

Last week online. Today with cleaning.

"Go home, Mason." I cross my arms and look at the floor.

He lets go of the elevator button and the doors open. I don't waste another second breathing the same air as him, so I snag my cart handle and drag that dumb thing with me.

"Leah," he practically begs from where he stands.

It's the look of utter rejection on his face that has me stalling. Bet he's never been rejected by a woman before. Bet he's never been told to fuck off, either.

My mouth forms the words, but they cram in my throat. I don't know why I'm being such a bitch. I should see how far he's willing to take this with me. A Sugar Daddy was never something I worked towards securing for myself. This baby makes her own damn sugar.

But…*What if?*

What if he's being sincere?

What if he really does like me?

What if he ends up being a blast?

Either Mason is the biggest Try Hard Pick Me Boy on the planet, or he's genuinely trying to work his way into my life. Maybe I'm the one being a shithead here.

I shove my foot in the door to keep it from closing. "Why?"

"Why what?"

If he doesn't know what I'm asking about, then we're done here.

Just as I pull my foot out of the door and it starts closing, he says, "I've never felt more like myself with another person before."

His confession robs the air from my lungs.

Mason slams his hand against the door to keep it open a little longer. "I thought we'd have fun together. I thought maybe I was your type, and you're *definitely* mine. And I thought, today, given how sore your hand probably is, you could use a little extra help." He shakes his head. "Guess I was wrong."

The elevator door shuts before I can change my mind.

Chapter 10

Mason

My entire life has been a series of reports. From grades to behavior to budgets. I've also had my fair share of publicity. When I started BanditFX, I used my connections in social media to propel my goals into becoming one of the most sought-after tech companies in Silicon Valley. I treat my employees like royalty, their pay is unmatched, and I diversified quickly, getting into every branch of the cyber world I could reach. There are articles and photos of me all over the internet. I've made friends and I've made enemies. I'm not a celebrity by any means, but there's always some competitor out there looking for dirt to use as blackmail.

Dating is a nightmare. Not only do I suck at it, but I barely have time for a relationship.

It's probably a good thing Leah rejected my sorry ass. I'd want to give her all my attention, twenty-four-seven, and I'm not at a place in my life where that's possible.

Yet.

I truly thought we'd have fun together. I

thought I found someone who is into the same things as me. But now that I'm sitting in my car, alone, without any distractions, reality sets in.

If I date Leah, social vultures will ask around about her. If it gets out that I'm dating a camgirl, my business deals could go south because a lot of folks in my line of business look down on that shit. Others will take advantage of it.

My social circle will eat her alive. They'd treat her like trash, and I'd end up beating the shit out of them, which will make parties and family dinners awkward afterwards. My parent's opinions and actions are a moot point. If they discover I'm with a sex worker, they'd act faster than I can blink. My disownment has always been imminent. I just want to be the one who pulls the pin on that grenade, not them.

"Fuck my life." A migraine's brewing. Leaning back in my seat, I pinch the bridge of my nose and close my eyes.

What possessed me to think it was a good idea to focus on my nonexistent love life today?

This woman has possessed me.

I'm not willing to walk away yet. I can't. We have a connection, an energy, a *something*, and I need to see where it'll go. She feels it too. I fucking *know* she does.

Four hours later, my ass is numb and lower back aches, but all that pain vanishes the instant Leah steps out of the building with a cell phone in her injured hand. She looks right at me, her eyes rounding like full moons, and storms over to my car.

I step out to greet her.

"What are you doing back here?" Her tone's high and shaky.

"I didn't leave."

"WHAT?"

"I can't just leave you stranded, Leah. How would you get to your next job?"

Her brows dig down. "Mak, I gotta call you back."

"No way! Big Tech Dick is still there?" someone shrieks from the cell phone.

"You're on speaker, Mak," Leah growls through gritted teeth.

"Hanging up. Oh my god." The line goes dead while Leah and I continue glaring at each other.

"Big Tech Dick, huh?"

"Shut up." Leah jerks her cart forward. "We weren't talking about you."

"Sure, you weren't." My ego is preening. "Is that in reference to my personality or the actual size of what's in my pants?"

"Neither. We were talking about my date I have later tonight. Which is, one hundred percent, not you."

"Mmm hmm." I open the trunk and put her stuff inside. "So, you're dating my competition, is that it?"

"Yup." Leah smooths out her Yankees shirt. "And he's hot. So hot and funny and has big hands."

"Big hands." I bite back a growl because even though I'm pretty sure she's teasing me with this bullshit, the idea of another man having his hands on her makes me feel territorial. Leah's mine, even if she's refuses to admit it yet. "Bigger than these?" I slowly wrap my hands around her waist and lean her against the trunk of my car.

"Mmm hmm." Her cheeks turn bright pink.

"Does this hot, funny guy with big hands give you a better necklace than this?" I gently wrap one hand around her dainty throat while keeping the other at her hip. "Answer me, Princess."

Her lips part slightly, while her pupils blow wide for me.

"I thought not." Instead of letting go, I lean in until our mouths almost touch. "Do his hands feel better than mine when they do… *this*?" I trail my fingers up her shirt and graze my knuckles along her ribcage.

Leah lets out a shaky breath. "Fuck, Mason." Her fingers dig into my shoulders, but she doesn't push me back.

"Tell me to stop," I whisper. "Tell me to go away."

"Would you listen this time?"

Fair question. "I'd stop. I might even leave. But…" I nip the flesh above her collarbone. "I really fucking hope you let me stay for a little while." Dragging my tongue along the taut muscle in her neck, I love that her knees buckle.

Guess I found her weak spot.

"Let me help you with this last job," I say against her ear. "The faster we get done, the sooner I get to spoil you with dinner tonight."

"I thought it was breakfast tomorrow."

"And I thought you had plans for the rest of your life."

She whimpers when I suck on her neck again. "Fuck, Mason. Why..." I lick her again and blow hot breath against her skin. "Oh my god," she squeaks. "What are you doing to me?"

"Negotiating," I kiss her throat. "Begging." I nip her earlobe. The sun set twenty minutes ago, and the streetlights finally turns on around us. "Want me on my knees, Princess?" Before she answers, I sink down on the asphalt.

"Oh my God, Mason. *What are you doing*?"

I already told her. "Negotiating." I spread her legs open a little wider for me. "Begging." Lifting the hem of her shirt, I kiss her fluttering belly. "Say yes to me, Princess."

"Yes to what?" Her knees nearly give out again when I nip the inside of her thigh. Looking up, I catch her scanning the area around us. Is she scared of getting caught or hoping we will?

Bad girl.

"Say yes to me."

Leah gives in with a sigh. "Yes."

I nuzzle her pussy, inhaling her scent through the flimsy cotton shorts.

I wasn't lying earlier when I told her I've never felt more like myself with another person before. This is who I am. This is who I've always had to hide from the world. But Leah? She gets it. She enjoys the way the world spins around us, always threatening to catch us, forever keeping us on our toes.

We might run in different circles, but we're the same in at least one thing: Putting on a show turns us on.

I shove my finger into her cunt, making her gasp. "What are you saying yes to, Princess?"

"You." She tips her head back, enjoying my touch. "You and dinner. You and… fuck…" Leah arches to give me better access. "You… just you, X."

X. I can't say I hate her using that pseudonym for me. If anything, it lets me know when we're in a game or not.

"Does my dirty little Princess like getting finger-banged in public?"

"Yes."

"Yes, what?"

"Yes, X."

I rise to my feet and pump my finger into her harder. "Such a bad girl, getting off in the parking lot where she might get caught."

"Y-you'll get caught too."

I lean in and suck the sensitive skin on her

neck again. "I know."

"Mmph." Leah turns to putty in my arms. "I'm so close."

I add a second digit, stretching her out a little more, filling her up. "Don't be too loud. I'm not ready to share your screams yet."

Leah goes rigid an instant before her pussy clamps down on my fingers, squeezing them, pulsing with a vice grip. "That's my good girl," Christ, feeling how tight she grips me is gonna make me blow my load. "God… *damn*."

Once she's ridden her climax and melts against my car, I slip my hand out of her shorts and suck my fingers off.

"Holy crap, Mason." She holds her chest, catching her breath.

"Kiss me." I lean down. When she doesn't take my mouth, I arch my brow. "Please, Princess?"

My good manners pay off. Leah closes the tiny distance between us and our lips fuse.

My girl kisses me with her whole body. I can't explain it, but that's how it feels. She's heavy against me, her lips supple as they press to mine. Her arms wind around my neck and tits push against my chest. We inhale the same breath while our tongues twirl around each other.

I swear I'm floating.

Then she breaks away slowly, shaking her head. "This is crazy."

Not gonna argue with that. "But it's fun,

right?"

"Yeah." Her cheeks redden when she giggles. "Okay, Buster. We have one more house to clean."

"Then dinner," I re-confirm.

"Yup. But I pick the place."

My victory smile goes a mile wide. "Whatever you want, Princess."

Chapter 11

Leah

The third cleaning job is a disaster and by the time we finish, it's late and I'm exhausted.

Mason loads my cart and looks like he barely broke a sweat. He's rolled the sleeves of his white shirt up, displaying yummy forearms, and his neatly slicked back hair is all disheveled. Strands have fallen into his eyes, making me bite back the urge to run my fingers through it.

He stretches, lifting his arms over his head, and groans. "How the hell do you clean like this every damn day? My arms feel like rubber noodles."

I pass him a water out of my little cooler. "You get used to it."

"I can't believe this place was such a wreck."

"The family bought the house to have somewhere to stay when visiting their son in college. He uses it way more often than they do and throws massive parties here. I'd bet ten bucks his parents will be arriving tomorrow morning." Saying that much about another client feels like I've violated the terms of my contract with the cleaning service, but oh well. Mason just polished their sink drains and did a hell of a job getting dust bunnies and condom wrappers from under the beds, so he should at least get something for it.

"I honestly do not miss college."

Me either. "Where did you go?"

"Yale."

"Fancy."

Mason arches a brow. "Is that code for boring, expensive, and pretentious?"

"Nope. Just fancy. I went to Penn State." It might just be my imagination, but I swear it looks like he's trying to hide his surprise. Standing up, I brush off my shirt and grab the cart so we can finally leave. "What? Can't house cleaners have a college degree?"

He stares at me for a few heartbeats, all playfulness gone. "Why do you do that, Leah?"

"Do what?"

"It's like you keep digging around, poking to see if I'll say something rude about your line of work."

His accusation is like a punch in the gut. He's right. I have no idea why I keep doing it when he hasn't once looked at me like I'm gum on his shoe.

"Sorry," I say, quietly.

Mason grabs my hand, pulling me towards him. "Don't be sorry. Be proud."

"I *am* proud." It's just that sometimes I feel

judged for my choices. And I'm no longer talking about cleaning, but he probably doesn't realize that.

"You're a hard worker."

"So? Most people are when they have bills to pay. That's nothing to be proud about. I'm adulting. Whoop-dee-woo."

"I admire you, Leah."

That's laughable. "You admire me for scrubbing toilets and getting beer stains off couches? Not likely."

"Yeah, I fucking do. This isn't easy work, and it's never ending. But this whole time you've been busting your ass with a smile on your face. You were even more lively at my house last week. You love this job. You're great at it. And it's really underappreciated."

Taking a step back, I'm not sure what to say. He must read the look on my face because Mason doesn't stop there.

"Love what you do, do what you love. That's the dream, right?" He cups my face. "But that's not the only thing that's got me awestruck by you."

"What else is there about me you like so much?" *Please don't say my tits.*

"Your drive," his gaze drifts all over my face, making me feel admired. "You seem to live so unapologetically. From your day job to your night job, you know exactly who you are, what you like, what you want, and fuck all else."

He's right. I'll never let another person's opinion steer the path I carve for myself. I almost cave and tell him my ultimate business plan but go with, "I imagine you're the same way."

His hand drops from my face. "I'm getting there."

"You're filthy rich, Mason. You're already there."

But is he happy? I hate how my heart clenches worrying that he isn't.

I'm suddenly in memory overload, ticking off the things I've seen about him so far. His condo is empty. It doesn't feel like a home at all, just a glorified hotel room, honestly. He has no pictures of family or friends hanging on his walls. He ate dinner alone, in the corner, at that restaurant the other night. He's here with me now, when one may assume he has plenty of better places to be.

My gut twists with sadness.

"It's hard being elite, Leah. Everyone either hates you or uses you. You don't get genuine admiration or respect. It's all a façade so they can get something out of you."

Cold words said in a frigid tone.

"I don't want to get anything out of you," I say in a rush, though why I'm defending myself, I have no clue.

"I believe that." His tone warms. "And I'm not trying to get something out of you, either. I'm not trying to *rent* you." He says in frustration.

"I'm genuinely drawn to you."

I get what he means because honestly? Same. I can't seem to pull back from this guy. Even when I made him leave earlier, it felt awful, and I spent the entire time rage-cleaning because I was mad at myself for letting my insecurities get in the way of having fun. I called Mak and vented to her about everything, and she helped me pull my head out of my ass.

But when I saw him parked in the lot waiting for me after that?

Words cannot express my shock and relief. No matter how hard I try to mask my true feelings, there's a chemistry here I don't want to deny. Mason is too perfect for his own good. It's scary because I don't get attached. Having one-night stands is my mode of operation. This man? He's not one-night stand material.

I have no idea what he is.

My heart skips when he reaches over and runs his fingers through my hair. Then he pulls out something from my frizzy tendrils and smiles. "You have a dust bunny in your hair."

Blowing out the breath I was holding, I smack his arm. "Come on. Let's get out of here."

I smell like sweat, bleach, and glass cleaner. My head hurts a little. I'm tired. Mason's not much better. We drive home in utter silence, but it's nice. Comfortable.

"How about..." He pulls into his parking spot. "I draw you a nice hot bath?"

"I really should get home."

"You promised me dinner, Princess."

"Mason," I sigh. I'm too tired to put up a fight, and too tired to eat.

He shuts the engine off and looks at me with a warm smile. "You pick the place. I'll have it delivered. Deal?"

"I really should get going."

"Why?"

"I'm exhausted."

"Which is why I want to draw you a bath. I have this wild invention called a bed too, so when you're tired, you can sleep in that."

His offer is a little pushy, but his bed is bigger, and his tub is *definitely* better than mine. It's hard to resist those pleading eyes, too. "Okay."

We make fast work of loading the cleaning supplies in my car and then head up to his place. Mason doesn't say a word, but the slight smile curving his mouth is a dead giveaway that he's happy.

I've never had someone like me enough to go through everything he has today.

It's nice to feel special and worth the effort.

That's my fault. I never let a guy get close enough to put in the effort. What makes Mason so special?

"After you," he says, holding the door for me.

We head straight to the bathroom, Mason

leading the way. He starts the massive tub for me, adding bath salts from a glass canister into the running hot water. Next, he pulls the hem of my shirt up and over my head.

Annnnd throws it in the trash.

"You've been dying to do that all day, haven't you?"

"You have no idea."

Well, he's not the only one who's been dying to do something all day. Clutching the back of his neck, I smash my mouth to his while he unfastens my bra. This guy kisses with his whole being. It's deep. Rough. Thorough.

I could easily get addicted to it.

"You're so fucking gorgeous, Princess." He hooks his fingers around my waistband and pulls my shorts and underwear down to my feet.

When he stares up at me from his knees, I swear the whole world stops spinning for a moment.

Then he kisses my soft belly, and I dig my fingers into his hair, relishing how good his hot mouth feels on my skin. Mason works his way up my body, licking, sucking, and nipping. When he draws my nipple into his mouth, I arch into him. "You feel so good."

"You taste so good," he counters, licking his way up to the spot on my neck that drives me insane.

It's the only erogenous zone I think I have, and it makes me useless, embarrassingly fast. I groan while he alternates licking and kissing that spot on me. One more drag of his velvet tongue and my knees buckle.

"I've got you." He picks me up and carries me over to the filled tub. "Step in carefully."

My legs are still a little wobbly, but the instant I sink into the hot water, my body melts. "This is it. This is how I want to die." I lean back and sigh while Mason turns off the faucet. "What a glorious way to go."

"Too hot? Not hot enough?" He even dims the lights.

"It's perfect."

"I'll get candles for next time. And bath bombs."

As if I'm going to be taking baths at his place more often? Doubtful.

The moment I close my eyes, he asks. "What are you in the mood for?"

Your fat dick. "Cheese pizza and Root Beer from Tony's Pizzeria."

"Hell yeah, that sounds amazing."

"With breadsticks."

"Now we're talking." Mason kisses my forehead and leaves me alone in the bath while he places the order.

I can't believe I'm taking a hot bath in Mason Finch's tub. Closing my eyes, I refuse to overthink anything else tonight and just enjoy the luxury while it lasts. When I finally get out, the water's cold and my fingers are wrinkly.

Holding onto the edge, I climb out of it, wincing when I accidentally press down on my cut.

Knock, knock. "Dinner's ready, Prin—shit!" Mason's rushing towards me with his arms out. "Wait. Whoa. Let me help you out. I don't want you to slip." He wraps me up in a huge fluffy towel and sets me on the step. "Let me see your hand."

The bandage is soaked and falling off. "I think I fell asleep for a second and my hand went in the water."

"Okay. Let's get you fixed up."

For all the freak out he had earlier, he's calm as a cucumber now. Pulling out a small box from under his sink, he digs around and gets out the supplies. "Chase left us some extra stuff. Let me just get it all laid out first."

He meticulously places tape, gauze, and ointment out on the counter. Kneeling before me, he carefully unwraps my hand and fixes me up in no time. The cut isn't nearly as bad as I remember it being earlier.

Wow, I'm such a drama queen sometimes.

After he replaces the butterfly strips, Mason gently kisses my palm. "Better?"

"Yes, thank you."

"There's a change of clothes on my bed for you."

Oh my god. "Okay. I'll be right out."

He leaves again, and I feel awkward and

confused as I head into his bedroom. Those feelings disappear when a giggle bubbles out of me next. A Red Sox t-shirt and gym shorts lay on the bed.

They're so soft and comfy. And they smell just like him. I think getting out of these clothes will be harder than getting out of that glorious bath. To be wrapped in Mason, smell like Mason...

He's waiting for you to eat dinner. Hurry up!

Pulling my hair into a ponytail, I head into the main living space and see Mason plating the pizza in the kitchen. He takes one look at me and licks his lips as if I'm what he wants to eat for dinner.

"How the hell do you do it, Leah?"

"Do what?" I slide onto a stool at his breakfast bar.

"Look so fucking good in a priceless Red Sox t-shirt that I'm seriously debating on ripping the damned thing to shreds so I can see what you look like under it."

Laughter bubbles out of me. This man is fantastic for my ego. "You already know what I look like."

"Exactly." He pushes a loaded plate towards me.

"*Priceless* Red Sox shirt, huh?" I pluck the hem. "You really think highly of your baseball team, don't you?"

"That's my lucky Red Sox shirt."

"Oh yeah? How's it lucky?"

"The day my grandfather bought it for me was the day the Red Sox won the World Series in 2004."

"So it's vintage?"

Mason freezes. Is he having a circuit malfunction? "That's the year they broke the Curse of the Bambino."

What the hell is he talking about? "So... Don't get pizza sauce on it?"

His eyes blow wide with shock as he stumbles backwards, gawking at me. "You really know *nothing* about baseball?"

"There's a stick, a ball, and some bases." I take a sip of my soda. "And hot dogs."

His jaw drops. "Why is my dick hard right now? What magical sorcery have you put me under that this can be turning me on?"

"The curse of the great Bimbino strikes again."

"Bam. *Bam*bino. Oh my god." He storms over and kisses me so hard, our teeth clack. Laughter tears out of me because it's like getting all the sport stuff wrong is his ultimate hot button.

Guys are so weird.

"This is crazy," he rumbles in my ear before giving me a nice hand necklace. "You keep driving me wild in the craziest ways."

Well, he keeps driving *me* wild, so we're both winning.

I've had a lot of men and women look at me like I'm a fantasy come to life. Part of my camgirl job is to give the illusion that they're my one and only. To make them feel like what they're saying or doing on the other side of the screen turns me on, gets me off. It makes them feel special.

I'm not pretending with Mason.

And that scares me.

We're having fun together right now because I'm his shiny new toy and he's convenient. What happens when the game ends? I can't imagine us ever getting serious, so I won't even go there hypothetically.

Before Mason can take things further, I pull back. "We're both taking a big risk here, Mason."

His dark eyes soften a fraction. "I know."

"Do you? Because you've thrown yourself at me pretty recklessly." The instant I say those words, guilt smacks me in the face, making my cheeks heat with embarrassment. "Not that I mean you're being a pick me or anything like that. It's just—" Shit, I don't know how to say any of this nicely.

"No, I get it." He steps back. "I go full throttle with anything I want."

"That's not a bad thing, but we're really playing with fire here. I could lose my job if the company finds out I'm banging a client. And you..." My words fade as I think of what his family will say if they find out he's dating a housecleaner who moonlights in the sex industry.

This is the first time in a long while I've felt shame for being myself and I don't like it.

"I'm a big boy, Leah. I know what I'm doing and what the consequences of each of my actions are."

Yeah, but you're not the one who could lose the job you love. You're not the one who will be seen as a gold digger in this relationship. You're not the one who's living a double life — sweeping floors by day and sticking their painted pink toes in honey at night.

Fuck, there I go again, letting my head do all the talking when I should let my pussy have a say once in a while. Why should I give a shit what people think about me? Mason and I are just having fun. This isn't forever, it's for now. Everyone else should mind their damn business.

Mason's right, he's a big boy. He knows what he's doing and can accept the consequences of his actions.

But I'm not sure I can.

"We gotta keep this a secret, X."

Disappointment spreads across his features and down his body until he's a hard-staring, rigid-shouldered, tragic-looking Greek statue. But in the end, he concedes. "Whatever you want, Princess."

Good. This is... *good.*

Right?

Chapter 12

Mason

Keep this a secret, my ass. The only time I keep secrets is when I'm in the throes of a major deal and I don't want anything fucking up my carefully chosen negotiations. Leah deserves to be shown off. Spoiled. Put on a pedestal and given the world.

Yeah, I just met her, but my intuition is never wrong. This woman is made for me. I just hope I'm also made for her.

She's perfection. From her bunny whiskers to her yellow rubber gloves to her fancy black dress to her wretched Yankees t-shirt.

My only concern is that bringing Leah into my life will put a target on her back. Women will be spiteful and jealous. Men will get hungry and aggressive. Everyone is petty. They'll find out what she does for a living and use it against her to make her feel small and worthless and treat her like she has no business in our world.

I'm going to do everything in my power to prevent that from happening.

So yeah, I'll keep parts of her a secret until

she lets me shout from the rooftops what she does and how proud I am of her for doing it. Fuck anyone who makes her feel less than. I'll knock their goddamn teeth out.

Keeping all this to myself — *for now* — I focus back on my girl. Her lips are red and swollen from how hard I kissed her. She's drawn a line between us by calling me X instead of Mason, too.

The name switch immediately flips the script — putting her in the control seat while I do her bidding. If she wants to draw a line between fantasy and reality, I'll indulge her for now.

Bending down, I kiss her gently. Little pecks at first. She nips my bottom lip, spurring me to go harder. As I bury my hands in her hair, the air between us seems to crackle and zip. My heart thumps hard in my chest and my body burns for her.

She's not a toy to play with. She's a deity to worship.

Dropping to my knees, I spread her thighs while she leans back, resting her elbows on the counter. My girl looks down at me and I wonder if she's drawn this line because she's trying to protect me or herself. There are a million things I don't know about Leah, but we'll get there.

I'm at her mercy. Whatever she's willing to give me — her time, her body, her heart — fuck, I'll take even the breadcrumbs of her lust, if that's all she's willing to risk. Eventually she'll see I'm more than an empty condo, flashy car, and baseball fanatic.

She'll learn I'm a man who's starved his whole life. Dining off silver plates, gorging on gourmet meals that do nothing to satiate the ever-growing hunger inside me. I've spent my life masking. Playing a role in my family's games.

I took a risk with Leah and gave her the real me. The man who enjoys simple things. The animal who loves to fuck a woman as much as he loves to spoil her. The guy whose love for baseball runs deep because my grandfather would take me to games and let me be a kid instead of a photo prop. I'm the one willing to blow off an important business meeting this afternoon just so I could sit in the parking lot to wait for her, even after she kicked me out and told me to leave.

"You look damn good in my clothes, Princess." I run my hands up her legs.

Leah lifts her shirt off and tosses it onto the stool next to her. Then she shimmies out of the shorts and kicks her foot, sending them flying over my head. "How do I look now?"

"Good enough to eat."

Fuck that pizza.

Her smile makes my dick throb. "Well, I'd be a terrible person if I let you go hungry." Perched on the stool, she places her feet on my shoulders and lets her knees drop wide, exposing her pussy to me.

"I think you'll find me to be a very…" I lick

her slit. "*Very...*" I lick her again. "Starved man, Leah." Latching on, I suck her clit for a few seconds before sliding a finger inside her. Her pussy clamps down on me immediately. God damn, her grip is going to feel incredible around my cock later.

Leah sighs as she leans back, enjoying my attention.

As she should.

I already know she likes her g-spot hit, but how about more clit work? Learning her body—and all the ways I can make her come—is quickly becoming my new favorite thing.

"You look so fucking hot like this, X."

My gaze lifts to hers and I obscenely flick my tongue against her cunt. "Give me your phone." Holding one hand out, I use the other to keep finger-fucking her.

She drops her cell into my hand without asking what I want it for. The screen's unlocked too.

Pulling up her camera, I make a video of me eating her sweet, swollen, needy little pussy until she's writhing.

"That's a good girl," I growl against her clit. "Give X your cum. I'm starving for it, Princess." Holding the phone below us, I get a great angle of my long tongue flicking her clit while my finger thrusts in and out of her harder, faster. "Let me taste you while you melt on my tongue."

Her body tenses, but it's still a few minutes

before she explodes.

When she does, her heels dig into my shoulders, and I have to choose between holding her balanced or capturing it all on camera. I drop the cell without hesitation and let her ride my hand while I hold her steady. Her cries fill my ears, making blood rush to my dick. I hit her g-spot over and over until she's finished. Then I dive in and lick all of her cum out, gathering it on my tongue. Still on my knees, I show her the arousal I've collected and then swallow it.

"Holy hell." She lowers her sweet ass back onto the stool and I grab her cell again, pointing the camera at my face and suck my coated finger into my mouth. Then I wink at the camera and hit the stop button before tossing her phone onto the counter. I give Leah zero warning before lifting her into my arms and carrying her into my bedroom.

I had the appetizer, now I want the full course.

"I'm going to fuck you into next week, woman."

"I have too many plans between now and then," she teases.

"Cancel them." I drop Leah onto the bed and crawl on top of her. "I'm telling you right now, if you can walk out of my room after I'm done with you, I'm going to hang my head in shame for life."

Leah's laugh is the best sound in the world.

Kneeling between her legs, I reach behind me and pull my shirt off, tossing it on the floor. Leah makes quick work of taking my shorts off me. "I love your ass, X."

I shudder when she scrapes her nails down my back. Then she slaps my ass, hard, and I groan with pleasure.

Kissing her neck, I rub the tip of my dick against her wet pussy.

"Condom," she says quickly.

I wasn't going to push in, but she's right to give me the reminder. I have a feeling I could lose my senses with this woman too easily. I grab one from my nightstand and pause.

Shit, how old are these?

Squinting in the dark room, I can barely make out the date on the package and fear the break in our action is enough to snuff the spark.

"Sorry." I rip the package with my teeth and pull the rubber out. "Just wanted to double check."

"We good?"

"Yeah."

"I have an IUD too."

Good to know. The conversation ends and we're back to feverish kisses and tangled limbs. I swear she matches my energy in every way. No matter how hard I go, she's meets it with equal enthusiasm. Which means my first thrust inside her has us both gasping.

"You're so tight." And she's so wet, my dick

is coated.

Leah looks down between our bodies to watch me pull out halfway before slamming back in. "That's hot."

Fuck yeah, it is.

My abs flex as I lift her bottom half and fuck her a little harder. She loses breath every time I bottom out. Switching positions, I flip her over so she's facing my dresser mirror. "Watch how well you take me."

I fuck her harder and faster. Bet this would be even better with a real audience, but I like having her all to myself tonight.

Kneeling behind her, I clutch her throat with one hand and press her against my chest. Then I angle my dick against her slick cunt and shove back inside her. Leah's tits bounce with every thrust I make. We're the perfect height for each other and the view of us in the mirror together is nothing short of show-stopping.

"You look so good getting fucked by me, Princess." I drive into her harder, savoring all the sounds she makes. "I'm gonna use this pussy until you beg me to stop."

Leah's throaty chuckle sends goosebumps down my arms. "I don't beg, X."

"We'll see about that." I push her down and grab her hair, winding it around my palm before tugging it. My thrusts deepen, but I go slowly — feeding her each inch of my cock, a little at a time. Then I retreat just as slowly and repeat. "Rub your clit for me."

Leah reaches between her legs...

And tugs my balls instead.

"Fuck, yeah." My toes curl immediately.

"You want to come, X? You want to pump your load inside me?"

My heart slams into my ribs. "Yeah."

"Too bad. You're not allowed to come until I say so."

This wicked woman rocks back and starts fucking me while I hold on to her hair and my fraying control. Her sweet ass bounces against my groin while our bodies slap together. "That's it, Princess. Ride my cock." Her cheeks clap as she rocks back and forth harder and harder. "Come all over me. I want my balls to drip with it."

Leah squeaks as she reaches between her legs and starts rubbing her clit. Our breaths come out in short punches. She gets wetter and wetter. Sweat drips down my spine and I slap her ass twice, leaving a bright red handprint on each cheek. "I want to come all over this perfect ass."

"Not yet," she grunts.

Leah snaps her head up and stares at me through the mirror. She looks frantic and flushed and desperate for release. Her mouth drops, but no sound comes out at first. Then. She. Detonates. With my name flying out of her mouth in a chest rattling scream, her body practically melts under me as her inner walls clamp down, milking my cock while her orgasm tears through her.

"That's my good girl."

Spreading her ass cheeks, I gather saliva on my tongue and let it drip right onto her puckered hole before I leisurely run my thumb in circles around the tight band of muscle.

"Oh my god," she groans.

One orgasm isn't enough. I want her to come until she can't move for a month.

"You want this hole filled?" I press my thumb against it, making her breath hitch.

Instead of answering me, Leah has another orgasm. "Oh, my *god*."

Climbing on top of her, I force Leah flat on her belly. "Raise your hips." She pops her ass up enough for me to slide back into the most magical place on earth and I deepen each thrust, deliberately drawing out her third orgasm while she screams beneath me.

My release is getting harder to deny. "You feel so good, Princess." She makes a bunch of incoherent noises, but her body turns languid beneath me.

"Come," she demands.

Cute. But I'm not about to take orders.

"I'm nowhere near finished with you, Leah." I lick the padded flesh between her neck and shoulder, relishing how her pussy squeezes my dick when I do. I swear she gets wetter. "You're not finished coming yet."

"I can't..." she squeaks. "I can't come anymore."

"Yes, you can." I roll her over and slide down her body, leaving a trail of hot kisses on her sweet skin. Licking her wet folds, I love how puffed out her pussy is.

"Please," she whispers.

Is Leah finally begging? "Please what?"

"I..." She arches her back, groaning when I suck on her swollen clit. Shoving her hands in my hair, Leah holds me in place while I eat her sweet cunt like dessert. She comes so hard, she squirts.

"Oh my god!" Her thighs shake as this next release takes her by storm.

I coat most of my face in her lust and ignore my throbbing dick. It's too much fun giving her all this pleasure for me to worry about myself.

"Stop!" she cries out.

I pull away immediately.

Leah's eyes are huge, her cheeks flushed. "Oh my god, Mason! I just..." She gawks at me with terror and embarrassment. "I just..."

"Gave me the biggest compliment ever?" I stick my long tongue out, licking the arousal off the tip of my nose. "Fuck right you did." Hooking my arms under her thighs, I drag her closer to me. "Do it again, Princess." I drive my cock into her pussy once more and rub her clit with the pad of my thumb. "Hold on to the headboard if you think that'll help."

Leah's hands fly up and she clutches the spokes of my headboard.

"That's my good girl."

Chapter 13

Leah

Well, I'm forever ruined. Not only was that the best sex of my life, but I seriously couldn't walk afterwards. Leave it to Mason to deliver exactly what he promises. Four days later and I'm still hobbling a little.

"I squirted all over his face. Like a sprinkler, Mak."

"Girl!"

"I'm ruined for all other men. Damn him and his big dick and stupidly big tongue."

"How big are we talking?"

"*Big*, Mak. Wait, his tongue or his D?"

"Both! I want all the details."

"Both are impressive in size and talent. But his tongue work is diabolical. Okay, his dick game is too."

Good grief, what have I become? Ever since I left Mason's house four days ago, my grey matter has obsessed over every detail of that night. How perfect. How fun. How unexpectedly simple and decadent.

How it'll never happen again because once

was enough to make me question things.

I've been dying to talk to my bestie about it, but this is the first time we've been able to catch up after days of playing phone tag. "I don't know what to do, Mak."

"What do you *want* to do?"

"Fuck him again."

"Understandable."

"I also want to run for the hills."

"No one said this was a commitment. He doesn't even live here for most of the year. He'll have to go home eventually, right?"

"Yeah." I don't know if I'm depressed or relieved about it, which is one of my many issues here. "What if he has a wife, Mak?"

"I'm sure if he did, you'd have seen that on the internet already."

True. It's not like I didn't go on another deep dive down the Mason Finch rabbit hole when I got home the other day. Or every day since.

"I like him," I confess. "He's fun and sweet and sexy as hell." I lost track of how many times I've watched that video of him eating me out. And each time I get to the end, where he sucks his finger clean and winks at the camera, I swoon.

It's so embarrassing.

What's even worse is that I have no clue why he let me keep that video. He must know I could use it as blackmail. Someone like him caught making a porno would likely destroy his reputation, right?

He trusted me with it, though. Without saying a word, he took a risk and let me keep that footage.

Why?

Shit, even my employer sometimes makes us sign NDAs. Mason, however, seems to have thrown caution to the wind with me. It's reckless of him to do that. He's not stupid. He made that video on purpose.

Was he giving me proof that he trusts me?

Is this his way of showing me he doesn't care about his reputation, even though I'm trying my best to protect it for him? Does he even know that's why I've drawn a line in the sand between us?

Christ, my overthinking is overthinking at this point.

"What if he's your penguin, Leah?"

Doubtful. "He's just a fun fuck, Mak. Don't make it anything more than that."

Her silence makes me antsy.

"Look…" she finally says, "why not see where it goes? It'll be a fun ride, whether it's short or long. You deserve to have some fun with a guy who will treat you right. Sounds like Mason wants to do that."

"I'm too busy for a relationship."

"Make time then," she claps back.

Between my job and my side hustle, I've barely had time for my best friend over the last few months. Dedicating any free time I have to this man sounds... okay, fine, it sounds amazing.

Wow, I'm a headfuck and a half today.

"I need coffee so I can overthink this more." Hands balled into fists, I speedwalk down the sidewalk. "This is a triple espresso day, Mak truck. Maybe a quadruple."

"Whatever it takes."

We change the subject and bullshit about other things until it's time for her to get to work. Once we hang up, I'm faced with the fact that I'm alone and I don't like it. That's new. I'm usually content chilling by myself. I work alone, eat alone, sleep alone... but today a hollowness spreads in my chest.

It feels suspiciously Mason-shaped.

Eew. What the hell is wrong with me? Do I actually *miss* him?

With a big fat cup of ambition warming my hands, I stare out the cafe window, questioning my life choices. I'm so close to starting my own business, I don't have time for distractions. Or a relationship.

Or a reason to second-guess what I want to do.

But the thought of Mason calling anyone else Princess makes me want to murder someone.

This isn't love I feel clenching my heart. It's not infatuation either.

It's something else that my heart wants to run from.

What the hell is the matter with me? How

could I let this guy get under my skin so easily? It's ridiculous.

Is it because he calls me Princess? No.

Is it because he gave me way too many orgasms that I had no idea I was capable of having in one night? No.

Is it because he's stupid rich and can afford to give me anything I ask for? Hell to the no. I can buy myself whatever the fuck I want or need.

I only know how he makes me feel. Safe, adventurous, proud, adored.

Real talk: You know what did me in the other night? It wasn't the sex—though that nearly sent me into my next life—it was afterwards. Mason spent the rest of the night bathing me, feeding me, brushing my hair, rubbing my feet, and cuddling. Time stopped that night. We talked for hours about our favorite foods, movies, music. I told him a little about my family, he shared stories about his. The conversation was easy. Effortless. We talked, laughed, and touched until we fell asleep as the sun rose. It was so natural and perfect.

Too perfect.

I woke up the next morning, and was so out of it, I didn't know what planet I was on. Mason was in the shower, and I straight up panicked. All I kept thinking was, *I don't belong here*.

So, I bolted and haven't spoken to him since.

X hasn't requested a private chat with me either.

I don't know what I was expecting to happen after that night. It's not like I thought he'd chase after me or anything.

"Leah."

I glance up from my stupor and blink a few times before my brain functions properly.

Mason sinks into the chair across from me. Decked out in another black three-piece suit, he shoots me a sly smile that, looking more weary than mischievous, plays on his lips. "Double espresso?"

My tightening throat makes it hard to say, "Triple today."

He whistles. "Sounds serious."

The joke lands flat because we're both staring at each other with mixed emotions. I want to hide under a rock, and he looks like someone kicked his puppy.

Brows furrowed, Mason leans forward with his hands clasped. "Leah, if I — "

"I'm sorry I ghosted you. That was immature and uncalled for." The last thing I want is for Mason to feel like he did anything wrong when he did everything right. "I'm just overwhelmed."

"Is this where you say, 'It's not you, it's me, Mason, and I wish we could be more, but my life is a mess right now and I don't think going into a relationship is something I can handle at this point in my life'?"

All I can do is blink at him.

"I get it," he says, tapping his finger on the table. "We kind of fell into each other a little too perfectly the other night."

I blink some more.

"You're not the only one who doesn't beg, Leah. I'm not about to get on my knees and plead for you to let me into your life. Nor am I the kind of man who walks away from something I really want." He looks out the window for a second and draws in a long breath, then exhales it slowly. "I'm leaving for California and won't be back for a few days."

My heart sinks to the floor.

"If you want to see me again, Princess, say the word and I'll make it happen."

What's that even mean?

"If I don't hear from you…" He regards me with steel eyes that don't hide rejection well. "You're incredible, Leah, and I'm happy to have had the privilege of spending a little time with you." He gets up and knocks the table gently with his knuckles. "Have a beautiful day, Princess."

I watch him leave, my flabbers gasted. When I snag my drink to chug it, my gaze falls on a business card he's left on the table.

My hands shake when I pick it up.

I have no idea how he found me here. I have no clue why I'm holding this piece of cardstock like it's the holy grail either. What I do know is that when I flip it over and see his message on the back, my heart expands painfully in my chest.

Take a risk with me.

Tears fill my eyes, which is preposterous. It was just a one-night stand. This isn't real. We're from completely different worlds. We're—

I bolt from my chair and out the door. "Mason!" I yell, expecting him to stop.

But he's already gone.

Chapter 14

Mason

It's been four days. Four days of getting my ass back in gear with my new merger. Four days I've resisted the temptation of logging into Daisy Motherfucking Ren's site and requesting a private chat. Four days of jerking off to the memory of her taste on my tongue.

Four days of pure fucking hell.

My torture finally came to an end when I saw her sweet ass marching down the sidewalk and swinging open the café door with so much gusto, she knocked an outside chair over.

It's like the universe smiled down on me with the worst timing possible. I'm on my way to the airport, running late because I was still catching up on paperwork, and then I derailed my plans, parked my car in the middle of the street because there were no empty spots, and gave Leah all the time I could spare before dashing out again, so I won't miss my flight.

Christ, what the fuck is wrong with me? She's just a woman.

A sweet, fun, breath of fresh air.

A gorgeous, wild, sexy creature.

The oasis to my suffering heat.

The other night was, hands down, the best sex of my life. I want more of it. More baths, more laughter, more orgasms, and foot massages. I want to spoil Leah, ravage her, and feed her from my lap. I want to take her places and buy her pretty things. Show her off. Get her off.

She's nothing like the other women in my life. I don't want to lose her yet.

Fuck, I don't want to lose her at all.

I'm pussy whipped already. It's not a good look for me.

I'm seriously debating calling off my meetings and staying behind just so I can convince her to give me a chance.

Wow, talk about uncharted territory. I've never had to persuade a woman in my life.

In my experience, it's the woman who always chases after me. Once someone learns how filthy rich I am, they start kissing ass or sucking dick. I know when I'm being used, and I decide how long to let the bullshit game last. But Leah is different. She doesn't seem impressed with my status. She's making her own way in this world, and I love that for her.

The other night, I worshipped her body and took care of her afterwards. The bubble bath, the pampering—it was the greatest night I've had with anyone. Brushing Leah's hair will forever be in my top five favorite experiences. Her long dirty blonde hair was so thick and soft, like fat silk ribbons I could run my fingers through. And she smelled so goddamn good. It was my shampoo, my soap, my clothes on her, yet Leah somehow morphed those fragrances and made them her own. Sweet and divine. Sugar and spice.

We talked for hours about all kinds of shit. I learned she has two sisters, her parents got divorced when she was fifteen, and she's closest to her mom. Leah's twenty-six, has a degree in business, and started cleaning houses while in college because she could pick her hours and work around her hectic class schedule. She ended up loving it enough to continue cleaning after college.

"I moved here and got in with a ritzy cleaning service. They pay a little better, but the clientele is easier to work with most of the time. Most of the houses I clean are a second or even third home to these clients, so I can bang through their houses in no time, and still charge the full amount," she'd said.

My girl is a genius. She saw an opportunity and worked it in her favor.

But Leah could make a fuckload more money working for a large company or even for herself. When I brought that up, she said she's got something in the works but wouldn't share with me what that was. I respect that. I don't tell people my business plans either until they're already signed, sealed, and complete.

Leah also said she'd rather do what she loves and be poor than do something she hates and be rich.

I've never met someone who says shit like that and truly means it. Leah fucking means it.

When I brought up her side gig as a camgirl she'd said, "I like being watched."

We have so much in common, it's scary.

I asked if she's worried about being recognized as Daisy Ren out in the wild. She told me, "I'm sometimes recognized when I'm all dolled up. Even though on camera, I've exaggerated my features or wear a mask, sometimes I'm still caught." Then she laughed and said, "The first one to spot me was a woman at a concert. She and her boyfriend were next to me in the merch line. It was so awkward because they totally called me out on being Daisy Ren, like I was some kind of celebrity. It caught me so off guard I didn't have the wits to lie and deny."

When she laughed about it, something inside me growled with possessiveness.

I'll never tell Leah to stop being a camgirl. If that's what she likes to do, so be it. Besides, I like when people admire what's mine. But there are some motherfuckers who can't separate fantasy from reality and that could jeopardize her safety if she isn't careful.

Before I went into a lecture about it, however, Leah started drilling me about my siblings and why I like baseball so much, and where I live since she knew this condo wasn't my primary residence. I told her my company is named BanditFX after the beagle I had as a kid. She told me daisies were her favorite flower and that she grew up on Renfield drive, hence the name Daisy Ren. The night flew by and we crashed sometime around six in the morning.

Then she ghosted while I was in the shower.

I can't say I blame her, but fuck if it didn't hurt. For the rest of the day, I was in the worst mood and had to suffer through three online meetings and an annoying dinner with the "pretentious posse" — aptly named because it was my brother Jackson and his nosebleed buddy who thought they could weasel their way into my good graces.

They didn't.

I've spent the majority of my days and nights thinking of Leah.

Leah, Leah, Leah. This woman is slowly taking over every brain cell I have.

As I drive away from the café, my stomach drops. Getting into a relationship with her will cause trouble — with my family, with her job, with the media. I should take her ghosting me as a sign. Maybe I freaked her out. Maybe I went overboard the other night, but I couldn't help it. I wanted to give her the best of me, even if it was just for one night.

Leah vanishing while I was in the shower was a smack in the face. A reminder that we aren't on the same playing field. Hell, we aren't even playing the same game if she can reject me so fast.

Pulling my cell out, I swipe up and open the app to see Daisy Ren's face. She has a variety of gorgeous photos on the front page of her site. Her sweet smile is the same, there's a subtle difference in the hollows of her pink cheeks. Her eyes are bright blue in most of these pics too, when I know their real color is cognac. Her lips are in a perpetual pout, which forces blood to flow straight to my dick.

My drive to the airport is both too fast and too slow. Smoggy air infiltrates my senses as I stuff my cell in my pocket. The riotous sound of heavy traffic, airplanes taking off, and people rushing around drowns the heavy thud of my heart.

Grabbing my carryon, I head inside when my cell vibrates. Foolishness allows me to hope that it's Leah already.

Disappointment makes me numb when I see it's not.

"If this is about giving Carmichael a chair on my board again, hang the fuck up, Jackson."

"It's about Nicole."

Fuck my life. "What about her?"

"Are you sticking with your decision?"

"Yeah. Why?"

"I just want to make sure I have damage control ready."

"There was no damage done."

"Tell that to Mom. She's still furious, you know."

"I don't care." Our mother is too controlling for her own good. Sometimes I wonder if she hadn't put me on such a tight leash growing up, I might not have rebelled so hard. "Nicole is a nonissue."

"She's a huge issue, Mase. Her family runs the charity Mom's gala is for. And if you're coming to it too, it'll be a problem before hors d'oeuvres are served."

This is the opposite attitude Grace gave me about the whole thing. "Then I won't come." I didn't want to go anyway, so this works out for everyone.

"Mom will be pissed if you don't show."

"Jackson, I'm a grown ass man." Slipping past a cluster of kids with a harried set of parents, I step onto the escalator. "I don't give a fuck who I disappoint."

"You do this shit on purpose."

No, I don't. But I refuse to let anyone dictate my life.

"God, you're such a selfish prick, Mason. Everything you do affects the family." My heart clenches because he sounds like our mother and Jackson's better than that, damnit. "This rebellious bullshit needs to end. Grow up."

"This *rebellious bullshit* is what you and your dog, Carmichael, were foaming at the mouth to be part of the other night. What was it he said? Oh yeah, he'd fuck over half of New York if he got in BanditFX. The fucker *bragged* about how he would throw his mutuals under the bus and burn bridges to secure his seat, giving me the monopoly. And you sat next to him with a self-righteous smirk on your face the whole time."

"So?"

"My company was built from the ground up not to be a slap in our family's face, but to be my own goddamn path to greatness. That's me being a man, not mommy's baby boy. You want great things for yourself, bro? Fucking *earn* it like I did and stop riding coattails."

"Earn it? You built BanditFX with your fucking trust fund, you cunt. You're no better than me, even though you keep acting like you are."

I didn't use my trust fund to finance my company. My parents wouldn't let me take out that much cash, no matter how many times I pleaded and showed them my proposals. Instead, I worked my ass off in college, made quick investments in stocks, traded, and diversified and took major risks until I had enough capital to start up my company by my damn self. My stellar networking skills and ethics got me the rest of the way. I've made millions without my family's support — financial or otherwise.

As the black sheep in our family, I'm the disgrace while Jackson's their favorite son who does the Finch name proud. Grace has even less freedom than me and my brother do when it comes to her life choices. Still, Jackson keeps making big mistakes and if I can help him, I will, regardless of if he deserves it or not.

I love him. I just don't like him very much. "Watch yourself. Carmichael is not your friend. He's going to drag you down with him and throw you under the bus if it'll save his own ass or put him in the lead."

"And Carmichael's strategies have to do with Nicole coming to the gala...how?"

"That's his cousin!"

"And she was your—"

I hang up and stuff my cell back in my pocket before he can finish that goddamn sentence.

Two hours later, I board my flight and take off for Cali. Once I'm in the air, I open a particular text thread and type, "You ever just want to get a new identity, pack your shit, and disappear forever?"

Their response comes through seconds later: *Every damn day.*

Resting my head against the window, I close my eyes. I hate my life. I hate my obligations. I hate that I'm leaving a city I love. And I especially hate that the first time I find a woman I really fucking like, she ghosts me and still I vie for her attention.

A flight attendant brings me a glass of champagne and offers an inviting smile.

"Welcome aboard, Mr. Finch. Anything I can do to make your flight more enjoyable..." She licks her lips seductively, "just press the call button."

"Thanks, but no thanks." That goes for the drink and whatever else she's attempting to offer.

Only one woman occupies my thoughts and she's a mile below me now, getting further and further away from my grip.

Chapter 15

Leah

Ever since Mason vanished on the street, I've been going a little crazy. The harder I try to not think of him, the more he fills my head. My pussy is in a constant state of neediness. It doesn't help that the past two days have been slow as hell with work, and I haven't had a lot of desire to go online as Daisy Ren or make new content.

A reset is in order. Whenever I'm in a funk, a long hot bath with all the goodies usually does the trick. Lighting a dozen candles around the rim, I drop a bath bomb in the hot water and start my little attachable jet that's clamped to the side. It smells so good in here already.

What should I play for entertainment? A podcast? Music? An audiobook?

I go with meditation songs because I think anything else will give me a headache or set my sex drive on full-throttle again and I don't want that.

The cut on my hand has healed fast. I feel like a big baby for making such a fuss about it the other day. It really wasn't worth all that attention and care. Images of Mason's worried face fill my mind—how he got all freaked out and ran for help when it first happened, the way he carefully redressed my bandage, the way he kissed it better.

The way he kisses my mouth... my pussy.

How he sucks on my clit.

Oh my god, I'm the worst. Why do I keep fixating on him?

I need to get this man out of my system.

But the thought of sleeping with someone else makes me queasy. Going live on camera and flirting with strangers doesn't sound good either. Damn Mason and his confidence, sweetness, and big dick. Especially his big dick.

And his mouth.

Sweet mother of God, no human should have a tongue like his. It's insane. And what he does with it? Unacceptable behavior.

I want him to eat me out again.

Fuck that, I want him to tongue fuck all my holes.

"Damnit Leah, get a fucking *grip*!" The back of my head smacks the inflatable pillow and knocks one of the suction cups loose. Every time I press it back against the tub, it pops off again because the suction cups are too wet. "Stick, damn you! STICK!" I try three more times. "You know what? Fuck this."

Fuck that pillow. Fuck this bathtub. Fuck the bubbles and candles and meditation.

I can't get out of this thing fast enough. Stomping my feet on the rug, I snag a towel and wrap it around my chest before marching over to my phone. Fury has me plucking that stupid business card out of the back of my cell and I hate-punch the numbers in. The phone rings six times and goes to voicemail.

"You've reached Mason Finch. You know what to do."

At the sound of the beep, my fury explodes. "No, you asshole, I *don't* know what to do. You've got me all fucked up and I hate it. My bath is *ruined.* I can't even enjoy the *one thing* that's always been my favorite because *you*… you just had to make everything different and now I can't think straight, and my stupid suction cup won't even work on my pillow!"

I hang up, storming into my bedroom next. I need to take the edge off. Instead of Mason giving me the best Os of my life and satiating me, he's turned me into a sex monster. I want him again. Badly.

I've never been so frustrated in my fucking life.

Shoving a vibrator between my legs, I go straight for the highest setting and hold it tight to my clit.

Seconds turn to minutes and all I've managed to do is get wet. My arousal coats my fingers and the vibrator. My pussy has puffed out like it always does when I'm too horny for my own good. But no orgasm comes because I can't turn my goddamn head off.

I can still hear the soft timbre of his voice when he talks in the dark. I miss the way his hands heat my skin when he runs his fingers up and down my thigh. I crave the bubble we created when time stopped and it was just us learning about each other, laughing, unfiltered.

Now I feel worse.

"FUCK!" My pulse pounds against my temples.

My stupid cellphone rings. One swift glance at the number and I'm too confused to dissect my feelings about it. A mixture of relief, anger, and joy has me answering. "What?"

"What's the matter, Princess?"

My eyes narrow. *You. You're what's the matter.* "Nothing."

"You sound frustrated."

"Gee, whatever gave you that impression?" I'm acting like a brat and can't find the fucks to give about it.

"Where are you?"

"My house."

"Where in your house?"

"Why, Mason?"

"X," he says in a dark tone. "You better call me X, Princess."

I don't know why, but my frazzled head calms. We aren't Mason and Leah, we're X and Princess, which means no feelings and all fun, in my opinion. "X," I repeat, before taking a deep breath and blowing it out.

"That's my good girl. Now tell me where you are in your house."

My eyes roll so hard I almost see my last working brain cell. "My bedroom."

"Go to your bathroom and fill your tub."

"It's still full. I just got out of it." And was too mad to drain the damn thing.

"Good. Get back in it."

"Why?"

"Do what you're told, Princess."

I don't know what it says about me that I'm following this fucker's orders, but here I go. Climbing back in, goosebumps erupt down my arms and legs, my nipples tightening from the chilled water. "It's cold," I grumble like it's his fault.

"Drain half the water and fill it almost back to the top. *Almost*, Princess, you got that?"

My heel stomps on the plug, and the water level starts decreasing.

"So, how was your day?"

Is he serious? "Fine."

"Doesn't sound like it was fine. What's got you so worked up?"

You. "Nothing."

"For every lie you tell me, that's two punishments you get once I see you again. Understood?"

Don't threaten me with a good time, buster.

"Mmm hmm." I plug the drain and turn the water on, full blast, as hot as it'll go.

I swear a growl comes from the other end of the line. It sets me on fire, but I'll never tell him that.

"How was *your* day?" I ask in the most fake ass happy tone I have.

"Not too bad until now."

"Should I be insulted?"

"You should be doing what you're told and make sure that water level isn't as high as it can go."

Oh. Right. I turn it off because it's getting close.

"I didn't say turn it off, Princess."

"What the hell, Maso… X? You said to not let it get all the way up."

"Turn the temp to warm, not hot."

"Why?"

"Are you disobeying?"

"I'm asking a question."

"If I was there, my dick would be in your mouth so you couldn't ask me a damned thing."

"Well, you're not here, so your dick is…"

"In my hand," he interrupts in a dark tone. "I'm stroking my cock, in my office, staring out at the city skyline, imagining you in that fucking tub."

My heart swoons.

"Now do what I say and change the temp of the water. Make it warm, Princess."

"Okay."

"Now slide that sweet ass of yours forward and spread your legs as wide as you can. Let the water flow over that needy cunt and aim it at your clit that I'm sure misses my mouth."

Is he serious? "I—"

"Do it."

I scoot forward. The warmth, constant pressure, and trembling flow of water, combines into a blast of pleasure that builds inside me until my head falls back and hips thrust a little as I ride the wave. "Fuck."

"That's it, Princess. Keep going."

My climax isn't strong, but it's a decent distraction from my frustration. Once I'm done, I turn the water off.

"Feel better?"

"A little," I admit.

"My tongue should be what's between your thighs, getting you off, not your tub."

Sighing, I lean back and sink into the hot water, imagining him stroking himself on the other end of the phone. I want to hear him come.

"Did I still ruin baths for you?"

"Yes," I lie.

"That's another two punishments. Wanna keep lying to me?"

"No."

"That's another two. Damn, Princess, you really must want me to put you over my knee and make that sweet ass bright fucking red."

Now it's my turn to play. I pitch my voice higher, like I often do as Daisy Ren. "Mmm hmm. I want your handprints all over my ass, X. Then I want you to shove your big, fat cock in my mouth and face fuck me until I choke on you."

Silence spreads between us, then he growls, "*Leah.*"

I feel like a child who just got in trouble. "Yes, Mason?"

"Don't fake it with me."

"I didn't."

"You just did."

Holy Hell, the sound of disappointment in his voice makes me feel emotions I refuse to acknowledge. "I'm just playing the part, X."

"I don't want you to play with me. I want you to be with me."

What's that even mean? "I'm on this call with you. What more to do you want?"

"You," he sighs. "Fuck, woman, I want you. All of you."

"And..." I lick my lips, leaning forward in the tub so I can hug my knees. "What would you do if you had all of me, Mason Finch?"

His ragged breaths punch out of him and my pussy clenches at hearing it. "I'd bend you over my desk and fuck you. Then I'd press you against the window and lick your cunt. I'd rim your ass and fuck that, too."

"Is that all?" I tease. "Why stop there?"

"What more would you like?"

"A hand necklace would be nice."

"Fuck," he groans.

"I want you to tongue fuck me. I want you to rail me like you did the other night. Make my knees shake and head spin. Have me come so hard I soak your face again."

"God damn that was—" his voice strains, "*Leah*."

The vision of him coming turns into a full-blown cinematic experience in my mind. Ropes of white cum jetting out of his throbbing cock, his big hand squeezing around the base, his legs stretched out before him with his belt unbuckled and balls lifting tight against his body as his cock throbs while he orgasms.

"Jesus Christ, woman." He sounds out of breath. "I just splattered cum all over the fucking window."

"Mmm, if I was there, I'd lick it up."

"Don't say shit like that unless you mean it."

"Oh, I don't say things I don't mean. I'd totally clean that window off for you."

"I wish you were here."

"I bet." I wish I was there too. I'd like to see his office. And I'd really like to be bent over his desk.

"I can have a jet ready for you by ten pm, Cali time."

His words hang in the air like a pendulum swinging. Or an anvil.

"Very cute, Mason."

"I'm not being cute. I'm being serious."

My brow furrows. "I can't just hop on a plane and come to you."

"It's a private jet and yes, you can."

My adrenaline spikes. "*What?*"

"You heard me, Leah. Say the word and I'll have it arranged. You can be to me in just a few hours."

"I..." This is ludicrous. "I can't just come there."

"Why not?"

I have no idea why not. This is all so sudden and crazy and... okay, I could call out sick from work if I really wanted to. But do I?

"We can tour a vineyard. Shop." I can hear Mason's smile. "Massages, fancy restaurants, you name it."

"I thought you were there for work?"

"I am. But I'll make time for you."

I don't see how. I barely make time for anything else besides my jobs, and his is far more demanding than mine. "I don't want to intrude. You're busy, and being a distraction will only make me feel like shit."

"You can come with me to my meetings if you want."

"Hard pass."

"I'll make the trip out here worth it."

I bet being anywhere with this man would be worth it. "Mason, this is a big step."

"It's a plane ride to Cali for a few days, not

a month-long vacation on a yacht through the Caribbean."

"That's… very specific." And now I'm fantasizing about going on one of those and what it would be like. Ugh, I'd never be able to afford that level of luxury. Damn him for even putting that thought in my overactive brain.

"What do you say, Leah?"

I say this is a very bad idea. "I'll come."

Mason laughs and it's music to my ears. "Yes. You. Will. Princess."

We hang up and a half hour later; he texts me all the information I need. He's also booked a car service to pick me up.

"I'm out of my mind."

After packing a carryon, I sit on my front porch and turn my brain off, so I don't back out of this plan.

Chapter 16

Mason

Sometimes I come on a little too strong and my ideas get big and crazy. This wasn't one of those times. But the fact that I'm already checking out what it takes to rent a fully crewed yacht to sail us through the Caribbean says I'm not far from going overboard.

Hmmm, wonder if she'd prefer Greece instead?

Step back, Mason. You're doing it again.

Anytime I like someone, I go crazy with it. Grace says I'm self-sabotaging. I don't want women to want me for my money, yet I flash it all over the place and get extravagant. She's wrong though. I like luxury and sharing my wealth with others. I've never let someone take anything from me I didn't want to give. I've never been played. And I steer clear of gold diggers.

Impatience has me at the tarmac an hour before Leah's jet touches down. I don't usually take a private plane when on business, but Leah's not business, and I wanted her to have a nice, comfy, low stress flight. A private jet was the best way to ensure that since I couldn't be on the trip with her.

I expected my nerves to settle once the aircraft lands, but my entire body turns into a live wire. I haven't been this excited in a long time.

The stairs drop and a few minutes later, Leah's head pops out of the plane. My heart explodes into fireworks. This much joy in seeing someone should be bottled and distributed across the globe.

"I can't believe I just took a private jet." She's wild with excitement, and I'm drunk off her already.

"I trust it was comfortable."

"I drank champagne and hot chocolate."

She's adorable. She's also trembling. Concern has me tensing. "Are you okay?"

"That was so scary, Mason!" Leah tosses her hands in the air. "I just kept thinking, what if a gust of wind blows us into a mountain? Or a storm takes us out. Or a *goose*! Have you seen La Bamba? Heard of Patsy Cline? These little planes are death traps."

"Did you experience turbulence?"

"No!" She looks over her shoulder at the attendant bringing out her bag. "Oh my god, I would have peed my pants if that plane started shaking. I'm not a good flyer. It's too high up. I have zero control. Oh my god, I could have *died*." She hooks her arms around me and buries her face in my chest.

I fold her into an embrace and kiss the top of her head. "You should have told me you have a fear of flying, Leah."

"Yeah, well, it's not like BanditFX has perfected teleportation yet." She looks up at me, her brow crinkling. "Or have you?"

"Nope. I'm not that kind of tech company."

"Didn't think so." She hugs me tighter and sighs. "I'll get used to it, maybe. Hopefully."

My heart swells because that must mean she's willing to fly around with me, or to me, again. At least I *hope* that's what she means. I won't let her fly alone again if I can help it. I'll be there to hold her hand and keep her safe.

Standing on the tarmac with my arms wrapped around this woman has me floating like a balloon. This is crazy, spontaneous, and I can't believe she came.

Leah pushes away from me and digs her cell out of her jeans. "I have to text Mak and let her know I made it."

While her thumbs start flying across her phone screen, I take a moment to appreciate Leah's outfit. She's in jeans, dark green Converse, and a black faded t-shirt that says, "Never better" with a skeleton on it. The contrast of her outfit, and me in my business suit, turns me the fuck on. I've never been with a woman who would board a private jet in anything less than Chanel.

Once she stuffs her cell into her back pocket, Leah looks up and smiles at me. "Ready to get this party started?"

"You have no idea." Cupping her face, I smash my mouth to hers and it's like getting a burst of air in my lungs after drowning for days. "I'm really glad you came."

"Me too. This is going to be fun!"

Escorting Leah to my rental car, I open the door and help her inside, then make quick work of shoving her carryon in the trunk. Once I'm in the driver's seat, I squeeze her thigh. "Welcome to Silicon Valley, Leah."

She smiles and buckles up. "I can't believe we're doing this."

Neither can I, but the instant I saw her step out of the plane, I felt drunk with elation. What is it about this woman that makes me feel like a kid on Christmas morning?

"I've never been to the West Coast before."

Suddenly, my gut drops and twists. I have back-to-back meetings all day tomorrow, followed by dinner, and the next day is a tour of my newest construction site. Jesus Christ, I've dragged this woman, who I barely know, to a place she's never been, and I can't even be with her for most of it.

My mouth runs dry as we fly down the road.

It sucks to think I might have made a mistake, but there's no way on this green earth having Leah with me would ever be a mistake. I just need to figure out how to give her attention while keeping my schedule tight and timely.

"Where are we heading?"

"Our hotel. I got us a suite at the Five Points Resort and Spa." I'd been staying at a different hotel but upgraded when Leah agreed to join me. This one's brand new and eager to gain members like me.

"Oh fancy."

Why does the word *fancy* always sound like an insult to me? "If you hate it, we can go someplace else."

"Uhhh, I can't imagine hating any place with Resort and Spa in the title." She leans back and smiles. "So how much time will we really have with each other during the next couple of days?"

A couple of days. That's all she can give me. I'd have loved three weeks out here to really spoil her rotten, but our schedules won't allow it.

Clenching the steering wheel, I confess, "Tomorrow is jammed with several meetings and a late dinner." Taking a right, I flick my gaze to her. Is she mad? Disappointed? Already regretting making the trip here?

"That's a bummer for you."

For me? What about her? "I swear I'll have more time the following day. We can go wherever you want. Do anything."

"Don't worry about me." She leans back in her seat. "I'll entertain myself while you're busy doing Big Tech Daddy things."

"Big. Tech Daddy. Things?"

Her laugh fills my chest with butterflies. "I still don't have a clue what BanditFX even does, Mason."

Soon, it won't matter. If all goes well, I'm going to sell BanditFX and make a lot of money. "It's boring work. All cybersecurity and mechanical robot shit."

"Cyborgs? You make cyborgs, don't you? Ohhhh *Sex* Cyborgs."

"Wow." I shake my head, laughing. "Sex Cyborgs is a leap. Did you read that in a book?"

"Finished the audiobook on the way here. It's how I kept my mind off the fact that I might die in a ball of melting metal."

My throat tightens with guilt for not knowing that she was so afraid of planes. "And what did these sexy cyborgs do, Princess?"

"Welllll." Leah reaches over and runs her nails up and down my thigh. "They had fancy equipment."

"Mmm. How fancy?"

"They have all these different settings and if you hit this one pink button on their stomach, they can do DP."

This is fascinating. "What's DP?"

"Double penetration, baby! Woop! Woop!" Leah raises both hands in the air. "A second dick literally extends, and she gets double the fun!"

"Sounds delightful."

"Hell yeah, it does. And they have other

buttons too."

"Go on." I love how excited she is about her books.

"This one dude had a purple one for his voice range. A black one for his stamina setting. And there was a blue one too. Guess what *that* one was for."

"I'm terrified to guess."

"Try."

"Speed?"

"Ohhh! That's a good guess, but nope. It's FLAVOR!"

"Flavored what? He can't possibly come."

"He totally could. Loads. I'm talking like the mega cream pie, dripping out for days level of cum. It was fucking hot."

She's so damn animated about this Cyborg Sex Machine Man that it has me considering building her one.

"What ever happened at the end of the book we listened to last week?"

"Oh, revenge was served, everyone makes up, there's lots of sex, and they lived *happily ever after*."

We spend the rest of the drive to the hotel talking about other books she's listened to this week. Leah's still cracking up at my shock over three dicks in one hole in a paranormal romance with vampires from outer space as we both get out of the car. I'm glad I can amuse her. Grabbing both our bags from the trunk, I refuse to let her carry her own things. "I've got it, Princess. You just let me follow that sweet ass of yours inside so we can check in."

I swear she sashays her hips on purpose to keep my mouth watering. When we get into the elevator, Leah's gaze eats me up. "Thanks for bringing me here, Mason."

All I can do is smile because all my words have jammed in my throat. She looks so beautiful, so carefree. This woman embraces life and I'm the privileged one who gets to watch her enjoy it.

The elevator finally stops, and the doors open. I lead the way to our suite and watch her expression as she enters the room. "Holy shit, this is incredible." Leah kicks off her shoes and bypasses the living room to head straight into the bedroom. Her ass looks delicious as she crawls on top of the plush, king-sized bed. "Oh my god, this feels like a cloud."

I finally get to pull my suit jacket and tie off. Sitting in a swivel chair across the room, I kick off my shoes and sit back. This has been a long day. Successful, but exhausting. I just keep reminding myself that I'm at the finish line. Having Leah here is the boost of energy I need to reach it.

"Before you get too comfortable, Princess, go check out the bathroom. I think there's something in there you'll appreciate."

Leah scrambles off the bed, and a few seconds later, she screams with glee. This woman is louder than life, and I love it.

I make my way to her and lean against the doorjamb with my arms crossed. Leah's hands cover her mouth, her eyes wide with joy as she looks at what I've done.

The huge soaking tub is lined with pillar candles. Rose petals float amidst bubble clouds in the milky hot water, fragranced with lavender. Steam rolls up, making the air thick and sultry. The heater in the tub does a nice job keeping the temp high, which is great since I had to set all this up before going to the airport to get her.

She grabs the remote from the sink and hits a button. Soft music plays through the surrounding speakers.

"Holy crap. This is heaven."

Glad she approves. "Get in, Princess. I'll pour us both champagne."

Then I'm going to fuck her until she screams my name across the Valley.

Chapter 17

Leah

Look, I live loudly and unapologetically. I spoil myself whenever I can, but this? What Mason's doing? He's gone next level. Last night was amazing. Hot bath, hot sex, hot room service eaten in bed. Once again, we stayed up talking until way too late and I think I fell asleep first.

I woke up to Mason's head between my thighs. When I stirred, he gripped my legs harder to make sure I stayed still for him. He had this wicked grin and my arousal shining on his mouth when he looked up at me and said, "Good morning, Princess."

A girl could get used to this.

Coming to California on a whim is turning out to be the best thing ever. I'm going to remember this trip for the rest of my life, and I haven't even left our suite yet.

But now Mason has work to do, which means I'm on my own for the day. It's cool. I plan to shop, explore, and check out the spa they have in the hotel. For now, I'm enjoying watching Mason get ready for work while I lay in bed like a fluffy, lazy cat.

"Take my black card," he says after I tell him my plans for the day.

"No way. I have my own money."

Mason glowers at me from across the room, clearly not happy. "I want to spoil you, and you're denying me that privilege?"

"Ugh, don't say it like that." I roll out of bed and wince.

Mason is on me in an instant, helping me stand. "You're still sore?" His mouth turns to a frown. "Damnit, I was too hard fucking you last night, wasn't I?"

"Easy, buddy, don't go inflating your dick's ego. I'm just stiff." My joints always hurt in the morning. It's another reason I take a hot bath every day. My bones hurt like I'm ninety-six, which sucks.

But honestly, I am a little sore from last night, too. Mason fucks like an animal and I love it.

"You'd tell me, right?" He's still holding my waist, worry making his brows dig down. "If I'm being too rough, you'd say something. *Promise* me you'd say something, Leah."

"Hey, whoa, chill." I boop his nose. "I like the way it hurts."

Mason stills. "I don't want to hurt you."

"It's a good hurt, X." My body's already craving his touch again. This chemistry between us isn't just fun, it's addictive. "I want you again."

Hooking my arms around his neck, I lure him back in the bed with me.

"I can't be late for this meeting, Princess."

"Then fuck me fast, X."

"Jesus." He peels his shirt off and unbuckles his belt while I rake my fingers through his hair and shove my tits in his face. "I swear you're going to break me, woman."

"Awww, poor baby."

He spreads my legs and dives his big tongue inside me. "We don't have time for your mouth!" I smack his head. "I want your dick."

"You get what I give you," he growls, before sucking on my clit.

I'm still overstimulated from last night and my clit is extra sensitive. He has me coming in less than a minute, with my eyes rolling back as my body catapults into pure bliss. I scream Mason's name.

He looks up from between my legs and smiles. "Say it louder. The penthouse didn't hear you." He peppers kisses all over my body until he reaches my mouth. "You're so gorgeous when you come, Princess." He slides his cock inside me, and I realize he's not wearing a condom.

We'd discussed this last night, but it's still a little freaky not using one.

I've got an IUD. I'm clean. He's clean. And it was my idea to go without a barrier. Great dick must make me stupid.

"You feel so fucking good," he groans in my

ear.

Mason fucks like a storm. He doesn't just piston his hips. He surges. The man's entire existence seems to laser focus on giving me pleasure.

"Turn over." He pulls out long enough for me to roll onto my belly, then he crawls on top and plunges into me again. His mouth is hot on my skin when he latches onto my shoulder. That body part is my absolute kryptonite.

He bites down.

"Fuck," I squeak. "Again."

I can't describe how good it feels to have my pleasure laced with a little pain. We tried it last night, and this only confirms that I definitely enjoy straddling the line.

Mason licks the spot he just bit, soothing it. "Your pussy clenches whenever I kiss you here."

He puts his mouth on me again, groaning because he's right; I do clench when he does that. It's an automatic response I can't control.

"You're so wet, Princess." His mouth works in wicked ways, driving my lust higher and higher.

With his arms bracketing my shoulders, I'm pinned in place. Keeping my hips tilted up and lower back arched, I let him drive me towards another climax. I see stars when I come this time.

"That's a good girl," he growls. "Grip my dick with your pussy. Make me come."

All I can do is whimper while he fucks me.

"Where do you want it, Princess?"

Inside me, I want to say, but I'm too afraid to go that far. Last night I took him in my mouth. "My ass," I grunt. "Come all over my ass, X."

"Ask me nicely." He bites down on my shoulder, and I nearly come again.

"Please," *shit, fuck, holy hell, he feels so good.* "Please come on my ass."

The instant he pulls out, I regret my decision. Mason unloads all over my spread cheeks and I wonder what it would feel like to have all that pumped inside of me instead.

I really need to lay off the Cyborg romance novels.

Mason kneads my ass, squeezing me roughly. "That looks so goddamn pretty."

Before I can move, he leans down and drags his tongue through the mess he just made on me.

I... I'm... ummm a new kink just unlocked, my friends. Rolling over slowly, I gawk as he stares down at me with heavy-lidded eyes and asks me, "Are you sore now?"

I shake my head.

"Good. Because when I get back from my meetings, I'm going to fuck you properly until dinner."

He stands up and grabs his clothes again, redressing as if he didn't just cause me to ascend into my final form. "Will you come with me tonight?"

"I came with you just now."

"Dinner, Princess." Mason works on his tie. "Will you join me for dinner tonight?"

I'm not sure I should. "It's a dinner *meeting*, right? Do you really want a date to that?"

"I want you. Hell, I'd have you on my lap for all my meetings today if I could. But there's no reason both of us should be bored to tears."

"I didn't pack anything fancy. All I have is a sundress and some shorts."

"Wear whatever you're most comfortable in."

"No way! You're going to go looking like…" I flick my hand in the air, "*that*."

His eyebrows raise to his hairline. "That?"

"Like sex on a stick! You can't go looking that good while I'm dressed like a tourist."

His laugh takes up the whole bedroom. "You're overthinking it, Leah. Who cares what you wear? It's dinner with a bunch of stuffy motherfuckers who should count their lucky stars that they get to be in your presence."

That's not true. "I'll look for a nice dress today while I'm out."

He digs his wallet from his pocket and pulls out his black card. I immediately object, but he rebuttals with, "It's a business expense. Please, give me the write off."

Like he needs it? This is just a poor excuse for me to accept his offer. "Fine." I pluck the card from his fingers. "But just so you know, I'm going to a thrift store, which means your deduction will be minimum."

"Mmm hmm." His victory smile is so sexy. "Just in case you can't find anything there, I'll call ahead and make sure a few other stores are ready for you." He starts listing a bunch that are way above my pay scale.

"Wow, Big Tech Daddy. You really know your fashion icons."

"My sister has accounts in all of them. Drop her name and I bet they'll give you free shit."

Laughter bubbles out of me, and I playfully smack his arm. "You better freshen up and get dressed. You're going to be late for work."

"I'm the boss. I can't get fired for being late." He's on me again, kissing me like I'm better than caffeine to get his mojo going in the morning.

"Keep this up, and you'll never see the inside of your office again, Mr. Finch."

"Keep looking this goddamn delicious, and I just might quit, anyway."

I know he's only joking, but it sounds like there's a hint of truth in those words.

Either that or I'm delulu.

Before I get to overthink it, Mason backs off and finishes getting dressed. "Is *that* what a nest would be like?"

It takes me a second to realize he's asking about what's in the smutty omegaverse novels I like. "Yeah," I say, curling up in the puffy pillows and soft blankets. "But add more blankets and creature comforts."

"Like snacks and fuzzy socks?"

"Whatever makes her happy."

Mason nods, as if he's making a mental note, and then crawls into bed to kiss me goodbye. "I'm really sorry I have to leave."

"Don't be."

"I feel like a prick."

"Why?"

"I lure you here, then abandon you."

"Someone's gotta make that money, baby." Speaking of which, I really need to log into my account and upload new material, or my patrons are going to get cranky.

Ugh, the thought of being Daisy Ren while I'm with Mason feels wrong on so many levels.

"Hey." He tips my chin with his finger. "What's wrong?"

"Nothing," I play it off. "Why would you think something's wrong?"

"You get this extra crinkle in your forehead sometimes."

I do not. "Nothing's wrong, I swear." The last thing I want is for Mason to leave the hotel room with any guilt, especially since I know he's already feeling bad that he'll be gone all day. "Get to work, Big Tech Daddy. Go forth and..." I wiggle my fingers, "make big security firewall cookies."

His laughter hits me in the chest.

We kiss goodbye again and he reluctantly leaves. Being with Mason is so easy. We have great chemistry, the sex is off the charts, and I don't feel like a disappointment around him.

And I'm not fake.

Just as I'm basking in post-orgasm bliss, my cell dings with a text.

Mason: Use that tub and bed to make some video content for Daisy Ren if you'd like. Give them something to hate me for.

That last bit throws me off.

Leah: Why would they hate you?

Mason: Because you're mine, Princess. And soon enough, everyone will know it.

My heart slips and falls on its ass.

Leah: Oh yeah? Going public, are we?

There's no way that will happen. I'll lose my job and what's worse is he'll be the laughingstock of the fancy pants richy-rich society he's in. It's too much to risk.

Although we're risking it right now, aren't we?

It doesn't matter if we're in another state. We're still together. He's still amidst his peers and mutuals. Something could go sideways and one or both of us will pay for it.

But part of me doesn't care. I like being with him. Mason is spontaneous and reckless, like me. He matches my energy. Do you have any idea how hard it is to find someone who can match *my* kind of fucking energy?

I thought it was impossible until Mason came into my universe.

Staring at the phone screen, I wait for him to reply. He doesn't.

The fucker left me on read!

Two hours later, I'm out of bed, freshly showered, and ready to explore the city. Mason still hasn't answered me, which pisses me off like you wouldn't believe.

You're gonna pay for that.

Plucking his black card off the bed, I smile wickedly.

Chapter 18

Mason

Mid-meeting, I glance at my cell to the text I haven't responded to yet.

Leah: Oh yeah? Going public, are we?

She has no clue how loaded that question is for me.

I haven't answered her because there's no response that doesn't give me away. But I hate keeping secrets, and I don't want Leah to ever think she's one of them.

Glancing around the room at my team, I realize just how close I am to having everything I want. It's like being on a tightrope, inches from the final platform, and I'm scared a gentle breeze will blow, threatening to knock me off and make me fall.

"—profits this quarter are the highest they've ever been. Projected sales look outstanding."

I glance up at one of my best friends, Kerrington. "Good call on the expansion, Kerr."

"Thanks."

"What's going on with the new

developments in—" My attention cuts to my cell again when a notification comes through.

Daisy Ren is live.

I quickly stand, my chair gliding away until it hits the windowsill. "Excuse me gentlemen, I have to take this."

They don't need me here, anyway. I know how successful our company is and I have no concerns with its future. Storming out of the conference room, I click on the app and log in.

All the blood rushes to my dick when I see my girl holding a dress up to her body. The camera's angled to focus on her neck down, but I'd recognize that hourglass figure anywhere. My hands flex on instinct, eager to touch every inch of her again.

Leah's in a dressing room I don't recognize. A cream-colored pouf serves as a chair behind her, and there are gold hooks with little birds mounted on teal walls. It's a vibrant backdrop. A perfect choice to go live in.

"You like this one?"

Several fuckers respond and it makes me wonder how many of them are watching from their offices just like me, and how many are jerking off in their mommy's basement right now. No matter where they are, their attention is on Leah, and I love it.

How she manages to angle the camera so no one can see her face is beyond me. I'm worried she'll slip up. It's not like she brought her bunny mask or all that extra makeup with her.

Or did she?

Leah dips down, her long waves falling over her shoulders, framing her beautiful face. Pink lipstick hooks my gaze and I stare at her mouth. Her perfect, full, plush, kissable, fuckable mouth.

She's got a white lace mask over her eyes that looks like something from a dollar store. "Mmmm, I think this dark purple one is my favorite." She pulls another dress out and holds it against her chest. "Or should I go with white?" She switches between the two fast enough for her audience to catch a glimpse of her bra and underwear.

I'm so turned on, my palms sweat.

She flashes off her creamy thighs and gives us a peek of her tits spilling out of her red bra, and I swear to God I could come just watching her tease us like this. I'm lucky enough to know how fun those tits are to suck on, how hard her thighs can squeeze my head when she comes on my tongue. How the taste of her is the single most exquisite flavor I've ever known.

But seeing how luscious she is on screen and knowing I'm the lucky sonofabitch who's coming home to her in a few more hours starts a war inside me. I don't think I can wait that long to see her again.

Another notification comes through, dowsing cold water down my spine.

Nicole: Got a minute?

Not for her. I swipe up and watch Leah unzip her dress slowly to shimmy out of it.

Another text pops up.

Nicole: Please, Mason. I need you.

God. Damnit.

"Mason."

I turn around like a kid with his hand caught in the cookie jar. "Yeah?"

"We just need you to sign off on a few more things, then we can get back to work," Landon says.

"Be there in a minute."

I glance back at my cell just in time to see Leah blow a kiss to the camera. "See you later, guys."

She cuts the live feed and I feel like the floor's turned to a waterbed. My legs are wobbly. Standing in the hall with a hard-on that could smash concrete, I look around to see if anyone's watching, prepared to readjust my cock before heading back into the conference room when my phone dings again.

Nicole: Ticker

My dick deflates immediately. Dialing her number, guilt slams me from all ends. Ticker is Nicole's safe word. Or, as she says, her emergency code word.

She answers on the first ring. "Hi."

"What's wrong?"

"Can you meet?"

"I'm out of town. What's wrong?"

"Have you had a chance to read over my proposal?"

Rage spikes in my veins. "Are you fucking kidding me, Nicole?" I could kill her for this. "I thought you were in trouble!"

"You said you'd help me." Her tone shakes. "You promised, Mase."

"I know and I will. I've just been preoccupied lately."

Her shaky voice turns instantly venomous. "With business, or pleasure?"

"Bye." I hang up on her before I lose my shit.

Marching back into the conference room, I feel the weight of three men staring at me with hope.

They're most likely thinking I left to take the call we've all been waiting for.

I shake my head and plaster a fake smile on my face. "Sorry, boys. That was just a personal one."

The wave of exhales and sagging shoulders makes me feel even worse.

I haven't told them that the deal is practically done. That the paperwork was drawn and most of it is already signed. And I won't say a fucking word until all parties complete the last documents and I have copies of everything in my possession. Disappointment hurts when things fall through at the last minute. That level of letdown is nothing compared to what we have riding on this deal.

If all goes well, I'll be a very rich man. And so will my three best friends, who took a chance and trusted me to make some bold expansions with my company, using their money to do it.

Gage, Kerrington, and Landon took every dime they had and let me work magic with it. They're tight lipped, trustworthy, and terrified that this big risk will cost us everything. I refuse to let that happen. BanditFX might be my company, but it wasn't built without the support of these three men sitting with me right now.

My cell goes off again.

I don't even want to look. If it's Leah, I'll crack. If it's Nicole again, I'll explode. And if it's my pain in the ass mother or sister, I'm going to toss my phone into on-coming traffic. Very few people have my personal cell number, so the list of possibilities is short.

"Answer it," Kerrington demands.

Sweat blooms down my back as I pull my cell out and stare at the screen. It's a New York area code.

But it's not my mother's number.

It's…

I answer fast and keep my head down. "Mason Finch." I stare at the table because I can't meet the eyes of my colleagues until I know for sure that we're golden.

"Mason, it's Harris." Loud music plays in the background, making him hard to hear. "The documents are all signed. My secretary should have emailed everything to you." More loud noises and people laughing and screaming fill my ears as Harris yells, "Anyway, everything's in order. It's been a pleasure doing business with you."

He hangs up.

Holding my breath, I pull up my email and open the documents, just to be sure. It's all there. Everything we've negotiated. Everything we've hoped for.

I look up and the first set of eyes I see are Landon's. "We got it." I look at Kerrington next. "It's done." I beam a big cheesy smile at Gage. "He's signed everything."

The four of us let out with a chorus of yells and howls—just like we used to after every success we celebrated together in college.

"Holy fucking shit, man. I can't believe we did it!" Gage falls into his chair and buries his face in his hands. "We're rich."

"Filthy rich," Kerrington laughs. "Jesus, I feel like I'm floating. Are my feet touching the ground?"

"I can't hear you, my ears are ringing," Landon drops into his chair. "I think I'm going to pass out."

A billion dollars will do that to a person.

Kerrington marches over to the sideboard, where glasses and a pitcher of water sit. "Why can't this be vodka? We can't toast with water."

"I think if I drink alcohol right now, I'll

throw it up." Gage pales. "I have no clue how to handle this level of success."

"We should buy a boat," Ker says.

"Fuck that." Landon grins. "We should buy a whole ass island."

"I can't feel my face." Gage slaps his cheeks. "Being rich is making me numb."

I grip his shoulders and squeeze. "Get used to it, man. Because this is just the beginning." Splitting a billion-dollar payout is only the start for us. My first taste of blood turned me into an animal desperate for more of it. Now my three friends are experiencing the same thing.

"Thank you," Kerrington says from across the table. "Fuck, Mason. Thank you."

"I'm the one who's grateful here. If you guys hadn't trusted me with your money, I wouldn't have had the resources to pull any of this off."

"Who would have thought BanditFX would go from a simple cyber company to…"

"A multifaceted tech empire that's about to give Google a run for its money? Me. It was me." Landon puffs up with pride. "Totally me."

Gage shakes his head, laughing. "Weren't you the one who wanted to invest in Facebook?"

"Don't talk about the book of faces in my presence," Kerrington fake shivers. "I'm still scarred from college."

Laughter fills the room and I'm so goddamn happy I could fly.

This deal didn't just bring us to the next level of business, it's opened doors and new possibilities for each of us.

And now I finally have the freedom I've always craved.

"Gotta go, boys." I beeline for the exit.

"Hey wait! Where are you going?" Kerrington tosses his hands up. "We have to celebrate!"

"I'll see you all at dinner tonight. Cancel everything for the rest of the day."

"What about a press conference?" Gage argues. "This deal is huge for the tech world, Mason. There's going to be publicity about it."

"You can handle it." I have every confidence in all three of them to say and do the right thing in front of an audience. "Besides, you're prettier than me."

"Mason, you're the owner of BanditFX. We're silent partners. We can't just show up and start talking."

Shit, they're right. BanditFX is my baby, not theirs. And this deal might have been for all of us, but it's my face, my name, my reputation that's been in the spotlight all along. "Set it up and send me the info. I'll be there."

Just as I swing open the door to leave, Landon shouts, "Dinner is still at eight, right?"

"Yeah!" I yell over my shoulder.

Running out of the building, I call Leah first, but it goes straight to voicemail. I try two more times and leave messages, plus a text, and still, I get no response. I've just had the best news of my life and I want her to be the first person I share it with.

Sounds crazy, I know. But Leah will be thrilled for me. Not jealous or petty or threatened or snobby or basically any of the things my siblings would be. Jesus, my brother is going to have an aneurysm when he finds out.

My cheeks hurt from the smile on my face. My chest is tight. It's hard to breathe. Generational wealth is great, but there are always so many strings. I'm cutting them all, immediately. I've secured my future and can walk away from my family now.

It's what I've always wanted. Yes, I love my family, but I don't like them. The feeling's mutual, trust me. Grace might be the only exception to that rule, but even she makes me question her motives half the time when she's being sweet.

Could I have ditched the Finch family and lived on an average salary? Yes. Did I want to? Absofuckinglutely not. I like having the finer things in life. And I am willing to bust my ass to get them.

My mother can officially take my trust fund, and all her stipulations that come with it, and shove it up her ass.

It feels like it takes a hundred years to get back to the hotel. The traffic is horrendous. The lobby is crowded. The elevator moves at a glacial pace. Reaching our floor, I jog to our suite.

The place is empty.

Only the faint scent of whatever Leah sprays on herself that smells so damn good remains in an otherwise pristine hotel room.

Sitting on the edge of the made bed, I dial her number, and it goes straight to voicemail again.

Fuck.

The excitement and adrenaline drain out of me. Sitting in the silent hotel suite, I stare at myself in the mirror and for the first time in a long time, I remember how truly, utterly, and painfully alone I am.

Chapter 19

Leah

The day drags by like a snail in molasses. The dress I bought is the only thing I found worth spending money on in the ten million gazillion stores I've been to. I did finish my audiobook though, so that's a win. Then my stupid phone died, and I realized I didn't have my charger with me.

What's worse? I couldn't get an Uber without my phone app, so I had to go around asking people if anyone had a charger I could borrow. No luck there. Everyone I asked acted like I was a weirdo with a disease they didn't want to catch.

After an hour of searching, I finally found a café employee who was nice enough to let me use their charging station.

Not wanting to be a big pain in the butt, I only charged my phone enough to order a ride and thanked them with my last ten dollars, which I put in the tip jar. As bad as I wanted to check all my notifications, I was still in the red for my battery and didn't want to risk draining it dead again.

Unlocking the suite door, it swings open hard, and I stumble inside, running smack into a big body. I drop my purse and dress on the floor as I scream. "Holy shit, you scared me!" What's Mason doing back already? "You nearly gave me a heart attack!" Slapping his arm, I clutch my chest. "For real. I think I'm stroking out."

He doesn't say a word. Silence stretches between us.

"You didn't answer any of my calls or texts."

I don't want him to think I left him on read –*ahem, like he did me* — but I also don't want him to think I'm at his beck and call either. "My cell died."

His brow pinches together as he stares at me. "I was worried."

"Sorry." Wait. Why am I apologizing? "It's been a sucky day."

He grabs my hand and leads me into the suite. When he drops into a chair, he pulls me onto his lap. "What made it sucky?"

Shrugging, I feel like a brat for even saying anything. "Meh. I don't think California is for me."

He huffs a laugh. "It's not for me either." Running his hand in circles on my back, his touch soothes me. "Did you find a dress?"

"Yes. I got the purple one."

"Mmmm."

He knows which one I mean because he was online earlier when I was showing off the choices. The instant I saw his profile pop up, I nearly choked on my persona and wished it was just him online with me. "Does it really not bother you?"

"Does what not bother me?"

"The Daisy Ren stuff."

"Not at all. I like watching. I like knowing others are watching you, too."

Watch, but not touch. "Are you... I mean, have you ever shared a woman with someone else before?"

"No."

"Would you?" My heart gallops nervously, waiting for his response.

Mason stops rubbing my back. "No."

I don't know what answer I was expecting. "But you'd let them watch me?"

"Mmm hmm."

"Have you ever been watched?"

Our gazes lock when I look over my shoulder. I hold my breath.

"Only by you," he finally says.

That's hard to believe. "Seriously?"

"Yeah. I don't normally put myself out there. But lately, I've been wanting to test my limits."

"With me?"

"Yeah. With you."

I don't know how to feel about that. "Explain what you mean, Mason." I'm all for exploring kinks, but we should at least be on the same page about them first.

"I've had to walk the line my whole life,

Leah. Do what I'm told. Act like I'm expected. Speak when spoken to. My sex life…" He shakes his head. "It's been lackluster at best."

I can't imagine that. This man fucks like a god.

"My enjoyments always fall flat because they're considered perversions."

My thighs clench a little. "What do you like?"

"Voyeurism." He pulls my collar down and kisses the flesh of my shoulder, where he knows it'll make me melt. "Exhibitionism too." He runs his hands over my tits, kneading them. "And I love knowing other people want what I have."

My breath flutters with my exhale. "Do you mean me?"

"Do I have you, Leah?" Mason pulls my hair to the side and continues licking and nipping my neck, driving me fucking wild. "Because I don't think I do. Not yet. But I will." He unbuttons my jeans and tugs them down. "Fuck, I've needed you all goddamn day."

This isn't the first time he's said something that sounds loaded with other meanings. I'm probably hearing things, right? Overthinking it? I mean, we just met. We're having a fun fling. There's nothing serious between us.

So why does it feel like this is bigger than a luxurious hookup?

Pull yourself together, Leah. You're being ridiculous.

Mason's hand sinks between my thighs. It's the distraction I need.

"At home," I whisper as he rubs my clit with his finger. "There are a couple of sex clubs. We could..." Fuck that feels good. "Go sometime. Together. If you want."

He pauses.

"Don't stop, X." I wiggle my bottom and can feel his hard dick under me.

"Mason," he growls in my ear, sending goosebumps down my arms. "Call me Mason, not X."

That line I tried to draw between us, to keep us a fantasy, vanishes with our next kiss.

This man's touch is transcendent. My body can't *not* respond to it. I grind against his hand as he plays with my pussy. "Did you think about me today, Mason?"

"I'm never not thinking about you." Before I'm able to ask another question, he lifts me off his lap and carries me to the bedroom. "I can't get you out of my goddamn head, Princess."

He might not like being X anymore, but I *love* being his Princess. "I'm truly sorry that I worried you. I didn't leave you on read or anything on purpose." I'm not *that* spiteful.

"I'm sorry I didn't answer your text this morning," he says, surprising me. "Because the answer is yeah, I want to be official. Public. I want the world to know you're all mine."

I'm not sure how this is happening so fast,

and it's terrifying. But I don't want to be alone anymore and putting my heart at risk of getting broken is better than putting it in a jar to keep safe. I'd rather Mason shatter me to pieces than never play with me at all.

Besides, what if this turns out to be the wildest love story of the century?

Okay, I really, really, *really* need to stop reading so many fast-burn romance novels. It's giving me way too many ideas.

Mason lifts my chin with his finger. "You have that extra crinkle between your eyes again."

I rub my forehead. "No, I don't."

He kisses me gently, leaning me back on the bed. "I had some really great news today."

I run my fingers through his hair and wrap my legs around his waist. "Oh yeah? What was it?"

"I sold my company and made a billion." He kisses my neck and works his way down my throat.

My brain short circuits. "Wait. Did you just say a billion?"

"Mmm hmm." Like that's no big fucking deal, he keeps kissing me while sliding his hand up my t-shirt to palm my tits.

"A billion with a b."

"Mmm hmm." He sucks one of my nipples into his mouth.

I slap his head. "A *billion*?"

He bites my hardened nipple. "With a b. We

180

just established that."

"Oh my god, Mason!" I squeeze his cheeks and pry him off my boob. "That's amazing! Congratulations!"

With his face squished until he has fishy lips, he smiles at me. "Thanks."

I smash my mouth to his.

He laughs and has finally lost that sadness in his eyes. He looks younger, happier, even lighter than he had just moments ago.

"Mason!" I scream at him. "Holy shitballs, we have to celebrate!" I wiggle out from under him and climb off the bed. "What do you want? My treat. This is incredible. *I'm so proud of you!*"

He sits on the bed, running a hand through his dark hair. "I just made a billion and *you* want to treat *me*?"

"Hells yes, I want to treat you!" I grab his shoulders and shake him. "Oh my *god*. How are you so calm? I'd be bouncing off the walls if I were you. Shit, I feel like I'm bouncing off the walls *for* you!"

He laughs again. "How about I treat you instead?"

"Nope. That's not how this works. You should be celebrated, not me."

He snags my hand and yanks me against his chest so he can play with my tits again.

"Ugh." I smack the top of his head. "You're incorrigible."

"And you're all I've thought about today."

He runs his hands up and down my back. "You drove me wild in that dressing room earlier. Knowing all those men were fantasizing about being the lucky fuckers to take you out in that new dress, when it's *me* who gets the honor." He unclasps my bra. "I want to fuck you in that dress. On live camera."

My heart stumbles to a stop. "Are you serious?"

"Yeah." He yanks my panties down. "May I?"

May he fuck me on camera during a live? I'm not sure about that. "I have to think about it, Mason. That's a big step." And I think he's still flying high on his good news, which is making him not think clearly.

The thrill of doing something so risqué gives me goosebumps. I absolutely love the idea of putting on a show for others to watch. To be the spotlight in the center of this man's attention and affection? To let others enjoy watching him fuck me until I come, screaming through a wild, vicious, head spinning orgasm?

It sounds amazing, but... "I don't think we're there yet."

I sense Mason closing up. The last thing I want is for him to think I'm kink shaming him. I have a feeling his other women probably have, and I'm not like them.

"I've never exposed my whole body on camera before." I confess. "And I've never had sex on camera."

"But you did it with me that first night," he argues, confusion in his tone. "You masturbated with me as X."

"That was the first time I ever did something like that."

Mason's eyes widen. He swipes a hand over his mouth. "You're serious?"

"As a heart attack." But I don't think he believes me.

His dark brow arches in challenge. "Why did you pick that night then?"

"Honestly?" I shrug. "I was hung up on fantasizing about fucking you, Mason. That night I left your condo, you were all I could think about. All I could talk about in the restaurant, too. When X showed up online that night, wearing pants that looked just like yours, and had a nice couch like yours, I totally imagined it was you I was getting off with, not X."

Why does it feel like I've somehow cheated on him? Wow, my braining is complicated.

Standing naked between his legs, I feel like I'm still shrouded in a mask because I've had a double life all along. I feel like I'm more Daisy Ren than Leah with Mason. We're all sex. All fun. All fantasy.

And he's trying to take that part of me, of us, to the next level.

I'm not sure we're ready for that.

It's one thing to do it in a club. There are no

recording devices allowed there. We'd have anonymity. But the internet is another monster. It stays forever. It could ruin us both.

No. It could ruin Mason.

One slip, one detail, one wrong move, and his identity could be revealed.

With that in mind, how on earth are we supposed to date at all? How can we make anything official without me losing my job or him being laughed at and looked down on for dating me?

As he sits on the edge of the bed, still in a three-piece suit, I'm suddenly very aware of how different we are.

He just said he made a billion dollars today.

I used my last ten bucks to get my stupid phone to charge.

He's a somebody.

I'm a nobody.

Yet, I feel this overpowering need to protect him. And when he stares at me like he is right now, like I'm the only person in existence, I forget it isn't true.

I want this man. For now. For however long I can.

"I'm really proud of you, Mase." Leaning in, I kiss him with every fiber of my being. From my toes to my roots.

The kiss is long, steady, strong, and possessive.

"Fuck, Leah," he groans when I finally pull

away. His gaze drifts over my face but doesn't lower to the rest of my body. "Kiss me like that again, Princess."

I give him what he asks for.

When I pull away again, I'm the one left breathless. "I've never kissed anyone like that in my life." It's only after his eyes widen and brow furrows when I realize I just said that out loud. Stepping back, I tuck my hair between my ears and clear my throat. "Wow, that was deep."

Stop talking, Leah, you sound like an idiot.

Mason stands up and slowly closes the space between us. "I hold everything close to my chest." Sliding his hand under my hair, he grips the nape of my neck. "I took the biggest risk of my life a few months ago and have felt like a ticking time bomb ever since." He cups my cheek with his other hand. "Today, everything fell into place. My best friends and I just had the biggest payout—better than we've ever dreamed of."

It's hard to swallow past the lump in my throat.

"And the first thing I wanted to do was share my news with you, Leah." His eyes get these little crinkles on the side with his tight smile. "I realized today how very alone I've been. And when I couldn't get a hold of you, it was all I could do to not rip the city apart to find you. I've been pacing this room for two hours, scared to death that you might not even come back. Then I thought of how crazy it is that we've clashed like this since the first moment I saw you."

My heart spins in circles.

Mason runs his thumb along my cheek, his tone softening. "On a fucking whim, because I craved you so badly, I asked you to come be with me and here you are."

"Here... I am." Is it getting hot in here? I think I'm having a hot flash or something.

"I don't have anyone else in my life to share happy news with."

My dumb heart grows a fat, pouty bottom lip and tears up.

"You're happy for me." His four words land like an anvil. It's as if the concept is so foreign, he doesn't know how to process it.

"Of course, I'm happy for you." I pull his hand off my cheek and kiss it. "Why wouldn't I be?"

He shakes his head with this look of complete confusion on his face. His breaths build in his chest, getting heavier with every exhale. His jaw clenches. His shoulders tense. He looks like he's going to shatter.

"Mason." How can having someone be happy for him make Mason this emotional? "Jesus, what the hell happened to you?"

We stare at each other for what feels like an eternity.

"You," he finally says, brushing the hair from my face. "*You* happened to me."

Chapter 20

Mason

People come in and out of your life for a reason. Some stay. Some you can't wait to get out. Others you're just kind of stuck with.

Leah danced into my world, and I'm determined to keep her. The way she makes me feel isn't something I've experienced before. Not to this level, at least. That's a scary concept right there, considering I know so little about her. But that will come with time. I'm going to learn everything about this woman, and I hope I never stop learning about her until the day I die.

Pull back, Mason. You're doing it again.

I've said it before, and I'll say it again. I'm a reckless, impulsive, over-the-top, wild card. But my instincts have never been wrong. No matter how big the risk, how expensive, scary, or crazy it seems, if my gut says it's a good move, I make it and don't second guess my decision.

Engage with confidence. Keep honest. Seal the deal.

In one conversation, Leah's shown me her true colors. Her sincerity. Her real self. We've blurred her two personalities a lot, but under both is the same genuinely sweet, amazing, smart, confident woman.

I need to show her that X and Mason are the same man, too. I want her to know that this isn't a one-way relationship where I get all the rewards.

Leah's eyebrows lift, making her big doe eyes even larger. "Can we go out before dinner?"

"We can do anything you want."

"I'll put on the dress now, just in case we don't have time to come back and change later."

"Keep your hair like this." That probably makes me sound like a demanding asshole, but I seriously can't help myself. Running my hand up the back of her head, I grip a handful of her long, beach wavy hair and tug it. "I can't wait to spoil you."

She smacks my chest. "You've spoiled me enough."

"Not hardly." I haven't even begun to treat her the way she deserves.

"You flew me here, got this suite, and paid forty-five bucks for the dress I'm about to put on."

She should have spent ten times that on herself. Next time, I'll make sure she does. For now, I'll sit back and enjoy watching her get ready for a night out with me.

When she's done, Leah's made a bargain outfit look like runway material. "God damn." I can't stop staring at her. Leaning against the doorjamb to the bathroom, I admire the way she puts on her lipstick—dragging the color across her fat bottom lip three times to get it completely covered.

Her tits and ass fill out the dress like it was custom-tailored for her body. She's got her music playing through her cell, sitting on the counter by a pile of cosmetics. Her hips sway to the beat, as if she can't control herself around good music.

I walk up behind her and wrap my arms around her waist. "Stunning," I whisper against her ear.

She flashes me a seductive smile. Leah knows she's gorgeous, but I'm never going to stop telling her.

Picking her phone up, I open the camera and hit video record. After propping it against the mirror, I kiss down her neck.

I've never known a woman who could be so instantly turned on by just a certain part of their body getting played with the way Leah responds to me when I kiss, lick, nip, or suck on her neck. The strap of muscle above her collarbone is her weakest point.

She melts immediately.

My greedy hands skate along her body.

Leah hooks one arm around my neck and we both stare at the mirror, watching as I devour her.

"You taste so good, Princess."

A breath shudders out of her.

"So sweet." I kiss her weak spot again. "So perfect." I drag my tongue along her throat column. "Tell me what you want and it's yours." I push her long hair over her shoulder and run my lips down the slope of her neck, all the while keeping my gaze fixed on hers in the mirror.

"How do you do that?" she whispers.

"Do what?" I nip her a little harder.

"Look at me like I'm the only woman in the world."

"Easy." I massage her breasts. "You *are* the only woman in my world."

Leah swallows hard. "I want to come all over your dick."

Does my girl understand she's about to make a sex video with me? Her gaze flicks to the camera, giving me confirmation that yeah, she knows exactly what we're about to do.

Maybe hearing my confession was too much for her to handle, so she'd diverted to sex. Maybe what I said turns her on so much she needs my dick. Maybe I should shut the fuck up and stop thinking so hard.

"I want to come inside you."

Her eyes round for a second. "Mason."

"Tell me no and I'll pull out." I grind against her backside. "But I want to unload inside you, Princess. I'll beg if you want me to."

Her breath releases in a short puff, as if I've just knocked the wind from her. "You'll beg to come inside me?"

"Absolutely." She has no clue what I'm willing to do for her. If my girl wants me to crawl like a goddamn animal, plead, scream, set the world on fire, all for just a kiss from her lips, I'll fucking do it. What she's done for me today, just by being her authentic self, has made me a goner.

I'm at her mercy.

"If I let you do that..." she says cautiously, "you have to promise me one thing."

"Anything."

When she arches her brow, an evil little smirk plays on her lips. "I want you to pump everything you have inside me. Then I want you to eat your cum out of my pussy."

Fuck. Yes.

My heart slams against my bones. "Whatever you want, Princess."

Leah smiles triumphantly into the camera. Pressing my head against hers, I unbutton my jacket, my vest, my shirt, and strip out of each piece of clothing, one-by-one. When I slip my belt off, I bend Leah over the sink and strike her ass with it one time.

The echo is loud in the bathroom. A pale pink mark stripes her ass cheek. "Fuck, that's pretty."

She looks over her shoulder at me. "Do it again."

I crack her ass three more times, then reach between her legs to feel how wet she is. "God damn, woman."

"Do it again." She bites her bottom lip, dragging her teeth over the lipstick. "It's the only way I learn."

"I didn't realize we were giving lessons today." I crack her ass again with the belt. My dick's so hard it hurts.

"I think we've both learned something today, Mason."

"What's that?" I unbutton my fly and drop my pants to the floor.

"That some risks are definitely worth taking."

My belt clanks on the tile floor when I drop it. Looking at Leah, I want to drive into her from behind. But more than that, I want to kiss her. Spinning her around, I do just that and take my fucking time with it. Hoisting her onto the counter, I nudge her legs open and sink my throbbing dick into her heat while our mouths stay locked.

We both inhale sharply when I go as deep as possible.

Then a frenzy starts between us. Hooking Leah's legs over my arms, I fuck her hard and fast. Our bodies slap together. I've been wound up tighter than a drum all day, so I'm not going to last long. Not with how good she feels. Rubbing her clit with my thumb, I make sure she comes first.

I'm a gentleman, even if I fuck like a maniac.

"Come on my cock again, Princess." I wrap my hand around her throat.

Leah's pupils blow wide.

I drive into her so hard and fast, my fucking legs lock.

My girl holds on for dear life. "Don't stop. Please, don't stop." Two seconds later, Leah's mouth opens, and my motherfucking name flies out.

I chase my release harder. Faster.

"Fill me," she pants. "Please, Mason. Fill me up."

I've never orgasmed inside someone without a barrier before. The thought of filling her pussy with my cum has me seeing stars. The way her body grips me. The way she digs her nails into my shoulders. The scent of us together. "Fuuuuck." My dick throbs, shooting my orgasm deep inside her. "That's it, Princess." I grunt. "Take it all." Fuck, I can't stop. "Keep every drop I give you inside that pretty little cunt until I'm ready to feast."

It's the longest orgasm I've ever had.

Eager for a taste, I pull out and squat down, latching onto her pussy with my mouth. The flavor is exquisite. Licking her folds, I go all in and suck. Our orgasms fill my mouth. I love how Leah's flavor enhances my own.

"Show me," she demands.

Staying on my knees, between her legs, I stick my tongue out as far as it'll go. She holds the cell phone angled down at me, catching it all on video.

"Swallow."

I obey, stick my tongue out again to prove I took it all, then go back for seconds.

"Give me a taste." Leah pulls me by my hair and drags my mouth to hers. When she sucks on my tongue, I grip the counter to keep upright. We both look like clowns with her lipstick smeared over our mouths. "That was amazing, Mason."

Her cheeks are flushed, and eyes look hazy. My girl is floating right now.

"We taste really good together, Princess." I can't believe she let me felch her. Part of me fears it's an act, and she's really grossed out by it. Any time I've tried to bring this fetish up to someone, they look at me like I'm a disgusting freak.

Leah looks at me like I'm magical.

"That's been a huge fantasy of mine," Leah says. "To have a man confident enough to eat himself out of my pussy or my ass?" She shivers and I see goosebumps rise on her arms. Her nipples harden in the dress she's still in. "It's the hottest thing ever."

"Tell me every fantasy you have, Princess, and I'll make them all come true."

"Ohhh I don't know, I have a depraved imagination."

"Test me."

"Only if you're a good boy."

I step back to give her space and we both fix

ourselves to get ready to leave for the rest of the night. There's no wiping the stupid smile off my face, no matter how hard I try. After getting dressed, I sit on the edge of the bed and Leah grabs her heels from a box.

"Did those cost forty-five bucks too?"

"Nope. Add a zero to that one."

"Please tell me you put them on my black card." I don't want Leah spending her money if she can spend mine instead.

"No way." Leah hooks the straps with her fingers and swaggers over to me, carrying her shoes. "I need business write-offs too, buddy."

She hands the heels over and lifts her leg, pressing her foot to my chest, and waits expectantly for me.

I think I'm in love.

Fastening her ankle strap takes me no time at all. I kiss the top of her foot before letting her put it down again. She switches feet and I fasten the strap and kiss that one, too.

"Ready, Big Tech Daddy?"

"Where are we going?"

"You'll see." Leah grabs my hand and yanks me out of the suite. "It's a surprise."

Chapter 21

Leah

If I could just wipe this dopey, lovey-dovey, freshly fucked smile off my face, that would be great. But I can't. And I really don't even want to. Is it preposterous to feel like we've been together forever?

I don't even know his middle name.

Hooking my arm with Mason's, I lead him down the sidewalk and no matter how many guesses he makes, I refuse to tell him where I'm taking him. Three blocks down and around the corner is a bakery I passed earlier this morning.

"Here we go!" I open the door and sweep my arm. "After you."

"Thanks."

I beeline to the display of colorful cupcakes. "Pick your poison." Practically pressing my face against the glass, I eye fuck every single one of these delicious treats. "Vanilla, chocolate, coconut." I look over at him, suddenly terrified. "Please don't tell me you're a carrot cake man."

Mason laughs. "What's wrong with carrot cake?"

"Veggies do *not* belong in sweets." I shiver dramatically. "I'm still traumatized from the time my mother snuck zucchini into our brownies one summer."

"Chocolate," Mason says. "The darker, the better."

Perfect. I knew he had good taste.

"Excuse me, may we have that one right there?" I tap the glass directly over a row of decadent looking cupcakes with shaved chocolate curls and edible gold leaf flakes on top.

The employee carefully boxes the treat in a pink container and rings us up. "That's seven dollars."

I tap my credit card and grab the box. "Thank you. Have a nice day!"

Mason follows me out of the bakery, and I clasp his hand, swinging it happily while we walk down the street. I take him over to a shaded bench and plop down first. Presentation is key when you have a cupcake, so I carefully dig it out of the box and hold it gingerly in my hands. The sucker is big and heavy and smells like a glucose overdose.

"Wait. What's your middle name?"

"Why?"

"I need to know."

Mason rubs the back of his neck. "Elijah."

"Cheers to you, Mason Elijah Finch." I raise the cupcake to his face. "May this be the beginning of many more successes to come your way."

I can't read the look on his face. Maybe what I've said surprises him. Maybe he's wondering why I'm making this dramatic and silly toast. Maybe he thinks he should have gone with vanilla.

"Thank you, Leah." A big, wonderful smile spreads across his handsome face.

We stare at each other for an awkward moment, silence like a blanket resting comfortably over us.

"Lick it."

Without asking why, Mason sticks his tongue out and drags it across the top, gathering a bunch of the gold foil and chocolate onto it. Some of the shavings fall on his lap and suit. He chuckles, brushing it off. "Why did I have to lick it?"

"You didn't," I shrug. "I just like watching you use your tongue for things."

Mason's laugh is so loud it startles the elderly couple crossing the road. "Are you obsessed with this thing, Princess?" Mason hooks his finger into the corner of his mouth, pulling it back and sticking his tongue all the way out. The curvature of it is impressive. Obscene. When Mason flicks the tip of his tongue in slow motion, my pussy clenches because I know exactly how talented that thing is. This man could give Venom a run for his money.

"Your turn, Princess." He drags his finger

through the icing, then holds it up to my lips. I make a lovely show of drawing it into my mouth to suck it clean.

"Christ, you are perfection."

"Because I'm so sexy?"

"Because you're so *real*." He leans back and peels the cupcake wrapper away. Breaking the treat in half, he hands the larger half over to me. "You live so carefree, Leah. It's inspiring."

"Yeah well, you get one life to live, so I'm living it." We sit back and devour the dessert. "My parents were very strict with me and my sisters growing up."

"You have two sisters, right?"

"Yup. I'm the oldest."

"I'm the oldest too. Fucking sucks, right? We somehow have to be role models for them when we really need role models for ourselves."

"Ugh. Yeah. I'm the fix it sister. If there's a problem, Leah will fix it. If they need money, Leah will send it." I don't mind helping when I can, but sometimes it's a strain on me. "I love my sisters, though. I'd do anything for them."

"You guys close?"

I lick the icing off my thumb. "We live in different parts of the country. Once we turned eighteen, we each hightailed it out of our house. My youngest sister, Bex, moved to New York and lives with two roommates in a tiny apartment. My other sister, Aly, is a DJ who travels a lot. We see each other on holidays, but that's about it."

I miss them.

"Does your mom know about your camgirl hustle?"

Mason sounds like he's concerned for me. Like if my mom or dad found out about this big taboo secret, they'd be disgusted.

"Yeah." I swipe more icing onto my finger and lick it off. "I told her about Daisy Ren last year after she freaked out trying to understand how I was able to afford plane tickets to her house, on top of paying Bex's portion of her rent for a few months, and also getting Aly some equipment she needed. I wanted to keep my side gig a secret from her, but in the end, I came out with it. She was shocked at first, but eventually got on board. She's pretty open-minded, actually."

"And your dad?"

"He doesn't have a clue. I doubt he'd care, anyway. When my parents got divorced, it was probably the best thing to ever happen to us." Unlike most of my friends, whose parents split up and they were sad about it, my sisters and I were relieved. "He treated my mom badly. She worked two, sometimes three jobs, and he was perpetually unemployed. He always talked down to her and made her feel like trash when really, he was the hot garbage in the house."

Mason looks stricken. "I'm so sorry you were in an environment like that."

"Meh. It could have been worse. At least he

never hit her." Mason looks horrified at my words. I don't blame him. The potential for disaster is the reason I think I've never been serious with someone before. Spend your childhood with a father who treats your mom like shit, and some part of you becomes wired to expect all men to treat you that way.

My mom said she kicked him out because she refused to raise her daughters in a house with a man like that. Sadly, the damage had already been done and I've never let a man into my life for longer than a night or two.

Mason shakes his head. "I can't imagine treating a woman with so little respect."

I can't picture Mason doing that either.

"The day she kicked him to the curb, we had a big party. It was the best night ever. My mom ordered food from all our favorite restaurants, and we blasted nineties hip hop so loud, the cops were called." I'll never forget how she answered the door wearing a glittery pink party hat. The cops let her off with a warning and we went right back to partying until we fell asleep in a big blanket fort in the living room. "She showed me what freedom was."

"Does that freedom include coming out to California on a whim with a rich guy you just met?"

"Yup." I pop the rest of the cupcake in my mouth. "Even if it means being terrified on a plane to get to him."

Mason kisses the top of my head.

We sit together for a few moments, people watching, then he says, "My parents hold the purse strings to our trust funds. My grandparents put in so many stipulations, it got exhausting to meet expectations just to get money out of it."

"That sucks. I thought when you turned eighteen or twenty-one or whatever that you just get it all."

"Not with us." He stretches his arm across the back of the bench, and I lean against him. "They tell us what our careers will be, where to have our primary residence, who we have to marry."

"Holy hell."

"It's crazy what people will do when there's a lot of money on the line."

"I guess so, but that's awful. So, you didn't want to go to Yale?"

He exhales loudly. "I didn't even want to go to college. I wanted to be a baseball player."

I can just imagine Mason in a white uniform on a baseball diamond. "The next Bambino?"

He groans. "I would *never* have been that legendary. But man, did I want to run bases and travel and be part of a team." Mason plays with my hair like it brings him comfort. "I wasn't even allowed to play in little league. Baseball was so far from my realm of existence it was a complete fantasy with no hope of ever coming true."

Hearing the sadness in his voice cracks my

heart down the middle. "I'm so sorry."

"It's not your fault."

"Still, I'm sorry. You probably never got to be a kid."

"It wasn't all struggle and strife. I had my grandfather on my dad's side. He's the one who took me to games. So even if I couldn't play ball, I still got to feel the magic of it."

"From the sidelines."

"I didn't care. I loved it."

A spontaneously wonderful idea pops into my head. "How much time do we have before dinner?"

He glances at his watch. "Two and a half hours."

"Good." I yank out my phone and start googling. "Will you take me somewhere right now?"

"Absolutely. Where do you want to go, Princess?"

"You'll see." I stand up and grab his hand again, leading him back to the hotel so we can get his car.

Chapter 22

Mason

Following the directions Leah gives—because she won't let me look at her map—we end up in front of an arcade and sports complex.

"Come on." She lets herself out before I have the chance to open the car door for her.

"You want to play arcade games?"

"Nope." She yanks the big glass door open and holds it for me. "We're going to the batting cages."

My heart slams to a stop. She's in a dress and heels. I'm in a stuffy suit. "We're not dressed for this."

"We've got clothes on, don't we? That's good enough."

She marches up to the counter. "We'd like an hour in two of your batting cages, please."

Be still my lonely heart. "You're swinging too?"

"Hells yes, I am. And five bucks says I'm totally gonna smoke you."

Happiness rips out of me. I think I've laughed more with Leah than I have in the past decade. "You're on, Princess."

We head to the batting cages and Leah takes off her heels. Dear god, she's seriously going to do this.

We pick out our bats and get in our cages. The feel of the bat in my grip, its weight and shape, is both comforting and foreign. It's been a long time since I've done this.

Leah blows me a kiss and twirls her bat around looking like she's a goddam professional athlete.

The balls fly.

I swing and hit mine. She misses hers.

"Ohhh, fancy Big Tech Daddy knows how to hit it!"

"You have no idea." I toss my bat in the air, letting it spin once before I catch it effortlessly.

The balls fly again. I swing and hit. She swings and misses.

"You can have a couple freebies," I say, winking.

"I don't need them. I'm just—ah!"

She dodges the next ball. "Holy crap, these things come quick!" Before I can tell her to get out of the cage and say this is a bad idea, she points her bat at me. "Stay over there, Mr. Finch. Worry about yourself. I'm not the kind of woman who lets a pair of balls scare her off."

God love her.

Leah gets all serious as she grips her bat and chants, "See the ball, hit the ball. See the ball, hit the ball."

They fly again and we both swing. She hits, I miss. "I get triple points for that."

"Why?"

"Pretty privilege, obviously."

In that case, she should be up by one million points.

We both swing again, and I miss. Leah hits hers but wasn't holding the bat properly. "OUCH! SHIT!" She drops the bat and shakes her arm.

"Hold it at the base and extend your arm when you swing." The balls fly again, and I hit a grand slam. "Out of the park, baby!"

Leah picks her bat up and tries again. "Full swing. Bat at the base. See the ball, hit the ball." Bouncing on the balls of her feet, she hits the next five and tips the sixth. "This is so fun!"

Her joy consumes me. Being here with a bat in my hand and my girl next to me makes this the greatest moment I've had in forever. I didn't realize how much I've been missing in my life until Leah came into it.

We have a blast taking turns trash talking, teasing, and hyping each other up. The hour blows by, and we finally hang our bats back up. Leah's out of breath as she gathers her heels and puts them back on. "That was way fun!"

"You did amazing." I kneel and put her foot on my knee so I can fasten the strap. "Total main character energy."

Leah's jaw drops and eyes widen. Clutching her chest, she leans in and says with all seriousness, "That's the single greatest compliment of my fucking life." Then she squeals and wraps her arms around my neck and kisses me.

With little effort, I lift her off the bench and keep kissing her even as I press her against the exit door. She runs her hands through my hair, devouring my mouth and my dick's been hard for the past hour, which means it's a throbbing, painful rod in my pants.

"Easy, Princess. There are kids around here."

"Right." She flicks me between my eyebrows. "Down boy."

"Hey!"

She flicks me again. "Granny panties. Think about granny panties."

"Are you in them? Because that'll still turn me on."

"You're a mess." Giggling, she straightens her dress and snatches her purse. "Ready to go?"

No. "Yup."

After freshening up in the bathrooms, we head out and I swear I'm walking on clouds. This head rush is amazing. On the way to the restaurant, we take turns story-telling our favorite memories and what's more important: queso dip or guacamole.

"Queso is the obvious choice."

"Ugh," she pouts. "I knew there'd be a flaw in you somewhere."

"Guac looks like orc snot."

"Mmmm so yummy." She taps her fingers to the beat of the song playing on the radio. "So, who is dinner with? You never told me."

"My friends." Who I can't wait for her to meet, or I'd have canceled dinner already and taken Leah back to the hotel for some real fun. I pull up and let the valet take my car. Escorting Leah inside is a motherfucking privilege. Several pairs of eyes turn to us as we step inside, and I love it. She's stunning.

And she's mine.

"Good evening, Mr. Finch. Right this way."

Leah makes a "Ohhh fancy" face at me and lets me escort her towards the stairs that bring us to the private seating area. It's much quieter up here than it is on the first floor, which is what Landon prefers.

"Mase," he says, standing up once he sees Leah with me.

"Landon, this is Leah. Leah, this mongrel here is Landon."

"Hi." She reaches out to shake his hand, but of course, he kisses it instead. *Show-off.*

"Great, now she probably needs a rabies shot. Keep your mouth to yourself."

Landon clutches his heart. "You cut deep, man. Real deep."

"Hi Leah." Kerrington also stands to greet

her.

"This is Kerrington. Don't let his calmness fool you. He's even worse than Landon."

"If by worse you mean better looking, then yeah." He also kisses Leah's hand. "It's nice to meet you."

"And last, by design, is Gage." I look around. "Who must be running late."

"He went down to get champagne and is probably talking to the chef." Landon slides back into the booth. "We've been pre-gaming for an hour."

"So have we," I say, letting Leah squeeze in next to Landon before I sit on her other side.

Kerrington cuffs his ears. "Please don't talk about your pre-game. I'll lose my appetite."

I flip him off.

Leah wiggles in her seat. "Don't let Mason get to you, boys. He's just mad that I beat him."

I gawk. "You did not. It was a tie!"

"Nope. I won. You miscounted."

"Are we talking orgasms or..." Landon leans in and waggles his eyebrows. "Orgasms?"

"Kerrington, come get your boy before I throat punch him for flirting with my future wife." The words fly out before I can stop them.

Everyone freezes, including Leah, who recovers fastest. "Who says I'd marry you?"

Her tone is playful, but underneath is a hint of something else I can't pinpoint.

I lean against her ear and say in a low,

grumbly tone, "I'd beg."

Kerrington snarfs his ice water, splashing it all over himself.

Landon leans back and stretches his arms over the top of the booth. "Gage, man, you're just in time. Mason here was just proposing to Leah."

"Oh yeah?" Gage holds out two bottles of bubbly. "This is good timing then, huh? Hi Leah, I'm Gage."

She leans forward to shake his hand and my gaze falls to the swell of her breasts in the low-cut dress. Landon looks, too. And so does Gage. "It's nice to meet you."

Gage pops the cork and pours champagne in our flutes.

We all lift our glasses and Landon says, "Here's to swimming with bow legged women."

"Christ, Landon, that's not it," Gage groans. "Here's to those who wish us well, and all the rest can go to Hell."

"Wow," Kerrington huffs. "You both suck balls." Raising his glass higher, he clears his throat and toasts, "Cheers to that long straight piece in Tetris."

"For the love of God, make it stop," I joke. Raising my glass, and also Leah's hand, I kiss her knuckles before saying, "Here's to a long life and a happy one. A quick death and an easy one. A good girl and an honest one, a cold pint and another one."

"Ayyy!" Kerrington and Gage clank their

glasses. Landon chimes his with mine. Then we all take turns hitting Leah's.

Dinner starts off with a variety of small dishes. Leah plucks an olive from Landon's plate and pops it in her mouth, smiling like the devil.

He rests his elbow on the table and has this dopey smile on his face. "Tell me about yourself, Leah."

I stab a crouton and eat it, waiting for her reply.

"Oh, there's not much to say."

"Where did you and our boy meet?"

She looks over at me, completely unfazed while my heart's pounding. I'm pissed my natural reaction is nervousness and decide to do something about it. "She works for a cleaning service."

"Nice. You like it?" Gage spreads bruschetta onto a toast point.

"Yeah, I do." Leah pulls a face. "Is that weird?"

"Doing what you like?" Gage frowns. "No. Why. Is it supposed to be weird?"

Leah looks up at me as if she hadn't expected him to say that. Winking at her, I sip my water.

"This place sucks." Landon flicks an olive off his plate. "I hate hoity toity food. Why are we here?"

"Because it's the nicest restaurant in the city." Ker slathers butter on his roll and shoves the whole thing in his mouth at once.

"You eat like an animal," Gage states.

Unbothered, Ker swallows and says, "I fuck like one too."

"Do you guys want to get out of here?" Landon asks. "Leah, doesn't a burger sound way better than this…" He pokes the food on his plate. "What the fuck even is this?"

"Pate." I stab another crouton on my plate.

"I'm game to leave if you guys are," she says happily.

"Oh, thank god." Gage tosses his napkin on the table.

"Where do you want to go, Princess?" We all turn our attention to Leah. She looks at each of us like a deer caught in the headlights. Then a devilish smile spreads across her lips.

"Dancing." She looks directly at me. "I think we should go dancing."

Landon wraps his knuckles on the table and hops out of the booth first. "You heard the lady. She wants to go dancing. And what Leah wants, Leah gets."

"Ohhh I like that." She shimmies out of the booth next. "Can we make that a thing?"

"Absolutely." I'll live by that rule for the rest of my life if she lets me.

Gage follows Leah and Landon down the steps, leaving Kerrington and me going last.

"What the fuck is going on, Mase?"

"What do you mean?"

"I haven't seen you this happy in... forever." Kerrington slaps a stack of cash on the table to pay for the meal we're not sticking around to eat. "And I know damn well it's not the money that has that goofy ass smile on your face." He tilts his head in Leah's direction. "She do this?"

"Yeah." My cheeks hurt from grinning so hard.

"I didn't even know you were dating anyone. Especially with the whole Nicole thing."

The mention of her name is like ice water poured down my back. "Do me a favor, Ker. Don't mention her name."

His pace slows down. "Fuck, Mase."

"It's a nonissue, and it's staying that way."

"How long have you and Leah been together?"

"Three days." Or is it four now? Wait... when did we first get together? "Maybe a week and a half?"

Kerrington freezes. "You're fucking *joking*."

My glower tells him I'm not.

"Shit." He looks over at Leah, who's talking animatedly with Landon. "You better know what you're doing, man."

I don't. But I'll figure it out.

Chapter 23

Leah

We hit two clubs before we find one that has a vibe we all like. An hour in, and I'm drenched in sweat and smell like way too many people's perfumes. The music is fantastic. Beat after beat, the energy on the dance floor spreads like wildfire and everyone's grinding and swaying in a huge mass.

I spot Mason watching me from the second-floor balcony with Kerrington. Gage is going strong, dancing all up on a woman in a tight red dress. He lifts his beer bottle up in the air when she spins around and drops it low, putting her face at dick-level.

Landon went to the bar.

It's so crowded, it's dizzying. Laser lights streak the club in blues and purples. The DJ's wearing an oversized mask that makes them look like a bobble head on the stage. They're mixing songs, driving the crowd wild with beats that hit us smack in the chest.

It's been so long since I've gone clubbing. I wish my sisters were here with me. Aly would really appreciate this DJ's skills and Bex would be a blast to dance with.

Once the song's over, I snake my way over to order a bottle of water. I need to hydrate before I die-drate.

"I've got it." Landon lifts his hand to the bartender. "Put it on my tab."

"No, no, I can buy my own water."

"Let me be a nice guy tonight, Leah." He puts his hands together like he's about to pray. "Pretty please, with cherries on top?"

"Fine." It's just a bottle of water. Still, I don't always like it when people pay for my stuff. It makes me feel like I owe them something in return, which isn't true, but whatever. My brain is not always logical.

"I'm not sure where you came from." Landon grabs the water and twists the top off for me. "But I've never seen Mason like this before."

"Like what?" I take a careful sip. The liquid pours down my throat, dousing my overheated body with icy goodness.

"Happy. Himself." He takes a sip of his drink. "Kerrington says you guys just met?"

This feels like a trap. "Yeah."

"And he flew you out here?"

"Yup." I don't think I like where this conversation is going.

"He's never done that before." Landon rests his elbow on the bar. "He doesn't date. He doesn't go clubbing. And he sure as shit doesn't talk about having a future wife."

"That was just a joke."

"No, it wasn't." He takes another sip, cautiously looking up to where Mason and Kerrington have secured us a table. "He's crazy for you."

"That's…" I shake my head. "No, he's just in a great mood because of the deal you guys secured today. A billion bucks would make anyone happy and talking crazy."

"Not Mason." He takes another sip of his drink before locking eyes on me. "He doesn't give a fuck about money like that."

"Well, he seemed thrilled when he told me about it. He was super proud. As he should be."

"Mase took every dime he had, combined it with ours, worked his ass off, and sold his precious company for a mint."

"Hence the happy mood." I'm not sure I understand the problem here. What's Landon getting at? "He made a lot of money today."

Landon's smile falls. "No, sweetheart. He *lost* everything today."

My gut twists. "What do you mean?"

Landon downs his drink and slams it on the bar just as Mason approaches. "I gotta take a piss."

"Could have lived my whole life without that knowledge," Mason says, letting Landon slip by him. Leaning against the bar, he runs his finger along my ribcage. "I thought you might need rescuing down here. Landon doesn't shut up after he's had too many drinks."

"Oh no, he's fine. He was drinking club soda."

"Really?" Mason's brow pinches as he looks in the direction Landon went in. Then he focuses back on me. "You wanna dance?"

"Always." I drain the rest of my water and place the empty bottle on the bar. Mason leads me into the crowd, his big hand engulfing mine. Even with his jacket and vest off, he must be sweltering. I'm melting in my dress, and it barely covers anything.

We easily find the rhythm, and I wrap my arms around his neck. We don't say a word, but our eyes talk plenty. It's hot, secretive, but there's worry in both of our gazes, too.

The night ends faster than I expect, and we head out to our cars just after the club closes.

"Leah, it was a pleasure meeting you." Kerrington drapes his arm over my shoulder. "You keep this fucker in line, mmkay? Spank him if you have to. It's likely the only way he'll learn."

"Gage, come get your boy." Mason looks over his shoulder. "Wait. Where's Gage?"

"Over there," Landon points.

Gage is against the wall with his shirt unbuttoned and back against the brick wall. His head is tipped up to the night sky and his eyes are closed. He looks like he's about to pass out.

"Awww, he can't hang like he used to."

Landon pushes out his bottom lip. "Don't worry, I'm driving them both home."

Mason's eyes narrow. "How much have you had to drink?"

"Nothing. I stuck with club soda all night." Landon puts his hands up. "Shocker, I know." He looks at me next and shoots finger guns. "I can't wait to hang with you again, Leah."

"*Leah*?"

I freeze at the sound of that voice. Turning slowly, I swear I'm hallucinating. "*Aly*? Oh my god! What are you doing here!?"

"Uhhh shouldn't I be asking *you* that?" My sister rushes towards me with her arms out wide. We hug and squeal, rocking back and forth.

"Fuck me, there's two of them?" Landon runs a hand down his face.

Aly looks him up and down. "Damn, sis. Who are all these pretty boys?"

Landon nudges Mason. "She thinks we're pretty."

"Those two over there are Kerrington and Gage. The blondie here is Landon. And this…" Pride swells in my chest for no good reason as I drag my man over to her. "Is my boyfriend, Mason."

"*Boyfriend*?" Aly snorts a laugh.

"Yeah. Boyfriend." I want to choke her now. Of course, Aly would find it hilarious that I have a boyfriend. I've never had one of those before.

She stops laughing immediately. "Well shit.

I… *damn*." Turning to Mason, she shakes his hand. "Hi, I'm Aly."

"The DJ." Mason's friendly attitude eases the tension that just crept into our circle. "Leah's told me all about you. She didn't mention you were in town, though."

"I'm only here for the weekend to work at this club."

"That was *you* up there?" I can't believe I was dancing to my sister's beats this whole time. She's really grown in her craft. And in looks. Her hair is bright blue with streaks of black in it now. "I didn't know you've gone incognito." How long has it been since I've spoken with Aly and checked in on her? Now I feel like a shitty sister.

Aly stuffs her hands in the back pockets of her ripped jeans. "It's easier this way. Wearing a mask makes me more intriguing. You know how hard it is making a name for yourself in any business. If you don't stand out, you don't matter."

A bouncer holds the door open and looks directly at Aly. "We need you back inside."

"So much for cooling off. Gotta go." She gives me another hug and whispers. "I'm really proud of you, sis."

Guilt and shame run through me, making tears prick my eyes.

We squeeze each other tightly, and when Aly lets go, I shove my emotions down and wave goodbye to her.

The ride back to the hotel is a bit of a blur. I have a lot running through my head.

Mason tosses his wallet and keys on the table. "You've got that extra crinkle again."

Ugh. Can he not be so perceptive for once?

"I think I'm going to take a hot bath."

Mason doesn't join me, and I don't know if I'm relieved or disappointed.

• • •

The press conference was at ten am. Mason had to cancel a construction site tour to make it in time and left the hotel in a rush this morning. I watched it in bed, on my phone, and have already packed my things to head back home.

By lunch time, Mason returns to our suite and looks utterly exhausted.

And sad.

What Landon said to me last night weighs heavy on my chest, and Mason's behavior only lends truth to his words. I want to ask about it, but it's not my place to pry.

I haven't told him what's on my mind, and I don't know if I should. Last night I didn't get a wink of sleep. Neither did Mason.

We didn't have sex. We didn't talk much. There's a weird chasm between us, filled with things I don't want to bring up because I'm worried it'll pop the bubble we've been playing in.

My sister saying she was proud of me last night did something to me. I hate it.

And Mason looked stoic and stiff on that podium at the press conference. He didn't smile at all.

If it's true he lost everything, why would he tell me he had the best news ever and wanted to share it with me first yesterday?

Something isn't right here.

I'm dreading getting on a plane again. I'm also scared that this fantasy is over. I'll go home and eventually Mason will too, and then what? At least I'm not taking a private jet home. He's put me on a regular big ass plane a goose can't take out. *Shit, or can it?*

What happens now? Do I say *goodbye?*

Thank you?

Call me?

You're amazing and I don't want this to end, but I also don't know how to have a relationship because I've never been in one before?

Commitment isn't something I've faced. No guy has ever wanted to keep me. And I've never felt compatible with anyone enough to make the effort. Not like I do with Mason.

Grabbing his packed bag, he hoists it on his shoulder. "Ready, Princess?"

Wait. I'm confused.

"You're coming with me?"

Mason tilts his head and arches an eyebrow. "Did you really think I was going to let you fly alone, knowing you're terrified of planes?"

Tears burn my eyes. "You're really coming with me?"

"Where else should I be if not with you?"

"But..." Doesn't he still have work to do here? What about rescheduling that construction visit?

"He lost everything." Landon's words from last night slither up my spine again.

Now I feel like a selfish bitch. I'm acting like a child when this man's going through some real-life shit.

Mason grabs my hand and gives it a tug. "Come on. We can't miss our flight."

• • •

Three hours later, we've boarded, and the plane takes off. Palms sweaty, I squeeze my eyes shut and hold my breath.

"Breathe, Princess." Mason puts his hand over mine.

I shake my head.

"You're going to pass out if you don't get oxygen."

We're flying first class, but I'm too terrified to enjoy it. When something soft hits my lap, I pop my eyes open to see Mason's placed the fleece blanket over me.

"It's chilly in here," he says with a wink.

No, it's not. I'm burning up because I'm so

nervous.

The plane dips for a second, and I squeak in panic. I grip his forearm and dig my nails in. "What was that?"

"Just getting past some clouds, baby. Don't worry." He holds my hand under the blanket, rubbing my knuckles soothingly.

I suddenly get a horrible, bad, brilliant idea. "Distract me?"

Mason's eyebrows rise to his hairline.

The panic squeezing my throat makes me squeak, "Please?"

He looks around to see if anyone's coming, then repositions himself. I spread my shaking legs apart enough for him to have access to my body.

"Unbutton your fly for me, Princess."

That requires me to unclench my hands, which isn't happening. "I can't let go of you."

His facial features soften. "Okay. Hang on." He quickly maneuvers my shorts down for me. "Stay quiet, okay?"

I squeeze my eyes shut again and nod. The plane tilts and I swear I feel like I'm going to fall out of the fucking window. "Mason."

"It's okay. We're just turning around to get on course." He sits forward and leans towards the window, his big body blocking us from the aisle. Then he slips his finger into my pussy and slowly fingers me. I'm not wet enough. I'm too scared for this. Mason notices the problem and pulls out.

"Open that pretty mouth for me."

I unlock my clenched jaw, and he puts his fingers in between my lips. Twirling my tongue around his digits while my stomach roils. I feel dizzy.

"That's my good girl." He gets back under the blanket again.

"It's a pleasure to have you with us again, Mr. Finch."

My eyes fly open. The airline attendant stands next to us with a tray of filled glasses. "May I offer you two some champagne?"

Mason doesn't turn to address her. "You thirsty, Princess?" He shoves a slick finger inside me and I gasp.

"N-no."

"We're all good, thank you." He plunges into me again while I stare awkwardly at the airline attendant. She looks down at the blanket, then back at me.

I'm immediately wet.

"If you change your mind, just let me know." She heads to the next person in front of us and Mason presses his palm to my clit. I can't take my eyes off the attendant. When she flicks her gaze in our direction again, Mason plunges into me deeper. My breath catches.

Her knowing what we're doing, us in a very public space, the adrenaline I have from the plane going higher, the scent of his cologne, heat of his touch, his closeness, his attention, my desperation to hold on to him for however long I can…

My orgasm blows my anxiety away. Tipping my head back, silently screaming with my mouth wide open, the only noise I let slip is a moan when he drags the last few pulses of release from me. Pulling his hand out, Mason sucks both fingers clean and looks at his palm that's also glistening. With a wicked smile, he drags his long tongue across it and cleans that off, too.

"Better?"

"I feel like I'm floating."

Mason chuckles and tucks me closer to him. "Try to get some sleep, Princess. We'll be home soon."

Home.

What happens once we get there?

Chapter 24

Mason

Leah slept the entire flight. Exhaustion has a chokehold on me, but I'm fighting it. I think we're both caught up in our heads. Aly definitely rattled Leah last night, and I think Landon did, too. I just don't know how.

I've got my own shit to deal with though, and as much as it pains me to say it, I need to focus on my problems, which will start as soon as my family hears the news about BanditFX.

I've lost my empire. I've lost my power.

I'm starting over.

The only thing that makes it bearable is that I've made my best friends filthy rich. I've also secured jobs for all my current employees. Well, former employees now. They'll each be getting substantial raises.

I have every confidence that the man who bought my company will do amazing things with BanditFX but…

My heart still hurts. That company was my baby.

My everything.

There's a new hole in my chest that makes it hard to breathe.

It was a good business move to make. The right one to make. And even though Kerrington and Gage will stay on as board members, Landon and I aren't part of it anymore, which terrifies me.

What if the one thing I built crumbles now that I'm no longer with it?

Get a grip, Mason. It'll be fine. BanditFX isn't your responsibility anymore.

I need to have faith that I made the right decision. Business is always a risk. This overwhelming need to take care of everyone, to make sure every employee's needs are met, will pass. They'll be fine.

My financial freedom was worth losing my company for.

My heart's still broken about it, though.

I could have kept BanditFX and continued to rake in millions, but it was time to let it go. I have more business ideas to invest my time and money into. This isn't the end. It's the beginning.

"Wake up, baby." Kissing Leah's forehead to rouse her, the scent of her shampoo calms me. "We've landed."

Her eyes flutter open, and she looks out the window, relieved because we're on the ground already. "I slept through touchdown?"

"You were out like a light." I stand and stretch. "The plane's just about empty, too."

"Holy shit." Leah looks mortified. "Why

didn't you wake me sooner?"

"I was in no hurry for this trip to end I guess." Mesmerized by her sweet facial expressions, the little noises she makes, the way her hand would twitch on my lap, it was a perfect distraction for my racing mind during the flight. "You talk in your sleep."

Her gaze narrows. "Do not."

"You said all kinds of things."

"Like what?" She stands up while I grab our luggage.

"Mason is amazing. Mason is so sexy. I love his big tongue."

Her cheeks turn crimson immediately. "I did not say that."

"You definitely did. It just kind of came out as 'mmmsehr mmmphrr'. Very mumbly, but I could totally tell what you were saying."

Her laughter fills the cabin. "Come on." She slaps my ass. "Get me off this flying metal death trap."

We head out of the airport in this suspended state of brittle bliss. Like we're both trying to hold on to the last remnants of the past couple of days when we both know some things are going to change any minute.

Lacing my fingers with hers, we walk out of the airport together. I don't want to let her go. Not even to get in my car.

"So, when do you head back to your home-home?" Leah's hair curtains her face, falling over her shoulders in dark blonde waves.

I need to touch her again. It's not sexual, it's comforting. "I'll drive home tonight."

"Drive?"

"Yeah, it's a bit of a haul, but I need time to think."

She shifts away from me a little. "Well, I hope you get home safe."

"I'll call you when I arrive. If you'd like."

That little extra crinkle between her eyes fades a bit. "Yeah. That would be nice."

"I'm not sure when I'm going to be back in town, but…" I pull out my key. "Take this. Enjoy the bathtub at my condo."

She stares at the key like it's going to bite her. "Ummm."

"Take it." Kissing her forehead, I add, "It's just temporary."

I've been planning to buy something bigger in the area because this is where I want to make roots and start a new company, but Leah's welcome to use my space for however long I have it. Except she pulls away from me and crosses her arms. I have no clue what her problem is. "Did I say something wrong?"

"No, Mason."

"*Princess.*" I try to put my hand on her thigh, but she tilts out of my reach. My chest tightens. "*Leah.*"

"It's just temporary. I know." Her voice shakes. "It's fine."

My mind's too exhausted to catch up with her words fast enough, but by the time we pull into a neighborhood of single houses, I think I get where the miscommunication is. "I meant my condo is temporary. Not us."

She keeps staring out the window instead of at me.

"Leah, look at me." My jaw clenches as I juggle driving, following the GPS, and giving my girl attention at the same time. "I'm keeping you."

She doesn't say a fucking word.

"Look at me, Princess."

She finally turns towards me and there are flecks of gold shining in her brown eyes from the sunset glowing through the windows. "How's this going to work, Mase?"

"I have no idea, but it will. I'll be traveling back and forth for a bit, but I plan to settle down here."

"*Here*?" She repeats that word like I'm stupid to do so.

"This city is starting to boom. There's a lot of potential and opportunities. Besides…" I lock my gaze with hers. "I love it here."

Holding out my key again, relief floods my system when she takes it this time.

"*You have reached your destination.*" Tapping *End Route* on Leah's phone, I park in front of a red brick rancher.

With her hand on the door handle, she looks back. "Do you have time to come in?"

I'll always have time for her. "Absolutely."

Her next smile is an arrow through my heart. We head up the narrow cement walkway and she digs her keys out of her purse.

The first step into her house and I'm smacked with Leah's scent. "It smells like you in here."

She drops her keys on a table in her little foyer. A fat black cat jumps down from the couch and starts meowing loudly. Leah picks it up and scratches the side of its face aggressively. "I know. I'm so mean leaving you alone." She holds it out to me. "This fat bastard's name is Wicklow. We tolerate each other."

I scratch his head until he starts wiggling and meowing louder. Leah puts him down and fur flies all over the floor. "Let me give you the grand tour."

Her home is pretty. Colorful and fun, like her. Pictures hang all over the walls and clutter side tables. Most of them have Leah with other people, but there are a few colorful art prints hanging too. We have very different styles. Hers is better than mine.

"I have a feeling my entire house could probably fit in your living room wherever you really live," she half jokes.

She's right. Leah's home is lovely, but her entire kitchen is smaller than my second pantry. "Your home is perfect."

Like her.

"Not hardly, but I love it. It's enough for me."

It's a *home*. There's no comparing what we have because no matter what house of mine you go to, it's the same. Stark walls, pretentious art prints I didn't even pick out myself, plain furniture with no comfort. Leah has one, two, three... *seven* blankets in the living room alone. I have a white comforter on my bed and that's it.

"Let me show you my favorite space."

I think she's going to bring me into her bedroom, but I'm lured into a spare room with bookshelves lining all the walls and a collection of mugs and candles on display.

"Welcome to my nest."

There's a gigantic bean bag in the center of the room. More blankets and extra pillows are piled onto it and scattered on the floor. Wicklow bumbles in and climbs up a cat tree, settling on the highest perch.

It smells like pumpkin spice and vanilla.

"These..." She fans her arms out dramatically, "are my book trophies. I listen to an audiobook, then buy a physical copy so I can look at it." She plucks one off the shelf and pets it. "So pretty."

There are more books in this tiny space than I had in my parents' library growing up. "And how many trophies do you have?"

"Whoa, whoa, whoa, we don't count. No, no. None of that. We just look at the pretties and love them. Numbers don't matter." She shoves the book back on the shelf and plucks a coffee mug up that says, *Talk Darcy To Me*. "This is my most favorite mug in my ever-growing collection."

She's adorable.

"I fucking love you." I don't care if she wants to hear it or not. I don't give a shit if it's too soon to say it—because it definitely is. I'm not holding back. I never have before and I'm not starting now. "You're the realest person I've ever been around."

Leah runs her hands up my arms and hooks them around my neck. Dragging me under a wave of lust, she whispers, "I want you one more time before you leave."

She's got me for life. It just hasn't penetrated her head yet. "Whatever you want, Princess."

We waste no time between kisses, nipping and teasing, as we strip out of our clothes. Leah drops to her knees and takes my dick in her hands. Looking up with those big doe eyes, she opens her mouth wide and sucks on my head.

I'm marrying this woman.

Not because of the wicked moves she can do with her tongue, or because she's the sexiest creature this side of the universe, but because she's *everything*. She's my missing piece. The secret ingredient to the life I've always dreamed of.

"Does my princess like sucking my cock?"

"Mmm hmm."

I wish I could get this on camera. Her cheeks hollow out when she sucks me and that little crinkle comes back between her eyes because I'm too big to fit down her throat, no matter how hard she tries.

Sinking my fingers in her hair, I grip a handful and rock my hips and fuck her pretty face. Then I pull out. "Your mouth is where I *finish*." Reaching between her thighs, I test to see how wet she is. My girl is sopping wet. "I want to taste you." Carrying her over to the beanbag, I toss her onto it. "Spread those luscious thighs for me."

Leah does no such thing. In fact, she holds her legs closed. "Beg."

Fuck, I'm so in love.

Dropping to my knees, I give her what she wants. "Please let me taste your pretty, sweet, messy cunt, Princess. I need it."

"How bad do you need it?"

"More than my next breath."

Leah spreads her legs. It's like opening the pearly gates to heaven.

I drag my tongue along her slit. Her arousal is sweet, tart, and addictive. I swallow it greedily, and go back for seconds. "You taste so good, Princess."

She reaches down and spreads herself wider, putting it all on display for me.

I devour her pussy, alternating between my

tongue and fingers until I have her writhing, begging me to make her come. Every time I sense she's getting close, I switch things up and prolong her release.

"Please, Mason." She lifts her head so she can watch me eat her out. "Please. I'm dying."

Dramatic little thing.

I shove two fingers inside her and drag them along her inner walls, watching her toes curl. "Fuck!" she squeaks. Her knuckles turn white as she clings to the beanbag. Her inner walls flutter and I double down, sucking on her clit.

Her orgasm rips through her. She screams like she's being murdered. "MASON!"

There's no relenting on my side until I'm sure she's spent. Then I shove my dick inside her.

"Oh my *God*." Her eyes flutter shut.

Hooking her legs over my shoulders, I fuck her hard. Pressing my hand on her belly, I relish the way my cock feels, sliding in and out of her body.

"Fuck... oh my god... shit... too much!" Leah gasps. "Too deep!"

I ease back and only push halfway in. "Better?"

Her hair's a wild bird's nest at this point. Cheeks flushed, and eyes heavy-lidded, she pants, "Give me a hand necklace. Please. Pretty fuck... fucking... holy shit that feels so good."

I'm buried balls deep again as I wrap my

hand around her throat and continue fucking her until I'm ready to come. "I want you to swallow me, Princess." Another minute of hard thrusts and I pull out. Leah immediately sucks me off like I've got some kind of magic elixir in me. "That's a good girl." Groaning and panting, I'm getting close. "That's such a *good fucking girl.*"

I blow my load so hard she chokes. "That's it. Keep going, Princess." It's too much for her to swallow all at once. My cum drips out of the corners of her mouth and down her chin and it's so goddamn hot I think I might come again.

Leah pulls back and sucks in a harsh breath.

Leaning down, I lick her mouth and kiss her. We're salty and sweet together. Perfection.

My cell rings from the floor. Leah's gaze falls to it and that crinkle is back between her eyes.

"Ignore it," I say.

"What if it's important?"

"Nothing's more important to me than you."

Her expression shifts and I think I've said something wrong again.

My cell won't stop ringing.

"Here." She reaches it before I can.

We both see NICOLE written across the screen.

Of all times for this to happen... *Shit, shit, shit.* I want to ignore it, but if I do, that'll lead to more problems. Hitting the answer button, I hold it up to my ear. "What?"

Leah slides off the massive beanbag. Her cat stares at me like he's judging me.

"You sold BanditFX?"

"Yeah."

"Jesus Christ, Mason. What are you *thinking*?"

"I told you I had everything handled."

"You didn't tell me you were handling it like that! Why didn't you tell me? I had to hear about it from the fucking news. Seriously, Mase?"

"I can't really talk about this right now." Leah's gathering her clothes from the floor, dressing faster than my mind can put together. She tosses my boxers and pants onto the beanbag and leaves the room. "I've gotta go."

"Mason Finch, don't you dare hang up on m—"

I hang up on her.

Stuffing my legs in my pants, I hop on one foot to chase Leah down. She's made it to the kitchen already. Wicklow runs past me, and straight to her. "Sorry about that."

She picks the cat up and hugs it. "Nothing to apologize for."

"Nicole's a… friend."

"Good for Nicole."

Is she jealous? "She's *only* a friend."

"Mason." Leah lets her cat go again. "It's fine. Why are you acting so guilty?"

Guilty? I didn't think I was, but… okay,

maybe I am. It's just that Leah doesn't know everything yet and telling her after fucking her seems like really bad timing. "She's a family friend and a nosy bitch."

"Okay." Leah puts her hand on her hip and leans against the counter. "And?"

"And…" My cell goes off again.

Leah rolls her eyes. "Answer it, Mason."

Without even looking at the screen, I take the call. "Yeah?"

"You've been busy, Mason."

My mother's tone triggers a trained reaction from me. My walls slam into place, and I keep aloof. "Always am." Leaving Leah glaring in the kitchen, I head into the spare room to grab the rest of my clothes. "What can I do for you?"

By now, she's received my letter attached to the paperwork drawn up by my lawyer.

"Do you still plan to attend the gala?"

"Of course. I gave you my word that I would be there." But I hear what she's *not* saying.

Her first-born son has no place at her side anymore. There will be no seat at the family table for me. I'm officially cut out.

"Fine." She hangs up.

Numbness seeps into my body, starting at my face and spreading down my chest, arms, and legs. I don't feel the fabric of my shirt as I button it. I don't feel the floor beneath my feet as I walk back into the kitchen. I don't feel my tongue when I say, "I'll see you soon" to Leah, and I don't feel the doorknob as I turn it and leave.

Risk is a wild thing. It can bring you everything you've ever wanted and take everything you have.

In both cases, you're left wanting.

Chapter 25

Leah

It's been a week since Mason left. I wasn't going to use his key, but tonight I am. We've talked on the phone, briefly. I haven't been online as Daisy Ren at all. Taking a couple extra houses to clean this week helped make up for the money I spent in California and did wonders for keeping me occupied, so I don't overthink.

"It's about damn time," Mak says when I answer my phone. "Shew. Playing phone tag all week was ridiculous!"

"I know. You work too much."

"Says the pot to the kettle."

"Fair."

"Sooo, how was the trip? Tell me *everything*."

"It was *wild*. Weird and wild. And fun."

"All good things."

"I saw Aly." For some reason, that's been weighing on me all week.

"No way! How the hell did that even happen?"

"She was DJing at a club we went to."

"That's oddly coincidental."

"Tell me about it. We'd been dancing for hours and when we came out at closing time, she was there. She recognized me before I even saw her."

"Holy crap, Leah. How's she doing?"

"We didn't get a chance to catch up, really. She looked good." I walk circles around Mason's living room. "Seeing her brought up a lot of shit, though. I'm in my head about it."

"Talk me through it."

Tucking hair behind my ear, I pivot and start walking circles the other way. "She said she was proud of me." Mak stays quiet. "I think she meant it. And that got me all fucked up, because why would she say that?"

"Did she say it out of the blue or…"

"I'd introduced her to the guys. Once I got to Mason, she was called back into the club. That's when she hugged me and said she was proud of me. I hadn't even told her about what I've been up to with my new potential business venture. And I know she's not all that thrilled about my Daisy Ren stuff."

Mak stays quiet.

"Say something, Mak. I'm feeling awkward and dramatic over here."

My bestie clears her throat. "How did you introduce Mason to her?"

"Uhhh as Mason."

"You were like, this is Mason?"

"Yes. No. Wait." Pinching the bridge of my nose, I think back to that night. "I introduced him as my boyfriend. To which she looked shocked out of her mind, snort-laughed at me, and then repeated the word *boyfriend* like it was a made-up word. Then she changed her attitude when she saw I was serious." I pivot and pace in the other direction again. "It felt like being hit with an anvil when she hugged me goodbye and said she was proud of me. I've been fucked up about it ever since."

Mak doesn't say anything again.

"Damnit, Mak truck, don't do this."

"I'm not doing anything, Leah."

"Yes, you are! You're making me feel worse!" I drop onto the sofa and tuck my legs in. Mason's condo sucks. There are no blankets or pillows or anything comfy. It doesn't even smell like him in here anymore. I hate it. "I don't know why I'm feeling so anxious."

"I do. And you do too, you're just being thick headed about it."

"Gee, thanks."

"Leah, I love you. You know that. We've been friends for how many years now?"

"A bunch."

"Mmm hmm. And you've never had a boyfriend. You only have hookups."

"And dates."

"Also just hook ups."

"I've seen a few of them more than once."

"Still hookups." Mak sighs. "Does Mason know about the camgirl thing?"

"Why?"

"Does he?"

"Yeah."

Mak's voice softens. "Remember when we talked about how this wasn't a commitment? That you both can have fun, then split off into your separate lives?"

"Yeah."

"Well. Do you still feel that way?"

"No," I confess quietly. "Oh my god, I'm broken. He's busted me all up. How am I attached already?"

"That's what happens when you fall for someone."

Oh god, what if she's right? "This is going to hurt." I feel sick to my stomach. "I don't want to get hurt."

Mak sighs. "Who says this won't last? There's no reason to think you'll get hurt, Leah."

Every man breaks a woman's heart. Only fictional book boyfriends are safe. There was a time when my mother was head over heels for my dad. They used to dance in the kitchen and hold hands in the grocery store. The bliss didn't last. Day after day, year after year, their love turned into hate, cruelty, and misery.

I can't imagine how painful it would feel if Mason did that to me.

"He said he loved me when we got back

from California."

"Holy. Shit." Mak pauses. "That's…"

"Fast. Stupid. Probably a lie." We're just in some kind of delirious happy-new-couple phase. It'll die down, eventually. He said it in a moment of excitement and probably wasn't thinking.

Except that doesn't sound like something Mason would do. The man is calculative and brilliant. Thoughtful and thorough. I don't think he'd say anything he didn't mean.

Mak clears her throat. "What did you say back?"

"Nothing." I bury my face in my hands. "I diverted the conversation by having sex with him."

"Okay, okay. So, if he said it again, right now, what would you say?"

I don't want to admit my answer. It's too insane.

"Holy fuckballs, Leah."

"What?" Defensiveness forces me to stand up. "I wouldn't say anything."

"Liar."

"I…"

"Leah, this is what your sister meant. I'm telling you right now, Aly saw in your face what I'm hearing in your voice. You're in love, girl."

"No. It's just good dick and fun."

"That can be part of love too, you asshat. Carson's good dick and fun. Look how fast we fell for each other."

"Yeah but."

"No yeah buts. Aly's proud of you for finally letting your damn guard down. For giving a man a chance to treat you right."

"All my guys have treated me right."

"No. They treated you like temporary entertainment. And you're no better. Look," she says, clearing her throat. "Mason isn't going to be like your dad was with your mom, honey. Don't put your past on him like that. It's not fair."

She's right. "Oh my god, I'm in love with him." My ass hits the leather cushion. "I... this is..." I don't know how to feel about it. "I'm in love with Mason." Saying it out loud makes me giddy. "I'm in love with Mason Finch."

"Yup."

My heart skips around like a child holding a balloon. "I am head over stiletto heels in love with Mason motherfucking Finch."

"Say it louder for the people in the back."

"I have a boyfriend."

"Sure do."

"And I love him."

"We've established that already."

My cheeks hurt from how big my smile is. "This is *crazy*, Mak."

"Love is crazy. Trust me. It makes you do wild shit you never thought you could do."

"Like get collared and chased in the woods?" I tease.

"Or get on a plane when you're terrified of

flying just to spend a couple days with each other because twelve hours apart was too long."

Holy shit. We did that. "I'm crazily, wildly, passionately, completely, happily in love with Mason Finch."

The way we fit, our personalities, our energy—we're the perfect storm together. Squealing, I rock back on the couch, kicking my feet. "I gotta go, Mak."

"Love you."

"Love you, too!"

My hands shake as I pull up my contacts list to find his number. I just want to hear his voice. I want to say something. Tell him... fuck, I don't know. That I'm over the moon for him. That I miss him. That I want to come see him.

"I heard you were in love with someone, Princess."

My heart stops.

Mason leans against the archway of his living room with his arms crossed. He tips his head and narrows his gaze. "What was his name again?"

"Mason," I walk around the coffee table with butterflies in my belly.

"*Mason.*" He puckers his mouth and saunters towards me. "There are a lot of Masons out there. You'll have to be more specific."

"Mason motherfucking Finch." I jump into his arms, wrapping my legs around him tightly.

His eyes widen. "Hey that's me."

Fireworks blast through my heart, lighting me up from the inside out. "It sure is, you lucky sucker."

"I've missed you, Princess."

"I didn't think you were coming back until next Tuesday."

"Yeah, well, that was too long to be away from you."

I agree. "This is nutty." I shove his hair back and kiss him.

"Nutty was thinking I could go without you so damn long."

Chapter 26

Mason

My plans changed drastically the instant I made it back to New York. I had everything in line, ready to execute, but my mind couldn't latch onto anything other than Leah. Texts and FaceTime calls weren't enough. I wanted to touch her. Smell her. Kiss and hold her.

I came back as soon as I could, even while the rest of my world has likely caught on fire.

The instant Leah's in my arms, I know I've made the right decision. She calms the frenzy in me. Doesn't seem possible, considering she's a ball of energy all the time.

Leah sounds so hopeful when she asks, "Are you staying here for good?"

"Yes and no. I still have to pack, and there's a gala to go to this weekend, but that's an overnighter. I'll have someone else handle selling my house."

"And how are my boys?"

She teased me the other night over the phone about Landon, Kerrington, and Gage being her boys. I love how she fits so perfectly in our found family.

"They're getting into trouble with their new money, I'm sure."

Leah laughs. "Well, if I win the lottery one day, I'll be going bananas for a hot minute too."

Why wait for miracles? "Say the word and I'll write you a check. You can pretend you won the lottery and go on a spree."

Leah smacks my shoulder playfully. We head into the kitchen, and she sits on a stool while I get a drink of water. "Not to ruin the mood, but I need to talk to you about something, Mason."

There's nothing she could say that would ruin my good mood. "Go for it."

"I haven't asked because I didn't think it was my business, but Landon said something to me at the club and it's been bugging me."

My body tenses. If he said something that made her feel bad or uncomfortable, best friend or not, I'll kill him. "What did he say?"

"It's about selling BanditFX."

I relax. "Oh?"

"He said you lost everything. Is that true? Because the math doesn't math. You told me you got a billion dollars. The news is all over the internet and there's no bad publicity. I don't get it."

It takes a few heartbeats for me to simplify my clusterfuck life and form it into an efficient explanation. "There's a clause in my trust fund that says if I don't follow all the stipulations, I'm out."

"Is owning your own company one of them?"

"Yes." I take a sip of my water. "And no." I dump the rest down the drain and place my glass in the sink. "It's fine to have our own 'side hustle' as long as it doesn't make the family look bad. And we can sell, merge, or dump whatever we want. But that money stays in the family, no matter what."

My chest tightens.

"I didn't use any family money to make BanditFX. I worked as a bookie in college, and took every dime I made, along with money that Landon, Ker, and Gage could spare, and threw it all into stocks. I day traded my ass off, which I do not recommend, by the way."

It gave me an ulcer and melted half my brain.

"I paid them back every cent, with interest, and took my portion to Vegas. In one game of roulette, I risked it all, and made a fortune."

I'll never forget the feeling of that payout for as long as I live. And I'll never go back and try it again, because that was a once in a lifetime break. A high I'll forever chase and never catch again.

"That's what I used to start up BanditFX. Then I brought in *your boys*," I tease, "and they got shares of the company. We expanded and diversified, and they helped me make the company successful enough to catch the attention of major players in the tech industry."

"That's incredible."

The awe and pride in her voice does little to staunch my bleeding heart.

"My parents didn't know how I got the start-up money. They, like my siblings, assumed I'd done it all with my trust fund. I haven't touched a dime in that account since I was eighteen. My grandfather, the one who took me to the baseball games?" She nods, following along. "He warned me that the minute I spent one cent from that account, they'd own me. He was right. I had my private lawyers look into it and there's language stating that anything bought with the money in the account is family property. That means my parents could control it."

I'd rather die than let them touch BanditFX.

"What about your house in New York?"

"Everything I have, I've bought with my own money."

Her mouth falls open. "That's incredible."

"It's pathetic. To be owned your whole life? Bought your whole life? It's suffocating and unfair." Dropping on the stool next to her, I steeple my fingers and look straight ahead. "There's more."

"Okay."

"Another stipulation is…" *Fuck me sideways, this is awful timing.* "Marriage."

"Do you have like, until the age of thirty, to find someone?"

"Something like that." My frown has my chin quivering. "It's arranged for us." There's nothing I can say to make this easier. "Our marriages are pre-arranged to keep bloodlines and business ties tight. To keep our secrets covered."

"What secrets?"

I shrug. "Financially speaking, there's a lot of grey area come tax time. Adultery and politics, too. It's ugly in my world, Leah."

"And where does Nicole fit into all this?"

She knows the answer.

"Oh my god." Her voice sounds so distant. I have to turn to see if she's even still with me, or a figment of my dying dreams.

My heart crashes against a concrete wall when tears slide silently down her face. I have to do something to make her understand. "Leah," I try to wipe her tears away, but she dodges me.

Hands falling to my lap, I shake my head. "She and I have been trying to find a way out of the arrangement for years. We prolonged it as much as we could. I finally told my parents that I wouldn't marry her. Shit got ugly between our parents. Nicole's been working on a business plan to secure her finances, but she doesn't have the capital because she spends a lot of her money on dumb shit. We got into it a couple months ago because I said she was self-sabotaging while crying about how unfair her life is. But she makes it worse when she's constantly doing retail therapy — blowing her money on purses and trips and jewelry. I cut ties for both of us by doing what I've done. I'm out of the Finch family, Leah. She can't have me." I raise my hand fast and add, "Not that she ever wanted me, or that I ever wanted her. Christ, I'd rather swim with sharks while wearing a meat suit than be in a relationship with that woman."

Leah doesn't speak for a long time. The silence spans across our bodies, spreading into the kitchen and coating the living room and hallway like a heavy residue.

"Say something," I whisper. "*Please*, Leah."

"I don't know what you want to hear."

The truth. "Tell me what you're thinking."

She remains quiet and my head screams for her to understand that yes, I lost a lot, but I'm gaining her and that's the biggest win ever. "I'll give us a good life." Whatever she wants, I'll make sure she has it. "Leah, I love you."

She silently grabs my phone from the counter. "Call her."

"Who? Nicole?"

"Yes. Call her right now."

Without hesitation, I dial her number and put her on speakerphone.

Nicole picks up on the fifth ring. "Ugh, what do you want?"

"I have someone who wants to speak with you."

Her tone changes instantly to a much

happier one. "Is it Leah?"

Leah's eyes widen in surprise. "Hi, Nicole."

"Hi! It's so nice to speak to you. Mason won't shut the fuck up about you, girl. It's disgusting. No offence."

"None taken." Her eyes lock on mine. "He's just explained to me the situation."

"You mean the one he's set on fire? Yeah. Thank God he did it. I would *die* if I had to be tied to him for life. I definitely mean that offensively, Mase."

"Feeling's mutual," I clap back.

"Are you coming to the gala with him this weekend? I'd love to meet you. Mase says you're drop dead gorgeous and fun as hell. Okay, well he didn't tell *me* that, but Grace did. That's his sister, in case you didn't know. Apparently, he kept her up all night talking to her about you. She overslept and missed her massage appointment the next day. Mason's inconsiderate like that."

Leah's brow pinches. "How's that Mason's fault?"

"It just is," Nicole says drolly. "I don't make the rules."

I flip her off, even though she can't see me. It makes Leah giggle quietly.

Nicole keeps yapping. "It'll be nice to have a fun night for once. Please say you're coming?"

Leah looks up at me and smiles. "I'll be there."

"Yay!" Nicole's happy tone turns to disdain

in a blink. "Mason. Will Gage be coming?"

"Yeah. They'll all be there."

"Fuck my life." Nicole groans. "Okay, well I gotta run. Leah, feel free to run him over with your car. Still come to the gala, though. Byyyye." She hangs up.

"I..." Leah cringes. "I think I like her."

My entire body locks. "No. No, no, no. She's awful. She's annoying!"

Leah laughs, but I catch the nervousness vibrating in it. Grabbing her hands, I kiss her knuckles and make sure I have her full eye contact. "I'm crazy in love with you, Leah."

"You must be." She pulls her hands out of mine. "You're giving up a lot."

No, I'm not. "I'm gaining everything I've ever wanted."

"Mason, your parents are going to hate me."

They might. But it's because they can't control her. "*You* might hate *them*."

"Oh, I think I already do. What kind of parent controls their kids this much? Geez. Cut the cord. Mind ya business, mom and dad."

God love her.

Leah's expression softens. "But is there some way we can help Nicole?"

"I've done all I can. Taking myself out of the equation permanently means she's not stuck in a loveless marriage." Yet. I dread to think who her parents will match her with now that I'm out. "My sister's in the same boat. It's probably why they're besties."

Leah's shoulders droop. "Oh wow."

"Mmm hmm."

"Well. There's only one thing left to do now."

"And that is?"

"I need a show-stopping dress that's easy to dance in. We're going shopping."

Chapter 27

Leah

It's on like Donkey Kong.

We arrived in New York late last night, fucked all over Mason's stupidly big house and crashed in bed around three in the morning.

"My dick's so hard it's going to snap off." Mason runs his fingers up my bare thigh. "Fuck I need you again, Princess."

I slap his hand away. "Eyes on the road, buster."

He growls but listens. There's something incredibly heady about having a man like Mason wrapped around my pinky. I think I could strut around in a potato sack, and he'd get turned on by it. The man's insatiable.

My cell lights up in my purse. Digging it out, I roll my eyes. "Ugh, it's Mr. C." He's messaged me six times today.

Mason's jaw ticks as he sails through a red light.

"He can suck it." I hit a button and put my phone in my purse again.

"What did you just do?"

"Blocked him."

"Poor guy."

"Daisy Ren's getting big changes soon, anyway. She has big plans."

Mason puts both hands on the steering wheel. "Intriguing. Care to share?"

"Not tonight. This idea of mine is so close to getting the green light, I'm too scared to jinx it by sharing it with anyone yet."

"I get it. I'm the same way."

The guilt I've felt holding this news so close to my chest eases hearing him say that. I haven't even told Mak about my big plans. No one but me and a few investors know about it.

When Mason brought up me being on camera with him again last night, while we fucked on his balcony, I almost spilled the beans. I want to tell him about my endeavor so badly it makes me giddy. But I won't.

Stay strong, Leah. It's not time yet.

We reach the hotel where there's a cluster of people and flashing lights on the red-carpeted sidewalk. I gawk at the crowd, reality setting in about how huge this event actually is, as guests climb out of their stretch limos and fancy cars. Mason told me it was a big deal, but I didn't think it would be *this* fucking big.

Holy crap.

Mason frowns as he looks at the guests ahead of us. "Jesus, she's pulled the big dogs in for this."

I have no clue who any of these uber wealthy people are, and I don't care. "Ready to play?"

Before I can pull the latch on the car door, Mason growls. "Don't you dare touch that door, woman."

I put my hands up like I'm under arrest.

"I've got one job and you're trying to take it from me." He steps out and swaggers around his car, looking like billion-dollar sex candy, and opens my door for me. "Princess."

I take his offered hand and the number of lights that flash and flicker in my face makes it hard to see. Mason warned me this could happen. Actual paparazzi are here tonight.

Some call out his name and ask questions about BanditFX, but he doesn't answer them. Smile, wave, walk—he acts more like a robot than a human. Wow, he's really uncomfortable here. It makes me want to protect him even more.

This calls for a diversion.

"Come on." I link my arm with his and feel the way he's tensing up. "Relax, Mase. We're going to have fun tonight." I'll make sure of it.

"This is the worst."

"How about I make it the best?" We get inside and after a quick scan of the lobby, I veer him off to the left.

"Where are we going?"

"I don't know." I keep walking. "I'm winging it."

We finally end up in a closet that's got a vacuum and a shelf full of trash bags, towels, and cleaning products.

The irony is not lost on me.

"Take a deep breath," I urge. "You looked like you wanted to crawl under the red carpet and disappear out there."

Mason's gaze eats me up. "I'd rather crawl under your dress." Chest rising, his heavy breaths punch out of him, and I swear he's going to rip his tux. Wrapping his arm around my waist, he pulls me flush against him. "I'm not going to be able to keep myself off you all night. I don't even want to try."

The instant his mouth lands on my neck, I groan. He always hits my hotspot on first contact and is absolutely relentless. "God, Mason." I sink my fingers into his hair, messing it all up. "You drive me wild."

"Good." He drops to his knees. "Because you do the same to me."

He ducks under my gown and rips my panties apart with one good yank.

"Damnit, Mase! Those are my prettiest pair."

"They're still pretty," he argues from between my thighs. "And now they're mine." He licks my pussy. "This is mine too." He licks me again.

"Ooof!" My legs give out with that one. Holy hell his tongue is talented.

"Hold still, Princess." Mason lifts my right foot and places it on his shoulder. Then he gives me an orgasm that has me groaning into the tablecloths hanging on hangers behind us.

When he crawls out from under my ballgown, he wipes his mouth off with my ripped panties. "I want to fuck you."

Samesies.

"We're going to play a game, Princess." He takes my underwear and balls them in his hand. "You're going to try to keep quiet, and I'm going to do everything in my power to make you fucking fail."

"Challenge accepted."

With a wicked grin, he stuffs the panties into my mouth.

He unbuckles his belt, yanking it free from the loops in one swift, hard pull. The sound makes me wetter. Mason grips my throat and pushes his big cock inside me in one thrust. "Fuuuuck, how are you so goddamn wet?"

Easy. I'm with him.

With one leg wrapped around his hip, the other barely touching the floor, I hang onto his shoulders while Mason lifts me off the ground with every thrust.

I know we're supposed to behave tonight, but I want everyone to hear us. See us.

Envy us.

"I want to fill you up. I want my cum dripping out of you all night." His speed picks up. The friction is amazing. Add to that the roar of people mingling on the other side of the door, the thrill of being caught, and my orgasm blasts out of me. I spit the lace out of my mouth and scream his name.

He slams me against the door, his pace quickening. "Fuck, woman. Say it again."

"Make me."

My man's eyes blow wide, and I have about one-point-two seconds to brace myself before he bites down on my neck, right on my hotspot. "Oh god, Mason!" My pussy clamps down on him immediately.

"That's my good girl. Let everyone know who you belong to." His thrusts deepen and body heat radiates through his tux. "Fuuuuuck." His cock pulses when he comes.

I'd give anything to have this on camera—the way he looks, how he sounds.

Too bad that can't happen.

Once he's spent, Mason lowers me to the ground and presses his head against mine. "Holy shit, my heart's beating so fast."

"Mine too."

He picks up my ruined panties that I'd spit onto the floor and puts them in his pocket, not bothering to scold me for taking them out of my mouth earlier.

"Ready?" He's back to being the Mason I know, instead of the intense, detached version I feared he was turning into outside.

"Yup."

Fluffing my gown, I follow him out of the closet, and we join the rest of the crowd for cocktails. He introduces me to a bunch of people, but their names go in one ear and out the other. He keeps up with polite conversation even as he scans the room constantly.

Who is he looking for?

"There she is!" A familiar voice chimes from the bar.

Landon swaggers over to us with amber liquid in his glass. "Damn, woman, you are looking good tonight."

"She looks good every night, asshole," Mason grumbles.

"Forgive me. Mason's right." Landon kisses my hand. "But you look exceptionally good tonight." He spins me around. If I didn't know any better, I'd say he was trying to get people to look at us.

"Stop being an attention whore," Gage growls, walking over with a hand in his pocket. He claps Mason on the back in greeting before grabbing my hand and kissing it. "It's wonderful to see you again, Leah."

Mason looks even more relaxed now. "Where's Kerrington?"

"He's here somewhere." Landon looks around. "I swear I'm gonna put a leash on him. He gets distracted too easily. Ohh! Bacon-wrapped scallops." He walks off.

Another man shows up to the party. "How dare you show your face here."

Who I can only assume is Mason's brother, Jackson, storms over to us. He's a slimmer, shorter version of Mason, but with lighter hair and a different shaped mouth.

Landon hands Mason his drink. "Here, you look like you need this more than me."

Mason takes a sip. "Jackson."

"You've got fucking balls, motherfucker."

My man doesn't seem fazed in the slightest. "You should get a pair yourself. They're pretty great to have."

"And so fun to play with," I add.

Kerrington snarfs his drink. "I really love her," he whispers loudly to Landon.

"Me too," Landon whisper-yells back.

Someone else joins the scene. Tall, thin, jet-black hair and bright... blue... *Oh my god. No way.* This new guy stares right at me and all the color drains from his face.

"Carmichael." Mason dips his head.

Jackson grabs Carmichael's arm and steers him away. "Come on, Jon. Let's go."

A small bell chimes. Cocktail hour is over, time for dinner.

Except I can't move, even as everyone else heads inside the large banquet hall.

"Hey, are you okay?" Mason grazes my arm, giving it a little squeeze. "That's just Jonathan Carmichael. He looks scarier than he is.

Trust me."

I watch Jon escort his wife—his very pregnant wife—inside. He looks over his shoulder, pinning me with another hard look before disappearing through the door with everyone else.

My mouth runs dry. "That's Mr. C."

Mason tenses and we both stare at each other for several measurably slow heartbeats. "You're sure?"

"Positive."

His jaw ticks.

"Who's Mr. C?" Landon asks.

I don't want to answer that question.

"What do you want to do, Leah?" Mason's hard stare hits me square in the heart. I think if I told him I want to leave, he'd take me home immediately. But we didn't come here to tuck tail and run.

"Come on, boys. Escort me into the lion's den. I'm starving." Hooking Mason's arm, I fortify my walls and remember what's important tonight.

The ballroom is decked out in elaborate floral arrangements, crystal, gold candelabras, and embroidered cloth. It looks like a fairytale.

And I'm the princess at this ball. Dressed in vintage haute couture, my confidence is through the roof, and nothing will dampen it. Especially not Jonathon foot-fetish Carmichael.

Head high, Mason escorts me over to our

table. "We're at lucky number thirteen." He pulls my chair out as I scan the room, feeling a lot of eyes on me at once.

Carmichael and Jackson are in an animated conversation at the table next to ours, and they both look over at us at the same time. Jackson grins this awful toothy smile right at Mason and my stomach sinks.

Fuck.

Chapter 28

Mason

Liberation is dangerous. Once you have no fucks left to give, your personality does a little reset.

"Have a seat, Princess." Pulling the seat out for Leah, I wait for her to descend gracefully into her chair before I push it in a little. She's the show-stopping centerpiece in this ballroom and everyone knows it.

Mr. C can kiss my ass if he thinks he can intimidate either of us with that dumb ass smirk of his. I have no doubt he thinks he can use my girl against me and blackmail me with Daisy Ren, but he can't. I'd have to be ashamed of being with her for that to happen, and I'm not. I'm proud as hell she's my girl and I love what she does for a living.

"Hey." I turn Leah's head with my finger under her chin. "Don't worry about him. If he says one thing to you, I'll knock his goddamn teeth out." I've been dying for an excuse to pop Carmichael in the mouth for years.

She shakes her head. "I'm not worried about

myself. I'm scared for *you*."

"Me?"

"He's just told Jackson I'm Daisy Ren. I know it. They're going to tell everyone here that I'm a…that your girlfriend's a…" She leans in and whispers, "*sex worker*."

I arch my brow, unfazed. "You're a hustler like me. You work hard just like me. You carved a path for yourself and have done amazingly well, just like me. You and I are the same."

"You don't charge people to…" She clams up and drops her gaze to her plate. "This is a huge mistake."

Fear spikes in my veins because I think she's going to run. Bolt out those double doors like Cinderella at the stroke of midnight. That's not fucking happening. I grab her hand and squeeze it reassuringly. "Stop doing that, Princess."

"Doing what? Pointing out the truth?"

Her cheeks redden more. Her eyes shine with tears she's trying to hold back. "Don't put yourself down again. You're a businesswoman, Leah. You found a niche, put in the hard work, and made a damn good life for yourself."

She grimaces. "I put peanut butter on my feet for money."

"Working smarter, not harder." I fail to see how this is a problem. Her feet are adorable. If they can make her money so she can have the things she wants, why's that an issue?

"He's married," she spits out. "And she's

pregnant."

I'm sure lots of people online are in similar situations, but I don't think Leah's faced the reality of who was in her audience before. It's easy to lie online. Maybe she fooled herself into believing the only ones paying to chat with her were single, lonely men and women. In my world, however, this is not earth-shattering news. Half the people in this room are likely having affairs. They're all in a club of some kind, all pretending they "would never" when in fact they "will always" if given the chance.

Nearly everyone here is just out for themselves. Carmichael is among the worst of them. Part of me keeps hoping Jackson will kick him to the curb, but I doubt he ever will. It makes me wonder if Carmichael has something on my brother and uses it against him every chance he gets.

"His wife is beautiful and sweet," I say. "She's also fucking at least two other men in this room." Probably more. I wonder whose baby is even in her belly. Hell, Carmichael offered her to me two years ago when he first approached me about becoming a board member for BanditFX.

I declined, of course, and it insulted him.

Boo fucking hoo.

Leah called this place the lion's den. It's not. It's a toxic cesspool.

The urge to dash out of here with Leah in my arms so I can protect her is strong. But I said I was going to be here tonight, and I don't back out of my word. No matter who I made that promise to or if they deserve my loyalty or not.

Besides, I'm untouchable now. Liberated. And like I said already, that's a dangerous thing. It's got me wanting to say and do all kinds of rebellious shit.

"If I hold him down..." Landon leans in on Leah's other side. "You can stab Carmichael in the eyes with this cute little salad fork."

Her laugh is fake.

"Hey." I make Leah look at me again. "No one except the people at this table matter."

Her brow pinches, and that little extra crinkle is back. I kiss that spot, and the scent of her shampoo and perfume fortifies me. "We can leave soon."

But first, I have a point to make.

Leah lets out a shaky breath. "I'm sorry. I don't know why I'm being like this." Worry and anger war in her gaze.

"You're being protective of me, Princess." Which is incredible of her. No one other than the three guys at this table have ever given a shit about me. Leah genuinely looks like she wants to burn the world down on my behalf. God damn, I'm the luckiest motherfucker alive.

It's not being called out as a camgirl that has her upset, it's that she's already imagining them spinning our relationship as something more scandalous. She's worried about what all these people will say about *me* dating her. I don't think she cares what they'd say about her at all. It's me and my reputation that she's getting paranoid over. "I promise you there's nothing to worry about."

I couldn't be prouder to have Leah by my side. She's incredible, smart, funny, sweet, and doesn't judge anyone. Her soul is so pure, it makes me think angels really exist.

"You're right." She rolls her shoulders back and changes her tone. "Fuck these bitches. And fuck Carmichael."

"Atta girl."

Kerrington sips his drink. "Your mom hasn't even looked over in our direction."

And she won't.

As the wait staff rush from table to table, placing chilled salad plates down, I keep my attention on my real family – the one I picked. Gage, Kerrington, and Landon didn't come with plus ones, which means our table is only half full. I'm glad. It makes us stand out more.

It will also make my mother suffer yet another bout of disappointment caused by me.

This night's turning out fantastic.

"What are they serving for dinner, anyway?" Landon frowns. "I hope it's not something too froo-frooy. I swear if they put a quail egg on my plate, I'm going to Door Dash McDonalds and eat it in front of all these pretentious pricks."

Leah cracks a laugh so loud it makes me jump. In quick recovery, she cups her mouth and ducks her head.

That's all it takes for the mood at the table to lighten back up. Looking behind my girl, I mouth, "thank you" to Landon, and he gives me a wink. My boys love Leah as much as I do. They'll have her back just like they've always had mine.

"I'm shocked they didn't sit us at the kiddy table, or the reject table in the back corner," Gage says.

Leah's brow furrows. "Why?"

"Because of what Mason's done. Personal success is a slap in their face. I expected us to be blacklisted or something, not front and center of the room at lucky thirteen."

I'd specifically asked for this table number and placement on the floor plan. You can't not see us where we're positioned. Nicole probably had to move the table numbers around last minute when my mother wasn't looking because I'd bet a million dollars we were shoved into the back dark corner of the room if my mother had anything to do with the seating plans.

"I'm sure your mom's not *that* vindictive," Leah says lightly. "She's still your mom."

My girl is about to learn a valuable lesson in how this world operates. "Do you play chess, Princess?"

"A little, but it's been a while. Why?"

"Because that's what tonight's game is."

Everything in this life is a game. Not a single meeting, brunch, wedding, or fundraiser is innocently benign. There are more frenemies than friends amidst the social circles spinning around us.

And my fucking mother is the ringleader and champion.

"Then I guess I'm the Queen who will protect her King." Leah lifts her champagne flute and blows me a kiss before downing the whole thing in one long pull.

Landon rests his elbows on the table, propping his head up on his fists and sighs. "I want a Leah."

"Well, you can't have mine," I shoot back.

Landon perks up. "Hey, maybe our next tech company should focus on cloning."

"Oh, Cyborg Leahs!" She waggles her eyebrows at me. "With flavor buttons."

My belly-laugh is drowned out by my mother's booming voice on stage. "I want to thank you all for coming out tonight," she says, with a grand sweep of her hand. All heads turn to the stage where a sixteen-piece band is set-up to play soon.

Scarlet Finch addresses the room like they're hanging on her every word. She's always known how to captivate her audience and demand respect from her mutuals. Too bad she rarely deserves it.

"Tonight's turnout is our best to date. As

you know, the Finch family has hosted a fundraising gala for twenty-five years. It's been an honor and a privilege that I, my wonderful husband Tom, and our two children, Grace and Jackson, take great pride in."

The last little light in my heart with my mother's name on it flickers and burns out.

She's just publicly cut me out.

I knew she would do something to make my presence inconsequential, like ignore me at cocktail hour, but the delivery of her message was perfect. Points to her, for that one.

I feel Landon and Gage's eyes on me. I'm sure Kerrington's shooting daggers at her from his seat.

"Landon," Leah growls, "give me that fucking salad fork. I'm going up there."

My heart lights up brighter than the sun when Leah looks back at me. "I *am* going up there."

Taking the fork away from her, I rest my hand on her thigh. "Don't waste your energy just yet, Princess. The game just started."

"The Greystone Foundation holds a very special place in our hearts," Scarlet continues. "They only just started this past year and have already made significant changes in countless lives. Helping to feed the hungry in low-income areas, they have given thousands of children three healthy meals a day, for free. This would not be possible without the brains, and compassion, of one amazing woman. Nicole, please come out so we can all give you a round of applause for a job well done."

Wowwww. Talk about blowing smoke up someone's ass. Nicole's charity foundation may be wonderful and helpful, but it's hardly the first of its kind. She's not Mother Theresa, for fuck's sake. Still, Nicole deserves some credit. She's more generous than most of the shitheads in this room. And her heart's in the right place.

Sometimes.

Nicole glides across the stage like a swan. Her white gown is practically painted on her. The diamonds dangling from her ears glint from the stage lights like annoying disco balls, and her smile makes her look like a Tasmanian devil.

Okay, that was harsh. She looks lovely.

The entire room stands and claps for her. Including me. Nicole holds her hand to her chest, bowing a little before taking the microphone from Scarlet. "Thank you all so much." The room quiets as everyone sits back down.

I lean forward and press my mouth to the slope of Leah's neck, relishing how her breath hitches. Both of us face Nicole, our eyes glued to the stage, but as I kiss Leah's neck, it feels like we're the only two in the building. "I can't wait to take you home, Princess."

"The Greystone Foundation could not have accomplished all it's done this year, or what we have planned next, without your support and generous donations tonight." Nicole looks everywhere but at table thirteen. "Tonight, we have raised over three million dollars and for that…" She holds her heart, "we are so grateful."

More clapping. More cheers. More fake ass compliments about how wonderful everything is.

The amount of money it took my parents to put this thing together should have been donated to the charity, not used to flaunt their fortune and be the center of attention. No one wants to be here. We're obligated to come because no one would dare piss off the Finch family. It's such a waste of time and resources.

"But there is one family in particular who stands out amidst all others with their incredible generosity," Nicole says, turning to Scarlet. My mother makes an "aww" face just as Nicole says, "Mason Finch, and the BanditFX team."

My mother's smile drops immediately.

I lean forward and whisper in Leah's ear. "Check. Mate."

Chapter 29

Leah

I'm so turned on right now. What's that say about me?

In a room full of wealthy, powerful, intimidating people, I'm awestruck by the way Mason and his boys have handled what Scarlet tried to make humiliating for them.

My heart breaks for Mason that he has a mother this ugly. But seeing her smile fall on that stage, and knowing it was Mason who stole the spotlight from her, makes me so damn proud.

And horny.

Ugh, I should be scientifically studied.

Scarlet takes the microphone from Nicole, recovering quickly, and gestures for the applause to die down. "Yes, well, this is a night for much enthusiasm, which I hope you'll use when bidding on the silent auction items in the lobby."

The room erupts in laughter. After Scarlet quickly closes the announcements, she and Nicole exit the stage.

I stab my salad. "The dressing's nice."

"Mmmm yes." Gage holds a forkful of

lettuce up to his nose and sniffs it. "I believe these leaves were picked at the peak of late spring, with the morning dew still dripping from the tips."

"I do say, the thinly sliced radishes are a lovely touch." Landon chimes.

Kerrington rubs his temples like he has a migraine. "When will any of you grow up?" He plucks a tomato out and eats it. "Pass the salt." Once Gage hands it over, Ker growls, "I can't believe how low Scarlet sank just now. I'm so disappointed in her."

"Why?" Mason laughs. "We knew she'd do something."

"Yeah, but damn."

"I can't believe Nicole did that on stage." Landon shakes his head. "That's probably gonna cost her, won't it, Mase?"

"No price she can't pay."

I feel sick. "Is this normal behavior?"

"For these people?" Mason looks around as if assessing the room. "Yup."

I can't imagine growing up in a world where everything is so double-edged and poisonous. "I'm glad you're out." The minute the words leave my lips, I feel bad about it. This isn't how life should be for anyone, but to say I'm happy that Mason has been disowned doesn't feel right either. "I'm so sorry."

"For what? You didn't do anything." Mason grabs my chair and slides it closer to him. "I like having you close to me."

How much closer could I get?

A terrible idea pops into my head. Guess Mason's not the only one feeling salty and rebellious tonight. And after seeing that stunt with Scarlet on stage, my fears about being Mason's downfall have burned to ash.

Fuck these bitches.

With a quick shift, I sit on his lap. "This close enough?"

"Fuck me," he says, banding his arms around my waist. "This is *perfect*."

I stab his salad and feed it to him, hyperaware that people are looking at us.

"Way to command everyone's attention, guys." Landon shakes his head, grinning like a Cheshire cat. "Damn, Mase, your girl is as rebellious as you are."

"I know," he says, preening with pride.

"Incoming," Kerrington coughs.

A flash of white appears in my periphery and the next thing I know Nicole sits in my chair. "Hi, Leah. It's nice to finally meet you."

We shake hands and I notice hers are freezing and trembling. "You were amazing up there."

"Was I?" She presses the back of her hand to her cheeks. "Oh good, I felt like I looked like a bumbling fool. My face kept burning, and I was sweating like crazy." She gawks at Mason. "But to see your mother's face when I said what I said will forever be one of the top greatest moments of my life." She blows out a breath and steals Landon's drink. "I've never felt so powerful before."

"You can feel like that whenever you want if you just break away a little more," Mason encourages.

"Ugh, I don't think I can handle it. I'd be unstoppable."

"Can I have my drink back, please?" Landon pouts.

"No." Nicole drains it. "Ew yuck, I hate bourbon."

Landon scoffs. "Then why'd you drink it?"

"Because tonight's the night, asshole. I'm feeling defiant and wild." Nicole stands and smooths her dress down. "Oh, and just so you know, Jackson is *pissed*. He's going around saying you're a camgirl." Nicole laughs like that's crazy. "He's so pathetic. I mean, come on. A *camgirl*? Mason would never."

When no one laughs with her, she sobers up. "Oh my god. Are you serious?"

I'm so uncomfortable I try to get off Mason's lap, but he pins me down. "Stay where you are, Princess."

I don't want to. I want to run. Hide.

Crawl under a rock.

Run into traffic.

Anything to save him from embarrassment.

So much for my confidence streak.

"Holy crap." Nicole drops back down in my

seat. "I mean, no judgement, right? You do you, but holy *shit*. Mason, if your mother—"

Inwardly, I'm squirming like a worm impaled on a fishhook. But Mason's calm, powerful demeanor makes me rethink myself. He's not ashamed of what I do. He fucking loves it.

And so do I.

"Scarlet," he says in a deadly tone, "can think and say whatever she wants. It won't change a damn thing. My girl is incredible, smart, and has more kindness and sincerity in her pinky than all the people in this room combined. Whether she flaunts her assets on camera, scrubs toilets, or is the CEO of a billion-dollar enterprise, Leah's got more integrity than everyone in this fucking room. Including me."

I think I'm going to pass out.

Nicole's eyes shine, and her cheeks turn pink, even under several layers of her foundation. "Wow, Mase." Her voice isn't chipper and sweet anymore. It's softer, more... real. "You've won."

Won what?

There's an exchange between them I don't understand. Before I can ask, a server picks up our salad plates and replaces them with the main course.

"Nicole?" A man in a pink bow tie taps her shoulder. "You're needed over at your table."

"Oh, okay." Nicole's attitude goes back to light and bubbly. Fake. "Well, duty calls." Before leaving, she kisses my cheek. "I'm really glad we met. Save a dance for me, will ya?"

She hops up and I'm back to trying to climb out of Mason's lap. "I think I better sit in my chair. Too many people are staring."

"Let them."

Of course, he'd say that. He likes when people want what he has. But that's not how this feels. "I don't like being a part of your game, Mason."

He stills under me. Then he drops his hands, silently telling me I'm free to get off his lap.

Except I don't.

We're all making a stand tonight, right? Staking our land. Claiming our titles.

Landon, Gage, and Kerrington are outcasts. They don't give a fuck about any of this and, yup, Landon's pulled DoorDash up on his phone already. Nicole just put a powerful woman in her place, slapping her pride by claiming Mason one-upped her at her own damn charade.

Mason, who has been dejected, humiliated, and disowned, still showed up because he kept a promise. He's front and center, so everyone sees that not only is he out of the Finch's good graces, but out of their family and their social circle. The table with only half the chairs filled, will be the talk of the night.

It's incredibly gratifying to see how little they care about the opinions of others.

So, I stay on his motherfucking lap.

I like it here. I like the way he holds me in this position. I love knowing that half the women in this room probably wish they were me. And if being a maid got me into Mason's life, and being a camgirl was how we both shared our favorite kinks, then so fucking be it.

I have no regrets.

I'm not ashamed of who I am or what I do.

I love my life. I've worked hard for everything I have.

I'm not going to be a part of this game. I'm going to be a player in it myself.

And I'll fucking win.

Mason must sense my change in attitude. "That's my good girl," he growls in my ear. "Know your place, Leah."

Oh, I do. It's on a throne. In the Mason-Leah Kingdom, I wear the crown and no one's taking it from me.

Okay. Wow. I need a romance novel intervention. Clearly, I'm blurring reality with fantasy again.

"I ordered pizza." Landon tosses his cell on the table. "And McDonalds. And cheesesteak subs."

"Jesus Christ." Kerrington looks up at the ceiling. "What am I going to do with you?"

"Love me till the end of time."

Mason takes a sip of his drink and traces his finger in little circles on my thigh.

A figure stands to my left and I look over to

see a stunning woman hovering over us. "Holy shit, I thought Mom was going to have an *aneurysm* up there."

"Grace." Mason doesn't sound thrilled to see her. "You probably shouldn't be here fraternizing with the enemy."

"She's busy with Jackson right now." Grace has black hair like Mason and the same shaped mouth. Dressed in all black, she looks like a dark fae queen.

Good grief. Someone please take my books away from me. I'm getting ridiculous.

Mason takes a sip of his champagne. "I'm sure she's scheming, but there's nothing left for her to hit me with. I'm out for good and it's staying that way."

"I swear the way you guys talk it's like you work for the mafia." I hold my hand out to Grace. "Hi. I'm Leah."

"My future wife," Mason tacks on.

My pounding heart almost explodes out of my throat.

Grace's mouth falls a fraction, but she recovers quickly. "Can we not have any more surprises tonight? My anxiety meds aren't strong enough for all this."

"Here," Kerrington slides over his glass.

Grace takes it and frowns. "What's in it?"

"Rum and coke."

She tips it back and starts choking on it. "Oh my god! That's all rum!"

"Nah, there's coke in there somewhere. Probably at the bottom." He takes it back and drains it. "Okay, maybe it was at the top." He goes into a coughing fit.

"I can't believe Mom cut you out for real." Grace shakes her head. "Dad said she was *livid* when she got your letter from the lawyer. She ripped the curtains off the dining-room windows in a fit."

Mason shrugs. "She'll survive."

I swear I'm living in a movie.

"Dad hasn't spoken to her since either. He's sitting at a different table tonight and Mom's made some stupid excuse for it." Grace looks over at me and I feel like shrinking again. She probably thinks I've wrecked her family and is blaming me for everything. "Is it true you're his maid?"

Wow, the camgirl *and* house cleaning secrets are both out. I can't even imagine how that's possible. I don't recognize anyone here. How could they possibly know these things about me already?

"I did clean his house, yes." I don't like the way she looks at me. "But I don't anymore."

"Mmm hmmm. Why would you? You've got a goldmine now. No sense in wiping down floors on your knees, when you can be on them doing other things."

Mason slams his fist on the table. "Grace, watch your fucking mouth."

"What? I'm just saying she won't have to

work anymore if she bags you."

"Actually, I plan to work no matter what." I pluck a green bean off my plate and pop it into my mouth. "I like earning my money."

"Yes, I'm sure. Daisy Red, isn't it?"

"Ren." I pluck another green bean and feed it to Mason.

He chews it with a wry smile on his face. It fills me with a stupid amount of pride.

Grace clears her throat. "Okay then." She gets up and fusses with her long hair. "I'm going back over to my table."

"Okay. It was lovely meeting you, Grace."

Once she leaves, Gage starts the slow clap. "Well done, Leah."

"She's officially one of us now," Landon says with pride, wiping a fake tear from his eye. "Our family is complete."

Mason chuckles, his chest vibrating against my side. "Well, Grace tried." He slides his hand up the back of my neck and tugs my hair, tipping my head back. Then he kisses me. "You did so good, Princess."

"This feels awful." My head is all mixed up. I wanted Grace to like me, but her attitude towards me was so ugly. "I acted like a bitch."

"You only matched her energy." Mason runs his hand up my thigh. "If she doesn't want to be put in her place, she needs to drop her high and mighty attitude and eat some humble pie."

"Speaking of pie. Our pizza's here." Landon

gets up and heads out of the ballroom, returning a few minutes later with a stack of boxes and bags. "Time for some real food, guys."

We dig into the pizza while Mason goes for a cheesesteak.

"We should just leave," Kerrington says. "We're being fake sitting here."

"Nah, I want to dance first." Landon stuffs a bunch of fries in his mouth. "I just need a partner." Scanning the room, he narrows in on the direction Grace went in and leaves the table.

"He's going to go poke the bear," Gage warns.

We all turn and watch him swagger over to the Finch family's table. His hands are clasped behind his back as he talks with Grace, and then she's up and following him to the dance floor.

Mason tugs my hair a little. "Want to dance, Princess?"

"Definitely."

We make our way to the dance floor and Mason twirls me around. "I had to take ballroom dancing lessons in high school," he explains. "Never thought I'd actually enjoy it, though."

I spin into his chest and push away to twirl in the other direction. I have no clue what I'm doing. I'm just following his lead. "Well, it all depends on the partner. I think that goes for all aspects of life, don't you?"

"Mmm hmmm." He grins as I keep my posture stiff and straight when he slowly dips me.

Mason gently presses a kiss on my neck again. Adrenaline and fizzy bubbles shoot through my bloodstream. Everything about this dance is what life is like with Mason. He leads, but I'm still the star. He alternates between fast and slow, always aware of what step to take next. His attention is solely fixed on me.

And he's winging every bit of it.

"Marry me." The words tumble out of my mouth. "Marry me, Mason Finch."

He doesn't miss a step as he guides me across the floor. "Aren't I supposed to be asking you that question?"

"Says who?"

"Social norms."

My stomach is a mass of butterflies. "Nothing about tonight is the typical 'social norm'. Look around us."

"I can't," he says, spinning us in a tight circle. "You're all I see, Leah."

It's in this moment the world completely falls away. The music stops. The floor vanishes. The room evaporates, along with the air and all the people. It's just the two of us. We're all that exists. We're all that matter. "Is that a yes, Mr. Finch?"

It's crazy, I know. It's too soon. It's too ridiculous.

But I don't care.

Mason dips me again, his mouth hovering over mine until I can't bend any further. "Yes."

He kisses me in the center of the dance floor, and it feels so right, so perfect, so real. "You just made this the best night of my goddamn life, Princess."

The joy, however, did not last long…

Chapter 30

Mason

As dessert is served, the ballroom becomes a mix of people mingling, eating, and dancing. The band's in full swing. My face hurts because I'm marrying the woman of my dreams and can't be happier about it.

Damnit, I can't believe she asked me first.

I had this whole elaborate plan in place for later.

"We could fly out to Vegas tonight if you want." The faster we're married, the better. I want Leah to be my wife immediately. It feels insufferable waiting this long. I get that most people take their time when it comes to a commitment like marriage, but I'm a fast-moving man who's never dragged my feet before. When I know I want something, I take it.

I've wanted Leah since the instant I saw her in those whiskers, singing into her mop.

She's the one for me. I know it with my whole soul.

"What? No." Leah shakes her head. "I want a beach wedding."

"Let's fly to the Virgin Islands tonight." I pull out my cell to start the process. "How long does it take to get a marriage license? Never mind, it doesn't matter." I drop into my chair. "We can just stay a month or two."

"Oh my god." She face-palms herself. "You're ridiculous."

"Vacay?" Gage asks.

"Leah's proposed. I've said yes." I swear to God, I could fly to the moon right now. "Is this what it feels like to win the World Series? Because I'm pretty sure this this is how it feels. Bases loaded. Bottom of the ninth. And I've just hit the grand slam."

Landon and Grace drop into chairs beside us, both flushed and out of breath. "What did we miss?"

"We're getting married." I grab Leah's hand and kiss it.

"*Mason*." Grace's eyes are huge.

"Grace." I shoot back. But then guilt slaps me. She doesn't have this luxury. Flaunting it only hurts her more and though my little sister is a brat most times, I want her happy. "Say you'll come to the wedding." I keep my upbeat energy rolling because I will not back down from this.

"Of course." Her brow pinches together as if the thought of not being there hurts. "I wouldn't miss it for the world." She stands up and looks shaky. Then she slaps on her cheery expression and acts all bright and bubbly as she kisses Leah's cheek and gives her a genuine smile. But it falters a little when she looks at me. "I'm really, *really* happy for you, Mase." A tear falls down her cheek and my gut twists.

"Grace!" I call out as she walks away from us in a hurry.

Ignoring me, my sister disappears into the crowd.

The band stops playing, making all the chatter louder.

"At this time, I would like to make a few announcements," Scarlet says from the stage. The noise dies down, and everyone turns to her. "My goodness, I'm just so excited." She touches her cheek. "First, a round of applause to you all. Your generosity knows no bounds." Everyone claps for a few seconds. "The silent auction has ended, and we have raised another two-hundred-seventeen thousand dollars!"

More clapping.

"Nicole, please come back up here." Scarlet covers the microphone with her hand and says something to the singer of the band.

My instincts go on high alert.

Looking around, I see my brother climbing the steps on stage right while Nicole climbs them on stage left.

Leah tenses next to me. "Why does this feel like that part of a horror movie right before acid rains from the sprinklers in the ceiling?"

"Tonight is a very, *very* special night

indeed." Scarlet looks out at the crowd. "Tom, please come up here to help me share this incredible news."

My father strolls up, reluctantly.

I've gone the whole night without seeing or speaking to him. His hair is slicked back, making the white hair by his temples stand out against his dark black hair. He's got his lucky bowtie on. With a scowl, he climbs the steps. He hates attention on him. And my father is, by far, the most docile man I've ever known. It's probably why he and my mother work so well.

Confusion wars with amusement on Nicole's face, but it's my brother who has me ready to bolt from my seat. What the hell is going on here?

"It has just been shared with me that my dear son Jackson..." Scarlet takes his hand, "and our beloved Nicole..." She snags her hand too, "are getting married!"

Nicole looks like the rug was just pulled out from under her. Beneath the riotous applause where everyone stands and cheers, I watch Nicole say, "No, no, no."

Jackson pulls her into his arms and says something only she can hear. Nicole presses her hands against his chest and tries to shove him away.

"This is painful to watch." Landon's tone isn't playful at all.

With a tight smile, Jackson backs off Nicole.

Fury boils out of me. They do *not* belong together. It's a match made in Hell.

I may not like my brother most days, but he deserves real love and happiness, just like the rest of us in this nightmare. Nicole's expression says it all. She's mortified and trapped. Their marriage was announced publicly. Stopping it will turn into a scandal for the tabloids to feast on. Her reputation will be destroyed instead of my brother's. My mother would make sure of it.

"What do we do?" Leah asks. "She looks like she's going to pass out."

Nicole's stoicism disintegrates. All color leaves her face. I think she's going to faint.

"We're so happy to have you as part of our family, Nicole." Scarlet announces. "The Greystones and Finches have been friends for so long. My heart is filled with joy."

"Ticker," Nicole says quickly. "*Ticker.*" She snatches the microphone and clutches it with both hands while Jackson tries to snatch it from her. "TICKER!"

I'm out of my chair in a flash.

Bolting towards the stage, I get two steps up the stairs before Carmichael jumps in front of me. "Sit back down, Mason."

I don't hesitate. Fist clenched, I clock him in the jaw, sending him sprawling. Fury propels me up the steps. "Enough."

Grabbing Nicole's shoulder, I guide her over to the stairs where Leah and Kerrington are waiting.

"What are you doing?" Scarlet sneers. "Mason, get off the stage."

"How about *you* get off your high horse." I snag the microphone from her and throw it on the dance floor, breaking it. "Look at you."

Stuttering, she points at the back of the ballroom. "Get out."

"Oh, I'm leaving. Trust me. I've been counting down the minutes since I stepped into the hotel." I stalk towards her. "But not before I've had my say."

"Son, this isn't the time for—"

"He's not our *son*!" Scarlet shouts at my father. "He's dead to us."

"He looks alive to me." My dad walks past her and straight to me. "And he's still *my* son."

"Thomas."

"Scarlet." He shoves his hands in his pockets. "You're making a fool of yourself right now."

Her cheeks are as red as her name implies.

"You are the most selfish fucking prick in the family," Jackson snaps at me. "You didn't want her. And now that I get her, you want her back? Typical Mason. Always wants, always gets, gets, gets."

I can tell he's been drinking. I also know what my brother sounds like when he's scared. To the rest of the world, he might sound like a manchild, but I know better. I grew up in the same house he did. I know what happens when one of us disobeys orders or embarrasses an authority figure in the house.

"That's right," I say cautiously. "I am selfish. I want a lot of things, and I'm not afraid to go after them." Flicking my gaze to Scarlet, I add, "No matter the cost."

"Let's take this conversation somewhere private." My dad tries ushering his wife off the stage and fails.

"You're a *disgrace*," she says to me. "A disappointment to the family name."

Her words don't affect me. Not anymore. "I can live with that."

Whatever she's about to say next must wedge in her throat.

"What I can't live with is being tied to someone I don't love. To be indebted to a family who I didn't choose."

Scarlet's eyes widen with indignation. "How dare you!"

"Money isn't everything, Mother." I point to Leah, who's escorting Nicole towards the lobby. "See that woman back there? She's worth more to me than every dime the Finch family could ever make. She's fucking priceless to me."

She cackles. "That bitch isn't worth the toilet cleaner she uses to scrub the shit off your porcelain."

"Jesus, Scarlet." Tom steps back from her.

"What? I'm only stating facts, Tom. She's

nothing. She's worth nothing. She'll always be *nothing*. If Mason would have just done what he was told and married Nicole, *none* of this would be an issue and I wouldn't look like the bad guy here. But of course, it's all my fault. Everything is always my fault."

I lean in and get inches from her face. "If the Jimmy Choo fits."

A hand brushes my shoulder, and I look over to see Leah. She's come back to me.

Holy hell, she's on this stage, in the middle of this nightmare, and I want to shield her from all the vile, toxic vitriol my mother is spitting. "Wait for me outside."

"I'm not leaving you." Her words are so firm, I know there's no persuading her otherwise. "I'm right where I belong."

I'm speechless.

"Everyone deserves love," Leah calmly says. "I'm sorry if that wasn't a priority for you, Scarlet. Maybe you didn't have a choice, just like you tried to take the choice away from Mason, and for that, I'm also sorry. But don't do this to your kids. You said you've been friends with the Greystone family for forever. Are you really willing to match Nicole and Jackson?"

Scarlet looks like she was just slapped in the face with a cold fish. "This is none of your concern, girl. This is Finch family business."

"I'm not family anymore," I shoot back. "You disowned me."

"You did that to yourself," Scarlet huffs.

"Yeah, I did. And I have zero regrets." I shake my head. "What are you going to do, Scarlet?" She flinches when I call her by name. "When Grace is matched with someone who hates her. Or *worse*."

She knows what I mean. We once housed the wife of a senator who beat her so badly, she had to have plastic surgery to fix her bone structure. After recovering, she went back to the monster out of obligation. My mother cried her eyes out every night for a month over it because that woman had been her best friend. I heard mom once say to Grace, who was only thirteen at the time, that her and Dad might not love each other like the couples in the movies Grace was obsessed with, but he never hit her so, that's good enough. She said Grace should hope to find a man as gentle as her father and count her blessings.

It made me sick to hear it.

"We've only ever wanted you to be happy, son."

"He's. Not. Our. Son." Scarlet steps back. "Leave now, before I call security and have them drag you out."

"Think of the publicity that will get you," I say at her empty threat.

"Mason," my dad frowns. "Maybe you should—"

"Is this my life or yours?" I stare down at my mother. "Answer me. Is this life I'm living mine or yours?"

The fact that she can't quickly answer is answer enough.

"I'm not property to own. I'm not a stock to trade. I'm not a chip to bargain with. I made my own success and I'll live my life how I see fit. Maybe one day, you'll be happy for me. Maybe you never will. But you've lost me." I stare at her, unblinking. "Don't lose Grace and Jackson, too."

Holding Leah's hand, I slip past my brother and leave.

All eyes are on us. The night is completely ruined. I never wanted the game to go this far. There is no winner here. Maybe that's a lesson I had to learn so I can move forward.

I eventually find my friends standing guard by a restroom door. "Nicole in there?"

"Yeah," Landon says. "And she's a fucking mess."

"Let me talk to her." Leah lets go of my clammy hand and pushes the door open.

Once it shuts, the adrenaline pumping in my veins starts fading and exhaustions sets in.

Landon's eyebrows shoot up to his hairline. "Think we're blacklisted now?"

Kerrington is the first to laugh, and it thaws some of the ice forming in my veins.

Running a hand through my hair, the tightness in my chest lifts a little. "Yeah. I think that did it."

The bridges are burning. It's over.

Chapter 31

Leah

Nicole desperately attempts to fix her mascara, but the more she wipes, the worse it gets. "For Pete's sake, how many layers did my makeup artist put on me tonight?"

"Here." I wet some napkins and hand them over. "Maybe blot?"

Her hands tremble and my heart cracks for her. What happened on that stage wasn't only dramatic, it was traumatic. I can't wrap my head around it, honestly.

Nicole side eyes me. "You're lucky."

"I know."

"Mason's…" She shakes her head. "He's going to love you with all he's got. And he's got *a lot*."

I don't think she's talking about his money. "I know. And I'm going to do the same for him."

Nicole tosses the napkins on the sink, her gaze fixed on mine in the mirror. "I believe you."

I don't care if she believes me or not.

The door flies open and Grace slips in. "Oh my god, are you okay?"

Nicole's chin trembles. "Please don't be mad at me."

Grace hugs her tight. "Aw honey, I could never be mad at you."

"I just ruined our families." She sniffles again. "But I *can't* marry Jackson. I can't." She holds Grace tighter. "It was bad enough to almost have to marry *Mason*."

Grace runs her hands up and down Nicole's back. "I don't think anyone's marrying anyone at this point." Her gaze lifts to mine. "You really showed up for him out there."

"And I always will," I say, backing up to give them space. I feel like an intruder here. Maybe I should leave.

Grace holds her arm out to me. I'm not sure what I'm supposed to do. When I don't move, she says, "Well, come on. I'm trying to hug you both at the same time!"

Once Grace can snag my dress strap, she hooks it with her finger and yanks me in. "I have *two* sisters from other misters now."

Nicole cries harder.

Guilt pangs my chest because Grace is acting so opposite of how she had at dinner. It's a little confusing.

"I'm sorry for acting like a stuck-up twat earlier, Leah." Grace rubs my arm. "I was just trying to figure out your intentions."

"Your tests suck, Gracie." Nicole pulls back and wipes her face again. Her red-rimmed eyes and pink-tipped nose make her look sadly adorable. "Leah's the greatest. Mason wouldn't have chosen anyone less than perfect to love."

My throat tightens.

"Oh my god, I look like trash." Nicole focuses on fixing her face.

"Here." Grace digs through her clutch and hands over a tiny jar of makeup remover. "Just wash it all off."

Leaning against the sink, I hug myself while Grace helps Nicole. Should I go now? Stay? I don't know what to do.

Scrubbing her face aggressively, Nicole grumbles, "I just wanted to get this gala over with, go clubbing, and get laid."

Grace shrugs. "Well, at least you made a ton of money for your new charity tonight so..." She shakes her fists in the air. "Success!"

"Psht. Yeah, and this will likely be the last fundraiser of this scale too, because tonight blew up in a bad way." Her eyes well with tears again. "Oh my god, my parents are going to be furious. So many famous people were here and they're never going to want to do business with us again."

"Fuck them," Grace snaps. "If they aren't proud of you for all you've done in the community, then they can kiss your ass. They can kiss mine, too. And screw the famous fuckers. They're not special, they're just good at acting. Whoopdie woo. We're all good at it. So, fuck them all."

A laugh escapes me. "You sound like Mason."

"Good." Grace tosses her hair. "He's a great role model."

Grace and I empty our purses so Nicole can choose what to put back on. Between the two of us, we have everything she needs to look flawless again. "Okay, I'm good." Nicole fluffs her hair over her shoulders and turns to check out her ass. "I'm really damn good."

Poking my head out of the bathroom, I see Mason leaning against the far wall with his arms crossed and a grumpy look on his face. His features soften when he heads towards me. "How's it going in there?"

"Good. She wants to come out."

"Okay." Mason looks left, then right. "Does she want to sneak out?"

Nicole swings the door open wider behind me. "Fuck no. I'm going out that front door."

"Okay then." He holds the door for us. "Let's do it, ladies."

Nicole rolls her shoulders back and heads out first. Photographers snap her picture and yell out questions that all lean heavily into a romance scandal. She handles it with dignity and grace, giving away nothing but not covering anything up either.

Mason puts his arm around me, and we walk out to another flurry of camera flashes and questions screamed at us. He remains polite and keeps walking.

"Leah, is it true you're his fiancé?" one of them asks.

The answer catches in my throat.

How on earth did they find that out so fast? Or is it speculation they're trying to confirm? Should I keep my mouth shut and head down, ignoring them? I don't know what to do.

"Well?" Mason grins, arching his eyebrow. "Are you my fiancé, Princess?"

My uncertainty vanishes. Okay, wow, we're doing this. On camera.

Tapping my chin, I playfully look up at him like I'm thinking it over. "Hmmm."

The way he looks at me has my legs weak. The adoration in his eyes, the confidence in his shoulders, the humor playing on his kissable mouth...

More flashes go off.

"Yes," I say with a huge smile. "I'm his fiancé." Talk about going public.

I feel so alive it's intoxicating.

Excitement floods the area, and more questions arise about wedding dates, where did we meet, blah, blah, blah.

"That's enough for tonight." Mason scoops me into his arms and carries me out of their range, and towards his waiting car.

"Holy crap." I'm out of breath and didn't even do anything. "Is it always like this for you?"

Because I honestly don't like it. It's scary and claustrophobic. I'm also now going over every single second of it in my mind, to figure out if I messed something up or not.

"Not always. But tonight was a special occasion with a lot of Hollywood stars and politicians in the mix. I'm just glad cameras weren't allowed inside for the real dramafest."

"Wait. Hollywood stars were in there?" How did I miss that? "I swear to god, if I missed my chance to meet Henry Cavill, I'm going to cry." I didn't even notice the other guests at the gala tonight.

"Nah. Henry couldn't make it."

"Phew." I hold my hand against my chest, dramatically. "A missed opportunity like that would have ruined this perfect night." My joke falls a little flat. I think we're both still shaky from the mess we left behind.

A lot of backlash may still come our way. And if the paparazzi do a little digging, they're going to find out about Daisy Ren and that I was Mason's maid. It's going to make him look bad.

My stomach flip flops.

After Mason drives off, his somber voice sounds as heavy as my heart when he says, "This was not how I thought things would go tonight." Silence between us falls like the first snow of the season. "You came back for me." He rests his hand on my leg. "On that stage, where you would become a target for everyone, you still came back."

"I told you, I know my place, Mason." I squeeze his hand. "It's right here, by your side."

He grips the steering wheel tighter. "I'm so sorry they said shitty things to you."

"I've been told worse."

"That's…" He strangles the steering wheel. "Not helpful. Now I want to tear the world apart and find every person that's ever made you feel bad about yourself and flay the skin from their bones."

"You say the most romantic things." I sigh dramatically and fan myself, hoping to make him laugh. "I'm swooning over here, you big sexy alpha."

"I'm serious," he growls. "I hate that you were dragged into my family's shitshow tonight. And it's my fault. I brought you to it."

"I came willingly, and I knew this wasn't going to be easy for you. But I'm really proud of you, Mason."

"Why? I was a petty piece of shit tonight."

I hear the regret in his voice. But sometimes you have to sink low for scum to hear what you're saying. It's not ideal, but Mason's message was loud and clear tonight. "You broke the cycle."

He stops at another red light. "I feel like I've blown up my entire existence."

"It might seem that way tonight because you're hurt, and the pain is fresh, but you broke a very toxic cycle and I think you've set an incredible example for Jackson and Grace. Your dad, too."

"He'll never leave her." Mason's voice drops in a gruff whisper. "He's trapped in a loveless marriage where she walks all over him. He must be so fucking miserable. We were just assets, not children to her. And I'm mad at my dad for never having the balls to stand up to her on our behalf." Mason scrubs his face with both hands and sits at the traffic light even after it turns green again. "I just couldn't sit back and let Jackson marry Nicole. It would make them both so miserable and it's not fair. And to think Grace is also on the chopping block." He leans back and shuts his eyes. "I can't believe we let Scarlet run our lives into the ground over fucking money and power."

"Which, again, is why I'm proud of you for breaking the cycle yourself." I want to hold him. Kiss him. Take away his pain and heartache.

Someone behind us honks, knocking Mason back into action. He waves apologetically in the rearview mirror and drives forward. "I have no regrets."

I don't think he's talking to me.

"I hope they see I did what was right and maybe follow in my footsteps."

He's definitely not talking to me.

"I hope they're happy." His voice cracks. "I want them to find their person. Like I've found mine." He clears his throat again, and the atmosphere gets a little lighter. "God damn woman, I'm so glad I found you."

"Took you long enough."

"Right?"

We drive in quiet comfort out of the city madness. New beginnings can also be happy endings, I suppose. And I'm here for all of it.

"We still should celebrate." The city whirrs past us. "Tonight was a good night. Messy, but good."

"What do you have in mind, Princess?"

I open the map app and get us directions to a bakery. "It doesn't have hours listed."

"It's probably closed, but let's see." Mason zips through the streets and barely slows down at the stop signs. I hop out of the car and dash to the door. It's locked. Damnit!

I strongly recommend bakeries be a twenty-four-seven convenience for those who need a little sweetness in their life. Everyone needs cake — they're the universal greatness. Want to celebrate? Eat cake. Just broke up with your red flag boyfriend? Cake. Pregnant? Cake. Bored? Cake. Rainy day reading smut? Cake.

Peering inside, I see movement in the back where the kitchen must be, so I knock loudly. A young girl cautiously walks out holding a piping bag. She's covered in flour and icing. "We don't open until seven am," she hollers.

Is she already baking cakes at this hour?

"Please, I just need a cupcake," I yell back.

"Or a slice of cake. Hell, I'll take a cake pop!"

She frowns and looks back at the darkened glass case at the counter. "Hang on a sec."

Hope bubbles inside me when she walks away and comes back with a hot pink box. Unlocking the door, she opens it and sticks the box out for me to take. "This is all I have left."

"Thank you so much! Here," I hold out a twenty.

"No, no. It's fine." She quickly shuts the door and locks it again, waving me off before heading back to the kitchen.

I cradle that sucker like it's a newborn kitten. Hurrying back to the car, I get in and present the dessert like it's the golden ticket to Willie Wonka's chocolate factory. "I got it!"

Mason chuckles. "How can cake make you this happy?"

"It's not the cake. It's you. Cake is just a bonus. A mystery bonus. I have no clue what's inside this thing." I pop the top off and we both look inside.

Dear God, noooooo.

It's carrot cake.

Mason laughs so loud he shakes the entire car.

Fucking carrots in my cake. And raisins! I have no words. "I don't appreciate the universe's sense of humor here." But I pluck that damn thing out of the container and hold it up to his mouth. "You first."

He chomps down on it and starts chewing. "Mmm. It's actually pretty good."

I take a little nibble, pleasantly surprised that it's nothing like I thought it would be. "Oh, this is kinda nice." Flicking a raisin out of the way, I chomp on a bigger bite. "Okay, it's really good."

Mason licks icing off his top lip. "You're adorable."

Shoulders lifting, I bat my lashes at him. "I know."

"And you're all mine."

My smile broadens. "I know."

"I'm going to make you so happy, Leah."

"I know." He already does.

"Do you know everything?"

"Pretty much." I drag my tongue across my teeth to get the icing off. "I'm well read. Ask me anything."

"What are we going to do next?"

"Easy. We're going home and you're going to fuck my brains out."

Mason acts shocked. "My God. You really *do* know everything."

"It's one of my many lovely and admirable qualities."

He kisses me and says, "I know."

Chapter 32

Mason

By the time we get home, my mind's calmer, clearer, and the peace I've longed for has settled in my system. They say people come into your life at just the right time. Leah came exactly when I needed her most and I will be forever grateful.

She drops her clutch on the first flat surface she sees. "I can't wait to get out of these shoes."

I scoop her up. There's no reason for her to walk another step. I'm frustrated she wore those damn heels all night if they hurt her feet so badly. Carrying her upstairs, I bring her into the bedroom and put her down on the side of the bed. Without a word, I kneel and bring her foot up to rest on my leg. Unstrapping her heels and removing them, I massage the back of her calf for a few seconds, before lifting her up to stand. "Turn around, Princess."

Gathering her long hair, I slip it over her shoulder and press a kiss to her neck while dragging the zipper all the way down her back. Hooking my fingers under the straps, the dress falls effortlessly to her feet.

I can relate.

I'll happily spend the rest of my life at this woman's feet. Worshipping her. Loving her. Spoiling her. Leah's happiness means everything to me. I didn't know love could strike as fast as lightning, but I'm proof that when the woman you're meant to be with walks into your life, your soul knows immediately.

Nipping her neck, I knead her breasts. They're full and soft, spilling out of my hands. Greedy for more, I run my fingers down her sides and across her belly. Leah's body is a treasure trove. From her golden, wavy hair, to her big heart, to her pretty little pink toes.

I'm the richest man in the world because I have *her*.

"Come on, Princess." I carry her into the bathroom and sit her on my lap while starting a bath.

She kisses me hard, hungrily, while taking off layer after layer of my tuxedo. First the tie, then the jacket, vest, and shirt. By the time she gets to my belt buckle, she's breathing heavily.

"Does my girl want to get fucked before or after her bath?"

"Before." She yanks on my fly. "And after."

So needy. I love it. "Whatever you want, Princess."

"Wait." Leah's eyes widen. "Can... can we record this?"

"Absolutely." I thought she'd never ask.

Dashing out of the bathroom, Leah squeals as she hunts for her phone. It's in her purse downstairs, which gives me time to work on a surprise I've been keeping.

The cat's out of the bag about Leah, and I'm relieved. There will be publicity spiraling round us, and they're going to use Daisy Ren or her cleaning career to tear us down. It won't work.

What a one-eighty tonight has been. A couple of weeks ago, I would have done anything to protect Leah from the ugliness of my world. Tonight, she showed me that staring in the face of those who would tear you down is the best way to build yourself up.

When Leah returns, she's flushed with excitement. "I've been wanting to discuss something with you."

The tub is halfway filled, so I pour bubbles in.

"Is it your secret business?"

"Yes."

Finally! I've been dying to know about it but didn't want to pressure her. I understand her desire to keep some news under wraps until the right time. "Let's hear it."

"I've had this idea for a while." She tucks her hair behind her ears. "It's a multi-faceted sex site."

I love it already. "Go on."

"I'm in the final stages of having the whole site built. It's geared towards women, with the content being slower and more sensual." She looks nervous. "Like the videos you've recorded of us—especially the one with you looking up at me from between my thighs." Her breath shudders and nipples harden. "It's those scenes that are most perfect. Every woman wants someone to look at them the way you look at me."

My heart pounds like a battering ram in my chest. Where is she going with this?

"I was wondering, if you… like if you're willing to… record more scenes like that with me." She looks so shy right now. "We can one hundred percent be masked, so our faces aren't recognizable."

Blurring our faces is a no-go if she wants people to see the way I look at her while I pleasure her.

I tip my head to the side. "Are you asking if I'd make porn with you, Princess?"

She bites her lip. Her little crinkle is back too. "Yes?" She waves her hand. "And it's totally okay if you say no. I won't pressure you. I just thought… well, I'm moving forward with this business, and I want to be the first to post something on it. If I can market it from the start to be a place where sex and sensuality meet in a combustive connection, there's no better example than the two of us."

The bubbles in the tub multiply, piling up like soft floral scented clouds in the water. The steam in the room builds and thickens.

Leah is starting a new business. I'm so fucking proud of her.

Of course, I'm going to support the hell out of it.

I make my way over to her slowly. For once, I'm not going to worry about the repercussions of my actions. I'm not going to overthink or fear what others may say about me doing something I enjoy, even if they think it's unconventional. I'm not holding back anymore.

My girl wants to bring her side hustle to the next level, and I will support her every step of the way. "Okay."

Leah lights up. "Really?"

"Really." I kiss her forehead. "This will be fun."

"And scary."

"Most new endeavors are." I wrap her hair around my hand and give it a tug. "I'll never say no to an opportunity to show you off, Princess. You have no idea how the thought of everyone craving you turns me on."

She moans against me. "I think you're the one they'll be dying for, Mason."

"And how does that make you feel?"

She grabs my hand, lowering it to her pussy. "Feel for yourself."

She's wetter than the tub.

"God damn."

Lifting her up, I carry her back over to the bath and put her in it. "Wait! I thought we were going to fuck first!"

"Honey, for the way I plan to rail you tonight, you're going to need your limbs loose. Heat helps."

She cups a bunch of bubbles in her hand and blows them at me.

After propping her phone on the tile ledge, I strip out of the rest of my tux and hop in with her. She leans forward and hits record, then falls back on my chest with a sigh.

"We look so good together." I pour water onto her tits. "But I think something's missing."

"If you say my bunny whiskers, I may just slap you."

"Careful, I might just like it."

She laughs, and it's so carefree and wonderful. Her joy sinks into my skin, setting me on fire.

Lacing her hand in mine, I bring it out of the water and kiss it. "I think we need one of these." I pluck a bath bomb out of a little bowl I put in here for her. "There's supposed to be a fortune in the center of it."

"Oh, I love those!"

It drops in the water with a splash.

We touch and talk until the bath becomes sensual and heady, with the scent of lavender perfuming the air.

The water has stained blue. "Is that fortune ready yet, Princess?"

"Let me see." She feels around the bottom of

the tub for it, and I know the exact moment she finds it because her entire body tenses. The vein in her neck pulses and flutters.

Leah pulls out the waterproof paper attached to a ring. "Oh my god, Mason."

The hefty diamond glints in the candlelight and looks spectacular when I slip it on her dainty finger.

But her smile is the real showstopper here.

"Read it." Kissing her temple, I pull her back to rest against my chest again.

Her hands shake as she unrolls the paper that says:

And they lived happily ever after.

Her big brown eyes shine with happiness when she looks up at me. "This is *perfect*."

As far as endings go, I'd say this is a damn good one.

Epilogue

Leah

One year later…

My instincts were right. The multi-faceted sex site, Brazen Bunny, I started six months ago has taken off. It's officially a one-stop-shop for all your kinky needs, and I'm really fucking proud to openly promote intimacy, sexual empowerment, and safe kinking on my platform. Daisy Ren hasn't just upgraded. She's gone next level.

I'd give credit to the massive publicity we got after that gala, especially since Daisy Ren went from one million followers to two million in less than a week. But that's not what sent me into the next stratosphere of popularity.

It was a video clip of Mason and me.

We only posted it as a test run.

And my site went viral two weeks later.

The five-minute video was of Mason kissing me. I sat in front of the camera, and he came up behind me and started sensually working his mouth down my neck. It started so sweet and innocent, but he knew my weak spot and used it to both our advantages.

The moment built—the intensity of his

touch, the way my body responded. My man took his time with open mouth kisses, licks with his fat tongue, tiny nibbles all along my shoulders, neck, collarbone, and lips.

By the time he finished, my hair was no longer up in a ponytail, but down in a wild mess of knots because he kept running his hands through it while making me melt in absolute pleasure with only his mouth and hands. My pretty lipstick was no longer in place, but all over our mouths, cheeks, and chins. My cheeks were flushed and splotchy from arousal. My neck red from where he nipped it. When Mason collared my throat with his hand, he looked straight into the camera and growled against my ear, "You taste so fucking good, Princess."

I've yet to recover from that scene.

Since then, I've had dozens of investors pour in. Custom sex toys, kink safety classes, videos, audios, artwork, and even smut segments with several romance categories to choose from where authors submit scenes they've written for anyone to reenact and post on the platform for others to enjoy.

Monster smut is currently the most popular, followed by mafia romances.

Happy endings are everywhere, am I right?

We've also joined a few sex clubs across the country because Mason absolutely loves performing in front of a live audience. So do I. The longer we're together, the better we fit.

"What are you doing?" Mason slaps my ass. "We have to leave in twenty minutes and you're in here cleaning?"

"I'm almost done!" Wiping out the stainless-steel sink, I finish cleaning the kitchen. "There. So shiny."

"You know we can hire a housekeeper."

"Not on your life. This brings me joy."

I no longer work for the cleaning service, but our massive house keeps me busy enough. It takes me half the day just to wash the floors. I love it.

"Mmph." He presses his dick against my ass. "Is cleaning the only thing that brings you joy, Princess?"

"Of course not." I playfully wiggle against his erection. "The Yankees bring me joy too."

He stumbles back, gasping and clutching his chest. "You cut too deep."

The baseball game starts at seven thirty, but we were supposed to go out to eat first. Racing up the steps, I press play on my cell phone and music blasts through the Bluetooth speakers in the ceiling.

I scream-sing while in the shower, scrubbing down in a rush. Scrunching my hair, I leave it wet and wavy and hurry to my massive walk-in closet. Digging out my latest outfit that will drive Mason crazy, I shimmy into it and grab my Chucks. "Ready!"

Mason's putting his baseball hat on just as I

hit the bottom step. He spins around to say something and freezes.

"What?" I tug the hem of my new dress. "No good?"

His keys drop onto the floor with a clank.

"If you don't like it, I can change." I playfully take a step back and Mason bolts forward, grabbing me by the hips.

"I'm going to get arrested if you wear this out of the house, woman."

"What for?"

"Fucking you in a fully packed stadium." He looks me up and down. "Jesus, Leah, my dick's so hard for you right now."

I knew he'd love the custom Red Sox mini dress with thigh high tube socks.

"We only have ten minutes left to get to the restaurant." I pat the top of his head. "Concentrate, Mason. We gotta go eat."

"I'm eating right here." He spins his hat around and dear god, the backwards hat on him is sexy as hell. "In fact, fuck it, we can miss the whole game. The Red Sox will be back in town, eventually. I'll catch them next time." He lifts my hem and sees I'm not wearing panties. Running a hand over his mouth, his eyes laser focus on my pussy, and he whispers, "I'm the luckiest man in the world."

He tongue-fucks me on the steps. Just when I'm about to orgasm, he stops and grins with his chin glistening.

"Don't stop!" I yell.

"Beg me."

"*Please* don't stop."

"Beg harder."

I shove my hand between my thighs and gather some of my arousal on my fingertips. "Please." I shove a finger in his mouth. "Make me come on you, Mason."

He nips my finger and unbuckles his belt, pulling his pants down. "That's my good girl."

We both look down to watch him drive in and out of me. The way his cock is wet from my pussy. The way my lips wrap round his base. The sound of our bodies slapping together. He yanks the top of my dress down so my tits fall out. Then he bites my nipples through the fabric of my bra, making my eyes roll back.

"I'm close." Hooking my arm around his neck, I drive my other hand through his hair and pull it.

"I'm not wasting a drop of us," he warns.

"Neither will I."

Mason roars with his release. Hearing it and feeling the way his cock throbs inside me, makes me orgasm too. He pulls out and licks my pussy, gathering our pleasure on his tongue and holds it out for me. I take him in my mouth and suck on his tongue. I will never get enough of how filthy we can be with each other.

Once we're both fully satisfied, I pull my dress back in place. "Ready?"

"Mmph." He's already pushing his dick back inside me for round two. "Ten more minutes."

"Mason!" If we don't leave now, he'll fuck me straight through the night. "We have to go. Your dad, Jackson, and Grace are waiting for us."

He droops like a wilted plant. "Well, that just killed my hard-on."

I figured it would.

He snags his clothes off the floor. "Never mention their names to me when I'm balls deep inside you again, Princess. I'll need therapy."

"I promise. Never again."

By the time we reach the game, we're a half hour late. Even with reserved parking, it's a nightmare getting inside and to our seats.

Grace is the first to greet us. "You guys missed the first pitch!"

"Traffic was a nightmare." Mason snags a hot dog from his brother and hands it to me.

"Traffic, huh?" Grace's eyes narrow. "Is that the story you're sticking to?"

"Yup." Mason shoves a hot dog in his mouth and winks at me.

"Aw come on!" Tom yells at the umpire. "That was a bullshit call!" He pats Mason on the back. "Good to see you, son."

They embrace in a quick hug before cheering when the next batter hits the ball and runs to first base.

"Go! Go! Go!" Mason screams.

The player bolts past first and slides into second.

"Here you go, Leah." Grace hands me a cold beer. "Jackson's beer bitch tonight, so whenever you're feeling thirsty, make him go on a run."

Jackson shrugs. "I lost a bet with her that you'd be on time. Never thought it was possible for Mason to be late to a baseball game."

"And what did I tell you?" Grace puts her hands on her hips. She looks adorable in her Gucci blouse, red shorts, and baseball hat. "I said Leah was priority numero uno. She could have said she wanted to fly to Paris for a macaron before they came here, and he'd have made it happen."

Jackson shakes his head, ducking to hide his smile.

My heart is so full.

Mason's slowly working on patching things with Jackson. Grace is helping with that. Tom has also put some effort into making changes to rebuild a relationship with his kids. Mason still doesn't speak with Scarlet, but there's no love lost there. Maybe that will change later down the road, but Mason's happy with the boundaries he's set.

I'm so proud of him.

"Atta boy!" Tom pumps his fists in the air. Everyone's cheering, but I missed why.

Mason grabs another hot dog and shoves it in his mouth.

Jackson huffs because it was the last one in the box. "Didn't you eat before you came, bro?"

"Yup." Mason chews with a big grin plastered on his face. Then he smacks my ass.

Jackson rolls his eyes. "Oh my god."

"You should lighten up a little, Jay-Jay. Get laid." Mason downs half his beer. "Remove that stick up your ass."

"But then what would he ride home on?" Grace snaps her finger. "Beer bitch, I need a drink!"

"You already have one."

Grace shoves her drink in my hand. "No, I don't."

"Ugh." Jackson scoots through the crowd to get her another one. "Excuse me. Pardon me. Sorry. Excuse me."

Grace is such a brat. I love her to death. "You're so bad."

"And I'm so good at it." She bats her lashes. "It's one of my greatest qualities."

Mason sits forward, exactly like his father, watching the game.

I still don't know much about baseball, or why there has to be nine whole innings, but seeing the happiness on my man's face when he goes to games makes me wish they lasted longer than a few hours. Besides, the food is pretty great. I'm a sucker for the cotton candy.

"Here comes the pitch!" the announcer yells.

The batter swings and hits, making the ball fly right out of the park.

Our entire section screams and cheers.

Mason shoots up from his seat, cheering and clapping. Carefree and happy looks damn good on my man.

He leans down and kisses me like I'm the one who hit the home run. The crowd goes wild, and it's only after we break away that we realize we're on the jumbotron's kissing cam.

I arch my brow. "Did you know that was going to happen?"

"Nope. We just have great timing."

Yeah. We sure do.

That's how love works. It comes when it's meant to. It's a risk, that's for sure. Putting yourself out there, handing your heart over and trusting they don't destroy you is a risk.

Don't hesitate to take it.

Other Books By This Author

For information on this book, other books in my
backlist, and future releases,
please visit: **www.BrianaMichaels.com**

If you liked this book, please help spread the
word by leaving a review on the site you
purchased your copy, or on a reader site such as
Goodreads.

I'd love to hear from readers too, so feel free to
send me an email at:
Briana@BrianaMichaels.com
or visit me on Facebook:
www.facebook.com/BrianaMichaelsAuthor

Thank you!

About the Author

Briana Michaels grew up and still lives on the East Coast. When taking a break from the crazy adventures in her head, she enjoys running around with her two children. If there is time to spare, she loves to read, cook, hike in the woods, and sit outside by a roaring fire. She does all of this with the love and support of her amazing husband who always has her back, encouraging her to go for her dreams. Aye, she's a lucky girl indeed.

Made in the USA
Monee, IL
16 April 2025

15869671R00184